DEVASTATE
PAM GODWIN

FOR ROSA.
WHAT IS THE PRICE
OF LOVE?

Pam Godwin

Tulsa18

If you have not read the first three books, STOP!

The books in the DELIVER series are stand-alones,
but they should be read in order.
DELIVER (#1)
VANQUISH (#2)
DISCLAIM (#3)
DEVASTATE (#4)

PROLOGUE

Four years ago…

Tate Vades reclined in a shadowed booth, glaring at a high-top table of women across the grimy tavern. They'd been stealing glances at him all night, winking and licking their lips and abrading his nerves.

There had been a time when he would've invited them over with a crook of a finger. But his hands didn't twitch. Neither did his cock.

He hardened for only one woman. A fierce woman with eyes of molten brown and fire in her soul.

What a cruel thing love was, silent and desolate in its torture. How ironic that loving someone was the thing that hurt the most.

He knew how to suppress the physical, psychological, and emotional repercussions of violence. How to tune out the echoes of his weakened screams. The unholy pain of his bludgeoned flesh. The sharp, bitter scent of blood.

He was a survivor of captivity and sexual torture, and despite it all, he still considered himself a proud, dominant man. But when it came to love, he was a victim, powerless and unbearably alone in its apathetic clutches.

Two years ago, Camila Dias rescued him from his ruthless captors. She'd appeared out of nowhere, stunningly beautiful with guns blazing as she murdered the man who had paid Van Quiso a million dollars for Tate's body. A man who meant to own Tate and use him in depraved ways.

But Camila saved him from that fate. She freed him. Then she stole his heart.

"Can I get you another beer?" A server stopped at the table, his tattooed fingers deftly collecting the empty bottles in front of Tate.

"No, thanks." He lit a cigarette but didn't inhale.

He wasn't a smoker. Not anymore. He just needed to keep his hands busy while he came to terms with what he planned to do.

His long-suffering patience with Camila had finally reached its end.

He'd helped her bring down Van Quiso's sex trafficking operation in Texas. Her small vigilante group—the Freedom Fighters—was her therapy, her way of consoling the wounds she'd collected during her own captivity in Van's shackles.

She, Tate, and five others—Ricky, Tomas, Luke, Martin, and Kate—lived together, fought together, and slowly recovered from their shared experiences as Van's slaves-in-training. After they escaped, Tate bided his time, giving Camila space to heal, to focus on her revenge, and to open her heart.

Two years later, she still didn't belong to him.

Of all her roommates, he was her closest friend. When they were alone, she spoke of her darkest desires and forbidden fantasies, her seductive voice leaving him endlessly hard and desperate. But he hadn't fucked her, hadn't so much as kissed her.

He thought he was being chivalrous, providing her a safe place to put her trust and with time, her love.

He was a fool.

She didn't want chivalry or patience or love. At least, not with him. She was holding herself back for something. Or, if his intuition was correct, *someone.*

But who? *Who* did Camila dream about when she slept alone every night?

He snuffed out the cigarette and tossed a wad of cash on the table. He was done waiting. Done being friend-zoned. It was time to introduce her to the real Tate Vades. The man who would compel her to her knees with a look, grip her by her stubborn throat, and demand her secrets, her submission, and her love.

Rising to his feet, he turned and collided with a rock-hard body. "Excuse me —"

"Have a drink with me." Hazel eyes and dark hair, the ridiculously attractive stranger gestured at the booth, his accent hinting at south of the border. "I insist, Mr. Vades."

He knows my name? What the fuck?

"Who are you?" Tate held the stranger's intense stare with one of his own.

"We'll get to that. First…" The man waved over the server. "A glass of *aguardiente.* Neat. And another beer for my friend."

Camila drank *aguardiente.* Always neat. She said it was the way Colombians preferred their soft vodka.

This man, with his accent, Colombian features, and choice of drink… He was connected to her somehow. Tate was certain of it.

"I'm sorry." The server scraped a hand through his

PAM GODWIN

hair. "You said ah…gwar…dee…?"

"They don't serve *aguardiente* here." Tate slid back into the booth, eyes on the mysterious man. "You're a long way from Colombia, *ese*."

"It's Matias." He held out a large hand in greeting.

Never heard of him. Tate stared at the outstretched fingers in silent rejection.

With a sigh, Matias lowered his arm, ordered vodka, and sent the server away.

"You've been taking care of someone extremely important to me." He sat across from Tate and rested a muscled, tattooed forearm on the table. "Someone who belongs to me. For that, you have my deepest gratitude."

Camila belonged to no one. She never talked about her Colombian roots or her cartel connections, never mentioned any names from her past. Except her dead sister. She spoke of Lucia with a longing that trembled her pretty lips.

Tate blanked his expression. He didn't know this man, didn't trust the purpose of this visit.

"You have feelings for her. This, I know." Matias hardened his clean-shaved jaw, his accent thickening. "Have you fucked her?"

Tate had been on his way to do just that. Of all the nights for his relationship with Camila to be questioned, why tonight? Why now? He narrowed his eyes into slits of suspicion.

"Answer me," Matias said, his voice as black as his scowl.

"I fuck a lot of women."

A lie. Tate hadn't had sex since…

His nude body in shackles.

Van's grunts. Musky sweat. Dry thrusts.

4

Stretching, ripping, violating his dark opening.
Blinding pain.
Shame. A lifetime of maddening shame.

"That's a *no* then." Matias visibly relaxed, briefly closing his eyes before whispering, "We both know that if you were fucking Camila Dias, there would be no other lovers."

A protective jolt of anger spiked through Tate's veins. "How do you know her?"

"We grew up together."

"That's funny." Tate balled his hands on his lap. "She's never mentioned you."

"I don't suppose she would." Regret clouded Matias' eyes. "I'm the one she calls to deal with the bodies."

Stunned by his candor, Tate flicked his attention around the quiet bar. It was late, nearing closing time, and most of the patrons had shuffled home. The small table of women remained, their glasses empty and eyes still drifting in his direction. They were out of hearing range.

Near the exit, two men occupied a booth, sipping… Water? Vodka? He hadn't noticed them before.

Black hair, dark complexions, and powerful physiques, they looked like they could be related to Matias. The way they subtly watched every movement in the bar left zero doubt they came here with him. Armed guards, most likely. Camila's cartel connections.

Tate removed the phone from his pocket. He didn't want to alarm her or involve her in whatever this was, but he needed confirmation—

"Set the phone on the table." Matias flashed his teeth, his grin devoid of amusement.

It wasn't the words that lowered Tate's gaze. It was the long blade of a knife pressing against his inner thigh, sharp enough to slash denim, skin, and muscle, with the pointy end a hairbreadth from his balls.

His pulse hammered. Would the bastard neuter him? Right here in the bar? The glint in those cold eyes said, *Yes.*

The server approached, dropping off the beer and vodka, oblivious to the tension coiling beneath the table. "Can I get you anything else?"

"We good?" Matias arched an inky brow at Tate.

"We're good." Tate placed the phone on the table.

When the server left, the knife retreated.

"Hear me out," Matias said, "and I won't kill you."

"Comforting."

"Two months ago, she called me to collect a body."

Van Quiso's body. Tate gritted his teeth through a torrent of conflicting emotions. Van was a sadist, a rapist, the very monster that inhabited Lucifer himself. But something had changed in him around the time he was shot and left to die. He'd withdrawn from sex trafficking, avenged the wrongdoings against his first slave, Liv Reed, and left her the money he'd earned through his vile operation.

Six million to be exact, which she split between Van's nine slaves. Tate received $666,666. A fitting number from the devil incarnate.

"As you know," Matias said, flaring his nostrils, "Van Quiso didn't die from that gunshot wound. I arrived to find him driving away from the house where he imprisoned and tortured my girl."

My girl. Tate's stomach hardened, every muscle in his body coiling with denial.

6

"She's mine, Tate." Matias flexed his hand on the table. "I know he enslaved you in that house, as well. By my count, nine captives total over the past six years."

"And each of those captives had buyers," Tate said. "All of which are dead and the bodies never to be found, thanks to you." That was as much gratitude as he was willing to give the man.

"Van Quiso should be among them. I wanted to gut the sick fuck when I saw him drive away." Matias sipped from his glass. "But he was my only lead to discovering Camila's whereabouts. She trusts me to dispose of the dead, but she doesn't trust me with her location. So I followed Van. He led me to Liv Reed, who unwittingly took me right to Camila."

Camila doesn't know she's been found. She'd been so careful about remaining hidden, evading the law and keeping her cartel connections at a distance.

"I've been watching her for a couple of months. Learning her habits, where she goes, what she does, who her closest friends are." Matias met his eyes.

If that were true, he would know how committed Camila was in her pursuit to abolish human sex trafficking. She was so passionate about it she didn't consider the danger she put herself in. But Tate did. Constantly. He adored her tenacity, marveled at her fearlessness, but keeping her alive and out of prison was an endless worry.

"You grew up with her." Tate cocked his head. "You know where she lives. Yet you haven't approached her."

"Puzzling, isn't it? I'm the kind of man who takes what he wants. As much as I want to *take* her — restrained and at my mercy — I won't. She suffered enough in the

7

hands of that despicable slave trader." Matias spat the words, his accent seething with venom. "I will not take what isn't given. When she comes to me, it will be of her own volition."

Yet he'd stalked her, invaded her privacy for months. Tate opened his mouth to argue the hypocrisy, but Matias raised a silencing hand.

"All bets are off when her safety's in question." Matias heaved a frustrated breath. "Now that Van's operation is dismantled, she intends to take down another slave ring in Austin."

Tate knew every detail of her plan and would protect her at all costs. "If you stop her, she'll never forgive you."

Against his expectations, Matias closed his eyes and said, "I won't stop her."

Then why is he here?

The thugs in the booth near the door surveyed the surroundings, not once making direct eye contact with Tate. Their dark jeans and bulky sweatshirts only partially obscured the sidearms they were clearly packing.

"What do you want?" Tate leaned back in the vinyl seat, watching with fascination as Matias struggled through whatever was darkening his expression.

After a long moment of silence, he spoke in a voice almost too low for Tate's ears. "I'm the capo of the Restrepo cartel. She doesn't know this. They"—he nodded at his companions near the exit—"don't know this. My enemies would bribe, torture, and butcher for that information."

"Why the fuck are you telling *me*?" Tate angrily whispered, jerking forward with forearms braced on the table. "You don't even know me."

"I know you love her." Matias raised the glass of vodka to his mouth, his gaze sharp. "I know you'd lay down your life to protect her. That works in my favor as long as you understand she's not yours."

"She's not yours, either."

"She will be, and you're going to help me."

Two hours later, Tate closed the front door of the five-bedroom house he shared with Camila and the others. He rubbed his eyes, his head pounding with the weight of Matias' crazy goddamn plan. A plan that would bolster Camila's pursuit while keeping her safe.

If Tate weren't so viciously jealous, he might've admired Matias' selfless devotion to her.

His heavy boots carried him into the kitchen — the only room still illuminated at three in the morning.

"Where've you been?" Camila looked up from a spread of maps and news articles on the kitchen table.

"The bar."

She leaned back in the chair, her seductive eyes stroking him from head to toe before returning to his face. "With a woman?"

It was an opening. An opportunity to tell her he hadn't been with anyone since she freed him from captivity. Because he loved her with a madness that choked his senses.

But the fact that she'd asked about another woman without a hint of jealousy or anger spoke volumes.

She doesn't care who I fuck.

Because I'm not the one she wants.

He stepped to the sink, filled a glass from the tap, and guzzled it. When the cool water failed to extinguish the fire in his chest, he refilled the glass and drank again.

"What's wrong?" The chair scuffed behind him, followed by the tread of her socked feet. "Tate?"

"Have you ever been in love?" He gripped the edge of the sink, keeping his back to her.

"What kind of question — ?"

"Yes or no." Turning, he sank into her dark gaze.

"Yes." Her throat bobbed.

"And now? Do you still love him?"

"Where is this coming from?"

"Do you still love him, Camila?"

"Doesn't matter." She looked away, shoulders hitching. "He no longer exists."

She denied him a view of her eyes, but the pain seeping into her posture confirmed what he already knew.

Her heart belonged to Matias.

Acknowledging it, however, didn't change his feelings for her. Love was love. It didn't just go away when it wasn't reciprocated. It endured, persisted, and waited like a pathetic, unwanted pussy.

He could tell her everything — Matias' surveillance of her, his plan to decimate the Austin slave ring, his desire to eventually lure her to Colombia where she could help him fight against the worst slavery in the world, and the biggest shocker of it all, his refusal to reunite with her until the unrest in his cartel was controlled.

Matias calculated every detail because he didn't want to endanger her.

Because he loved her.

Tate could tell her all of this. Declare his own love. Make her choose. But it would benefit no one. She would run headlong toward Matias, straight into the kind of danger Tate wouldn't be able to protect her from.

"I'm going to bed." He cupped the back of her head and pulled her into a hug, relishing the warm softness of her petite body.

The kitchen window felt like a spotlight on his back. Was Matias watching from the street? Were there cameras in the house? During the meeting at the bar, the cartel boss had described — in vivid, gory detail — all the ways he would remove limbs and organs if Tate touched Camila in a sexual way.

Tate didn't scare easily, but a man in love wasn't a force to be taken lightly. Especially when that man was the king of a cartel.

"Why don't you call it a night?" He released her and stepped back.

"I will…soon." She stared longingly at the scatter of papers on the table.

With an aching hunger, he left her with her outlined maps of revenge and climbed the stairs to his room.

He hadn't agreed to help Matias with his insane plan to win Camila, but they'd exchanged phone numbers before parting ways.

A month later, curiosity led him to Colombia at Matias' request. He wanted to learn more about the dangerous capo and the anti-slavery raids he supposedly operated. It was on one of these raids, in a dilapidated barn, where Tate saw the horrifying goodness in Matias Restrepo.

He watched from the safety of a barn window as children — naked, beaten, and bloody — were auctioned off, one by one, for the wretched pleasures of men. Then he watched Matias save them all, leaving a bloodbath of

11

wrath in his wake.

It was on that night that he knew he would do anything for the man who held Camila's heart.

After spending weeks with Matias in the slums of South America raiding slave operations, he gained a friend and lost all hope of requited love from Camila.

He might've been her closest friend, but Matias... He was the counterpart to her passion, the mate to her vengeful soul. They shared a spirit Tate couldn't begin to understand.

So he consented to Matias' plan. He would watch over her, protect her, and call Matias every day with every detail of her life.

But he wouldn't, *couldn't* stop loving her.

"You need to return to her." Matias eyed him from across the table at his Colombian estate. "Her safety is my number one priority."

"I'll head home tomorrow," Tate said, distracted.

He scanned the floor of Matias' veranda, every inch of it covered with piles of papers, maps, and photos of warehouses and slave traders.

When he left Camila in Texas three weeks ago, he told her he was going on a soul-searching journey across the States. Now he found himself in the luxury of Matias' home, poring over an unsolved mystery.

"There's nothing there." Matias rose from the table and stepped toward the interior door. "I searched for Camila's sister for two years. She's dead, Tate."

"She's *missing*."

"For *six* years."

"You don't know she's dead." Tate stared at a photo of Lucia Dias, hypnotized by the huge brown eyes of a girl who looked so much like her sister.

"I know she was inside a transport of trafficked slaves that crashed in Peru. No one survived. That's where the investigation ends."

"You gave up."

"I prioritized." Matias gripped the door jamb and straightened his spine. "My priority is—"

"Camila." Tate swiped a hand down his face. "Mine, too. But there's no harm in digging further, to see if there's something you missed."

"Camila can't know. If you get her hopes up, I'll cut your—"

"Yeah, yeah, I know. I won't tell her." Tate lifted a photo of Lucia and Camila embracing each other in an orange grove.

In their teens, their likeness was uncanny—long black hair, delicate bones, stubborn chins. Yet there were notable differences. Lucia was two years older, her features sharper with maturity, her smile more relaxed, carefree. She was even more beautiful than her sister, if that were possible.

"I'll make copies of the documents." Matias blew out a breath. "I can digitalize everything and send it to you."

Tate nodded, his gaze glued to the image of the lost girl.

He might not hold Camila's heart, but could find her sister—dead or alive. He could bring her closure. It would give him purpose, a distraction from the persistent ache inside him. He desperately wanted to do this for her.

Because he loved her.

CHAPTER 1

Present day...

The electronic beats of Ke$ha's "Take It Off" followed Tate through the dimly lit halls of The Velvet Den. The worn wallpaper, creaking wood floors, and faint scent of perfume evoked a tantalizing nostalgia for his old stomping grounds. But beneath the swell of sentimentality lay a prickle of unease. Not all his memories of this place were pleasurable.

Stepping out of the final corridor, he lingered at the entrance of the main room. Settees and lounge chairs surrounded an empty stage. The rich textures and dark decor was designed to make club members feel relaxed and safe, and the exceptional service catered to their upscale tastes. Then, of course, there were the girls. Scantily dressed and easy on the eyes, they served drinks and sex with alluring smiles.

Nestled in a suburban border town in southern Texas, the invite-only establishment was older than his twenty-five years. It hadn't always been a swinger's club, but as laws cracked down on prostitution, The Velvet Den evolved. Money still exchanged hands after a sweaty fuckfest in a private room, but no one spoke of those transactions. A narc would lose more than his membership.

The club owner didn't just enforce the rules, authorize the contracts, and hire the well-vetted staff. She set the mood, simply through the elegance and grace of her presence.

As he scanned the room for her long blond hair and voluptuous body, her husky voice caressed his back.

"Your guest has arrived, darling."

"Lela," he breathed, turning to meet the sharp green eyes of his oldest friend. "It's good to see you."

"Is it?" Her plump, red-painted lips pouted her disapproval. "You never visit. I'm under the impression you don't miss me at all."

"You know that's not true." He wrapped his arms around her and smoothed a hand down the corset's lacing along her spine. "I've missed you more than you know."

Hard to believe she was in her forties. She didn't look a day older than thirty. He could still picture her towering over him and pommeling his ass for the mischief he'd stirred up as a boy.

She framed his face and caressed her lips against his. The lingering kiss, the exotic aroma of her shampoo, and the press of her fingers against his jaw—all of it filled him with warm memories.

The Velvet Den was his home, and while Madame Lela Pearl wasn't his mother, she was the closest thing he ever had to one.

"Thank you for letting me hold my meeting here." He glanced over his shoulder, searching the crowd. "Where's my guest?"

"I set him up in the Cognac Room." She trailed a

blood-red fingernail down the placket of buttons on his shirt. "Unless you prefer a room with more *privacy*."

"It's not that kind of meeting."

"No?" Disappointment creased her pretty features. "I hoped you returned to work for me again."

"Lela—"

"You're even more handsome than you were as a boy. Stronger. More virile." She petted his bicep. "The ladies would empty their purses to experience your dominant nature."

His stomach buckled. The clientele tended to be older, with marriage, careers, and kids behind them. Too old for the downtown club scene, they came here with unique proclivities, looking to quench darker appetites.

It didn't matter. Young or old, male or female, locals or out-of-towners, no one would be paying him for sex. Never again.

"I don't need money." He caught her arm and gently set her away. "There's more to life than getting off."

Her eyes bugged. "Shut your mouth. I raised you better than that." She propped her fists on the flare of her hips. "Have you forgotten what it feels like to fuck without commitment or strings—?" She snapped her teeth together, eyes growing wider. "Oh shit. Are you in love?"

That was only part of it. She didn't know what happened to him when he disappeared from The Velvet Den's parking lot six years ago. He was nineteen when Van Quiso took him at gunpoint and raped him for ten weeks in a soundproof attic.

She assumed he ran away, and he let her hold onto that belief. The truth would wreck her.

"Yes, there is someone." He averted his gaze, unable to hide the resentment in his expression.

"But?"

"She's engaged."

"So? Win her away from her fiancé."

"They belong together, and I love her enough to let her have that. To let her go."

It'd been four years since Matias approached him in that Austin bar. Four of the most miserable years of his life. After going along with Matias' plan, watching Camila reunite with him, and losing her completely when she moved to Colombia, Tate no longer wanted to stay in the Austin house he'd shared with her.

Visiting her a few times in Colombia hadn't helped his miserable jealousy.

So he came here.

Home.

But it wasn't the same.

No, *he* wasn't the same.

"My guest is waiting." He kissed the top of Lela's head. "I'll stay a few days, maybe longer, okay? We'll catch up."

"Very well." She fussed with the collar of his shirt. "I'll have a room prepared for you. Stay as long as you want."

"Thank you."

He turned back down the hall, slipped into a stairwell, and exited one floor below. The same dark furnishings adorned the Cognac Room, but the pungent aroma of cigars deterred non-smokers from using this space.

A bald man reclined on a couch, his trousers unzipped beneath the bobbing head of a young woman.

Nearby, several other couples engaged in various forms of fornication and sexual orientation. Across the room, a topless dancer writhed on a pole, grinding to the low volume of club music.

An attractive man sat alone at a table a few feet from her. He was the only man in the room who could've been Cole Hartman. Tate's guest.

Black leather jacket, short brown hair, early thirties, he watched the dancer with a strange expression. It wasn't curiosity. Definitely not desire. His furrowed brow and pinned lips hinted at displeasure.

Maybe it was shock. Especially if he'd never been in a place like this. And fair enough. Swingers were a peculiar breed. They paid outrageous fees for the convenience of ogling, sampling, or boning other people's partners. There weren't a lot of life experiences that prepared a person for a room full of naked, oversexed strangers.

Tate had deliberately withheld the nature of The Velvet Den when he suggested it as a location to meet. He wanted to hire Cole to help him find Camila's sister. But if the big, leather-clad guy couldn't handle an open display of sex, he wasn't up for the task.

Since Cole didn't appear to notice anyone but the dancer, Tate remained in the doorway, studying him, searching for anything that might've raised a red flag.

After four years and five private investigators, Tate had made zero progress on locating Lucia Dias. So he did the one thing he thought he'd never do.

He asked Van Quiso for help.

Liv and Camila had both been enslaved by Van, yet they'd found something redeemable in him. Something they trusted.

Van had connections with unsavory people —
slavers, drug and weapon dealers, assassins, and bounty
hunters. People with specialized skills in shady
situations.

People like Cole Hartman.

Tate didn't know how Van was connected to Cole
or if that was even his real name. All he had was Van's
unwavering conviction: *If Cole Hartman can't locate
Camila's sister, no one can.*

On the far side of the room, Cole shrugged off his
jacket, tossed it in a nearby chair, and crooked a finger at
Tate without removing his eyes from the dancer.

Evidently, he was more attuned to his
surroundings than he let on. *Good.*

As Tate crossed the room, Cole lifted a beer from
the table. Heavy ink tattooed his forearm, but the lighting
was too low to make out the artwork.

He didn't move or meet his eyes until Tate reached
the table.

"You're drinking Bud Light in the Cognac Room,"
Tate said in greeting.

"Am I breaking a rule?"

"No. But the cognac's free."

"So is the beer." Cole tipped the neck of the bottle
in the direction of the dancer. "Tell her to leave."

"You have a problem with dancers?" Tate
pointedly looked at Cole's tattoo.

From wrist to elbow was an inked silhouette of a
woman swinging on a dance pole.

"I've seen better." Cole brought the beer to his lips
for a hardy swallow. "Much better."

On the surface, Cole seemed relaxed. But with each
rotation the dancer made on the pole, his jaw grew

harder, the cords in his neck pulling tighter. For whatever reason, the dancing put him on edge, and it undoubtedly had something to do with the woman tattooed on his arm.

While Tate didn't know the dancer, all of Lela's employees knew him. His history at The Velvet Den gave him the authority to send her away, but how did Cole Hartman know that? Maybe he'd done his homework?

Approaching the dance pole, Tate touched the girl's shoulder, his voice low. "Take a break, sweetheart."

"Thank you, Mr. Vades." With a small smile, she sashayed toward the exit.

Christ, she had a great ass. Big and round, it jiggled in her thong, sending provocative messages to his cock.

With an inward groan, he returned to the table, lowered into a chair, and caught Cole's eyes. "How do you know Van Quiso?"

"Client confidentiality, pal. He's *your* friend. Why don't you ask him?"

Van wasn't his friend and had been annoyingly cryptic on the subject of Cole Hartman.

"I requested this meeting because I need you to find someone." Tate clasped his hands together on his lap. "A woman."

"How long has she been missing?"

The answer tried to stick in his throat, but he forced it out. "Eleven years."

Cole didn't grimace or flinch like the other investigators Tate had hired. He simply nodded and sipped the beer.

"Aren't you going to ask her name, age, last place she was seen, all the usual shit?"

"Nope." Cole leveled him with an incisive look.

"We're going to discuss *you*, the reason you're looking for her, and the price you're willing to pay."

"Money isn't an issue."

"I'm not talking about money."

Tate rubbed his head, losing patience. "I don't understand your meaning."

"Why did you choose this place to meet?"

"If you were good at your job, you'd be able to tell me."

"All right." Cole leaned forward, keeping his voice soft. "Let's start with your childhood."

This should be interesting. Tate had never told anyone about his past, not even Camila. "Go on."

"Tate Anthony Vades. Son of a prostitute. Father unknown. After your mother died from a drug overdose, you became a ward of the state, all before your second birthday. But her friend, Lela Pearl, took you in, kept you hidden and out of the system." He took a swig of beer and lowered it without looking away. "You were raised by whores in a brothel, *this* brothel, until you were old enough to turn tricks and earn your keep."

Jesus. Tate didn't know whether to be pissed or freaked out that he'd dug up so many buried secrets. But Cole's ability to elicit a vulnerable reaction was a good thing. If he could arouse fear in people, taunt them with personal information and provoke them to talk, maybe he really could make headway on Lucia's case. Because somewhere, someone knew what happened to her.

"I'm impressed." Tate tilted his chin down, measuring his words. "So I was raised among whores and earned a living as one for a while. What of it? You going to turn me in?"

"Rumor is, generations of sheriffs, judges, and

mayors have kept this place in operation in exchange for VIP treatment." He glanced around the room, watching topless women serve cigars and cognac. "To be honest, I'm waiting for the girls to break out in song, a la *The Best Little Whorehouse in Texas*." A smirk stole across Cole's face. "I work outside of the law, Tate. Your secrets are safe with me."

"I appreciate that." He narrowed his eyes. "Not sure how any of this helps you find the woman I'm searching for."

"I'll find her, but it won't bring you any closer to the woman you want."

He stopped breathing, and his heart flew against his ribcage. He didn't care if Cole knew he lost his virginity to a man at age fourteen or that he'd sold his body to female clients for a few years. Hell, he didn't even care if Cole had gleaned what happened to him in Van's attic.

But Camila was off-limits. In her crusade against slavery, she committed the kind of felonies—kidnapping, torturing, and murdering criminals—that would earn her a death sentence if caught. He didn't want Cole near her, asking about her, or investigating her in any way.

"This was a mistake." Tate moved to stand.

"Camila Dias is safe." Cole gripped his wrist, holding him in the chair with a cutting glare.

"She's none of your concern." He yanked his arm away and sat back.

"True, but she's in your head, messing with your thoughts. Isolating you. That's why you're here. You came back to the beginning, to the one place that gave you a sense of belonging."

"What are you? A fucking psychologist?"

"No." Cole laughed, a hollow sound. "Nothing like that. I just know from experience that a broken heart is the worst kind of hell, a goddamn lonely path from which you can never recover."

He touched a thin chain that hung around his neck, lifting it from beneath the t-shirt and letting it drop in full view. A tiny silver ring dangled at the end. A woman's wedding band.

If he was married or engaged, he wasn't any longer. Not with her ring in his possession and no ring on his finger.

Tate removed a pack of smokes from his pocket, lit a cigarette, and inhaled deeply. "What happened to her?"

"I let her go." Sadness whispered through Cole's voice, but an admirable amount of fortitude sharpened his eyes.

"Let me guess. She's with someone else?" At Cole's nod, Tate repeated the same words he gave Lela upstairs. "They belong together?"

"Yeah."

The air around them agitated before settling into a quiet hush. Cole did a good job tucking away his feelings. But Tate knew how deep that well could go and how hot and relentless the turmoil could burn within it.

"We're in the same hell, then."

"I don't think we are." Cole rubbed his whiskered jaw. "I watched you check out that dancer. You'll have her on her back by the end of the night."

Her or one of the other girls who worked here. Tate wasn't picky, as long as she was restrained and trembling beneath him. "I'm a man, not a saint."

"I'm a man, but there isn't a woman out there who compares to the one I had."

Given the tattooed silhouette on his arm, his ex-fiancé…wife…whatever must've been a dancer. That explained his displeasure with the dancer earlier.

"What's your point?" Tate asked.

"If you truly loved her, you wouldn't be fucking every tight ass that crossed your path."

He wanted to deny the accusation, but after Matias walked into that bar with a claim on Camila, he'd reverted to some old vices, such as smoking cigarettes and fucking anything in a skirt.

But that was beside the point.

"You did your research." Tate tapped the cigarette in the ashtray. "Which means you knew my background and the reason I asked you here before you walked in the door."

Cole nodded. "You're looking for Lucia Dias, because you think you're in love with her sister."

He did love her, but the dickhead could believe whatever he wanted.

"What I haven't figured out…" Cole studied him for a moment. "What is the price you're willing to pay?"

Back to this again. "How about we start with your fee?"

"A hundred grand."

His pulse raced. "A hundred—?"

"She's been missing for eleven years. It'll take time, but I'll get you the location of her body—dead or alive. That's the *finder* fee. It doesn't include retrieval. If she lives and *wants* to be removed from her situation…" Cole folded his hands on the table and exhaled slowly. "You can't afford it."

"How much?"

"Depends on the level of risk, the location, and

whether she's being held against her will. Extraction jobs can last months, man, and the expenses add up — surveillance technology, specialized weapons, informant bribes, recruitment of resources, hush money, travel costs... The bill would run higher than the six-hundred thousand sitting in your bank account."

Tate's stomach bottomed out, and it wasn't only from the outlandish price. Knowing Cole had hacked into his finances, the fucking pity etching his face — all of it made Tate want to slam a fist into the wall.

"Let's just...slow down." He took a drag on the cigarette and squashed it out. "We need to find her first. I doubt she's even alive."

"You believe that?"

Did he? With a deep inhale, he mentally probed his gut and found the hope he'd held onto for years. "I know she was abducted from her home. Her parents were tied in with cartel. Both were murdered after she disappeared. And justly so. They gave her up to spare their own lives."

When Matias had learned they'd sold their daughters — both Lucia *and* Camila — he'd killed them. Camila had eventually escaped Van Quiso, but Lucia's kidnapper died eleven years ago, taking her whereabouts to the grave.

"Her last known location," Tate said, "was in a sex trafficking transport in Peru. It crashed. No survivors, but her body was never identified. I traveled to the crash site myself a few months ago. Talked to the locals in the village. No one knows anything, or so they claim." He met Cole's eyes. "To answer your question, I believe she survived that crash and is being held somewhere against her will."

"What will you do when I confirm your

suspicions? When I give you proof of her life? Since you can't afford my retrieval fee, will you ask Matias Restrepo for help? We both know he has the power and resources to assist."

Fucking hell. Since Cole was privy to Tate's relationship with Camila, it shouldn't have been a surprise that he knew about the man she lived with. While the cartel capo could fund his own operation to find and extract Lucia, he'd already looked for her. And failed. Because he'd given up.

Tate wouldn't be asking Matias for shit. He was doing this, in part, as a gift to Camila. He didn't want Matias involved.

"No?" Cole's gaze pressed against him, probing too close for comfort. "Okay, so what's your plan? Will you try to retrieve her on your own and get yourself killed in the process? Or maybe you'll ask your roommates to help you? Are you willing to risk their lives?"

What the hell was this guy's problem? Tate just needed to know if Lucia lived. If she did, he'd figure it out from there.

"I don't care what you do, man." Cole leaned back, drummed his fingers on the table. "But before you go down this rabbit hole, you need to really think hard on why you're doing it and the price you're willing to pay. Right now, you can assume she's dead and walk away. If you hire me, it'll be too late to turn back."

Cole was right. If he found her, if she was still alive, it didn't matter how dangerous the situation, Tate would do whatever it took to reunite her with her sister. He ached to see the relief on Camila's face. To know that he was the one who put it there. That he had given her

27

something Matias couldn't.

That was the fucked-up part, wasn't it? His motivation was perverse, bordering on obsession, because dammit, he still wanted to win her heart. He wanted to be the one Camila belonged with.

So when Cole asked what price he was willing to pay, what he really wanted to know was how much Tate loved Camila. The answer was easy.

"I'll send you everything I have on Lucia Dias." Tate pushed away from the table. "Find her."

CHAPTER 2

Five weeks later, Tate woke in an unfamiliar bed to the muffled chirp of his phone. Blinking away grogginess, he pushed a feminine arm off his chest and scanned the moonlit room for his pants. A trail of women's clothing led out the door and into the hall, where he spotted his shoes and shirt.

"Where's my—?"

"Here." A naked woman sat up beside him and dragged his jeans from the floor, bringing the sound of his phone closer.

While searching the pockets, he slid off the bed and shuffled through the room. *1:13 AM* glowed from the clock on the nightstand amid a clutter of empty beer bottles and condom wrappers.

Fuck, he hadn't meant to fall asleep here— wherever *here* was.

The blonde he'd gone home with rolled to her stomach, her mascara-smudged eyes roaming his naked body. What was her name? Alicia? Allison? Did it matter?

Jesus, I'm an asshole.

His fingers bumped against the phone in the

pocket, and he connected the call from an unknown number. "Hello?"

"It's Cole."

His pulse spiked. He hadn't heard from Cole Hartman since he wired the finder fee. After five weeks, he started to wonder if he'd been scammed.

"Hang on." He shoved on his jeans and slipped into the hall, shutting the door behind him. "Did you find her?"

"Yes. We'll talk in person when I get back to the States in about…" A pause. "Fifteen hours."

"Is she—?"

"I'll come to you."

"Is she alive?"

Dead air.

"Hello?" He glanced at the phone, and the call was disconnected. "Motherfucker!"

After spending a week at The Velvet Den, Tate had returned to Austin. Evidently, Cole didn't need to be told that. But Tate had a million questions, so he hit redial. When the call wouldn't connect, he tried the contact number he had for Cole.

No answer. No voicemail.

Frustration roiled through him as he grabbed the rest of his clothes and left the woman's apartment without a word.

Over the next twelve hours, he tried to sleep between attempts to contact Cole. If Lucia were dead, wouldn't Cole have just told him on the phone? They wouldn't need to meet in person. The same could be said if she were alive and happy and safe.

His insides twisted as he dug through the laundry on his bedroom floor, sniffing each shirt in his hunt for something clean to wear. If Cole was coming to him, he needed to get out of the house. Two of his roommates, Tomas and Martin, were home. He didn't want them volunteering for a dangerous retrieval operation. Their untrained vigilante group, the Freedom Fighters, wouldn't hesitate to help him. But this wasn't their fight.

An hour later, he pulled into Liv's driveway and parked beside Kate's car, knowing his timid little roommate would be there. When Camila moved to Colombia, Kate started spending more time with Liv. Not that he blamed her. She was the only girl living in a house with five overprotective men who monitored her every move.

As he knocked on the front door, he didn't have to worry about Liv or Kate risking their necks for his cause. Liv's husband would never allow it, and Kate... Well, she was still recovering from her time in Van's attic, which made her painfully guarded and cautious.

The door opened, and Josh's bulky frame filled the entrance.

Tate had been Liv and Van's sixth captive. Kate came next. Then Josh—the last one. The one Liv fell in love with. While Camila and the others had helped Liv free each slave, it was Josh who had been the nail in the slave operation's coffin. Somehow, he achieved the impossible and broke through Liv's cold mask.

"Hey, man." Josh's smile lit up his green eyes. "What are you doing here?"

"Is Liv around?"

"Yeah. Come in." Josh retreated, leading him through the house. "She's back here with Kate. Everything okay?"

"I don't know yet. It's about Lucia Dias." As he

passed the living room and kitchen, there were no signs of Liv's teenage daughter. "Where's Livana?"

"She's at a friend's house this weekend." A sheen of perspiration slicked Josh's nude back, his feet bare and hair mussed.

Christ, had he and Liv been fucking? With Kate here? Surely not. But they were into some kinky shit, and he was headed straight toward the master bedroom.

"Hey, uh…" Tate paused in the hallway, unwilling to be part of anything that involved Liv's whips. "If I'm interrupting something…"

"I wouldn't have been able to answer the door." With a wink, Josh disappeared into the bedroom.

Wouldn't have been able to because he would've been tied up. Literally.

Tate exhaled a sharp laugh. Of all the men Liv had captured and trained, Josh was the only true submissive.

Since Tate had spent ten weeks in her restraints, he was intimately familiar with her dominant nature. The whole Mistress thing was a total turnoff, but when she'd had him naked and chained to the wall, she found ways to arouse him, torturing his cock until he begged for release. Unlike Van, she never fucked him, but there had been times when she'd taken pity on him and relieved him with her hand.

He rubbed the back of his head and tried to clear the memories. Over the past six years, he and Liv had become good friends, and he rarely dwelled on those dark hours of his life. But he'd never been in her bedroom, and as he stepped into the room, his stomach cramped.

Josh knelt on the bed, messing with a chain that connected to the headboard. Liv stood behind him, directing the work. In the corner of the room, Kate was curled up in a chair, her gaze drifting to the doorway.

A toolbox sat open on the floor. A drill on the nightstand. A package of heavy-duty eyehooks on the bed. Hairline cracks splintered the frame of the headboard. If he looked closer, he'd find more hooks and bolts. Probably a hidden rig of chains. Maybe a ball gag and a cock ring. The usual.

That explained why Josh was shirtless and sweaty. He was fixing the bondage equipment he'd built into the frame, which clearly hadn't held his powerful physique.

"You're doing it wrong." Liv parked her hands on her hips. "Stop."

Goddamn, that commanding tone took Tate right back to the attic. His spine tingled with echoes of pain, the burning lashes of leather on his back, the skin-crawling feel of Van's touch, and the fucking rules. *Kneel. Eyes down. Bend. Suck.*

The memories pissed him off, heating his face and clenching his fists.

Something moved in Tate's periphery, and a moment later, Kate's slender arms encircled his waist, her head tucking beneath his chin.

He pulled in a calming breath, ruffled her blond, baby-soft hair, and sent her back to the chair.

Liv smiled at him in greeting, and the scar that bisected her cheek pulled taut. The same scar that marred Van's face. The matching lacerations served as permanent reminders that Van and Liv had suffered as much as Tate and the others before they escaped.

"Josh said you were here about Lucia?" she asked.

As Josh packed up the tools, Tate updated them on his search. They all knew he was looking for Camila's sister. They just didn't know the extent in which he'd gone with the private investigators and Cole Hartman.

"Cole found her, but I don't know if she's dead or alive. He said he'd come to me…" Tate glanced at his watch. "Anytime now."

"He'll come here?" Josh sat on the edge of the bed and pulled Liv onto his lap.

"Is that okay? I can leave."

"Stay." Liv hooked an arm around Josh's shoulders. "If Van referred you to him, I trust him in my home."

At the mention of Van, the room fell quiet. They'd all been there during Van's reign of cruelty, but in the past few years, they'd watched him transform into something more human.

Still, there were things a person couldn't forget.

While Josh and Kate had been forced to participate in intimate acts with Van, their buyers had demanded virgins, saving them from the worst of Van's depravity. Tate and Liv hadn't been so lucky. Ricky, Tomas, and his other roommates had likely been raped by Van as well, but they didn't talk about it.

"Van seems hellbent on redeeming his transgressions," Josh said, breaking the silence.

"Transgressions?" The whisper came from the chair in the corner. Kate shifted to the edge of the seat, gripping the armrests, her voice soft. "He's a monster. There is no redemption for him."

"Kate." Liv's cold tone cut like a whip. "I was a monster, too."

"You saved us." She pulled her knees to her chest and angled her face away.

"In the end," Liv said, "he saved us in his own

way. The money he gave—"

Tate shook his head at Liv. He knew Kate hadn't touched her share of the six million. Despite his protests, she waited tables at a local diner in order to contribute to the household bills.

With a tug on Kate's hair, he guided her out of the chair and toward the living room. There, he continued the conversation with Liv and Josh, outlining his speculation on Camila's sister.

If Lucia had survived that crash, she would be thirty years old now. If she'd maintained a youthful appearance like Camila, she could still be valuable as a sex slave. She could still be alive.

Talking about it with his friends reignited the flame of hope he'd carried for so long. They didn't ask him why he was so gung-ho about finding her. Maybe they knew. Hell, Van's wife, Amber, had called him out for the way he looked at Camila. They all knew.

When a knock sounded on the door an hour later, he leapt to his feet, his heart hammering like a piston.

"I'll get it." Josh crossed the room and opened the door. "Can I help you?"

"Cole Hartman." A tall silhouette hovered on the dark porch. "Tate's expecting me."

Josh stepped to the side and let him in.

"Is she alive?" Tate asked the instant Cole entered.

"Yes."

Relief sang through his nerve endings and loosened his chest. Good fucking God, he didn't realize how badly he needed to hear that. "Is she safe?"

Dressed in black denim and a wrinkled t-shirt, Cole looked like he hadn't shaved or slept in days. As he slid a backpack off his shoulder, his expression was pensive. Solemn. "Take a seat."

Not good. Not fucking good at all. She'd been missing for eleven years. Was she enslaved all this time? Beaten? Raped?

He shut the door on those thoughts and gathered his composure to make introductions. "This is Liv and—"

"I know who they are." Cole gave the empty side of the couch a pointed look. "Sit down, Tate."

Dread held him in place until Kate gripped his hand and pulled him down beside her, holding tight to his fingers. Josh settled in the side chair with Liv on his lap.

"She's in Caracas." Cole sat on the other side of Tate, removed a laptop from his backpack, and woke the screen.

"Venezuela." Tate released a breath. "That isn't that far away."

Cole narrowed his eyes at him.

"What?" He straightened. "It could be worse, right? At least she's not chained in a dog kennel on the other side of the world." At Cole's silence, Tate set his jaw. "Tell me she's not in a dog kennel."

"She's not."

Returning to the laptop, Cole opened a photo of a dingy alley with overflowing dumpsters, laundry on clothes lines, and bars on the windows. Sagging balconies hung from the buildings, and graffiti covered the brick walls.

"I shot this from the second-floor apartment I rented." He pointed to a battered red door among a dozen others in the picture. "She lives in that one. Alone. In the largest slum in South America." He glanced at Tate. "In the most dangerous city on the planet."

"Why?" Tate had so many qualifiers for that question, he didn't know where to start.

Why was she alone? Why did she live there? Why didn't she come home? Why hadn't his other investigators been able to find her? Every cell in his body buzzed with urgency to go to her, to get her the fuck out of that hellhole.

"Why is it the most dangerous city?" Josh asked. "Drugs? Cartel?"

"It's the most weaponized city with the highest homicide rate. A gun for every two people, and a murder every twenty-one minutes. Street gangs and crime lords are in charge. There's political corruption and drug trafficking, but those aren't the only problems."

"It's the kidnap capital of the world," Tate said quietly, recalling a headline he'd read somewhere.

"That's right." Cole flipped to a new image — another view of the slum with a huge iron gate dominating one side of the road, surrounded by armed guards in street clothes. "This compound is the main hideout for Tiago Badell, the man Lucia works for."

"Works for?" His head pounded as every assumption he'd made about her over the years unraveled. *Armed guards. Iron gate. Main hideout.* "Who the fuck is Tiago Badell?"

"One of the wealthiest crime lords in Venezuela." Cole met his eyes. "His specialty is kidnapping."

CHAPTER 3

A chill crept over Tate's scalp. Aside from Cole, every person in the room had endured their own personal hell at the hands of a kidnapper. As unease vibrated between his friends, he wanted to shelter them from it.

He turned to Liv. "I can take this conversation elsewhere."

"How does it work?" She asked Cole, ignoring Tate's concern. "Are they trafficking humans?"

"No. Badell leads a gang that targets tourists, missionaries, Venezuelan middle class, anyone who is too ignorant to avoid Kidnap Alley and not wealthy enough to travel in armored vehicles. He grabs people off the street and gives their families three days to cough up the ransom. If payment isn't received, the victim is murdered."

Lucia was part of this? It didn't make sense. How could she go from being abducted and sold into slavery to working for a man like Tiago Badell?

He was certain he wouldn't like the answer, but he asked anyway. "What does she do for him?"

"You won't believe me unless I show you." Cole clicked on a video file and hovered the mouse over the play button. After a moment of hesitation, he leaned around Tate to speak to Kate. "It's graphic."

Tate twisted at the waist to see her face. She'd watched Josh kill her buyer and had spent weeks, bloody and broken, beneath a whip. She didn't look it, but the girl was tough as hell.

She wrapped a tiny hand around Tate's bicep, shoulders squared. "I can handle it."

Cole pushed play.

On the screen, a naked man lay on his back on a concrete floor. Eyes swollen, nose busted, and chest heaving, he jerked against the ropes that restrained him. He was skinny, pale, and *hard*, his engorged dick pointing heavenward, and he didn't look happy about it.

Whoever held the camera handed it off to someone else, changing the angle to show at least two other men in the windowless room. The footage stayed below the necks, capturing dust on black boots and blood stains on pants. Assault rifles hung across their torsos, their tattooed fingers resting on the trigger guards.

"Who are they?" Tate asked.

"Badell's men. And that"—Cole pointed at the screen as a woman walked into view—"is Lucia."

The camera lowered, keeping her head out of the frame. A tight miniskirt exposed the curves of her perfect figure, and a black bra bared her flat stomach. Her hair was either pulled up or cut short, putting all that satiny, bronze skin on display. Her shoulders, arms, chest...every inch of her was toned, smooth, flawless.

No, not flawless. He leaned closer to the image. "Is that—?"

"A scar." Cole paused the video and zoomed in on her abdomen. "See how it zigzags like that?" He traced it on the screen, following the jagged white line from the bottom of her breastbone to her hip. "Blunt force trauma. It's pretty faded. Old."

"Eleven years old?" He inhaled sharply. "Is it from the crash in Peru?"

"Yes. She barely survived. Badell's men pulled her out, and his personal doctors saved her. I know there were multiple surgeries because I've heard Badell discuss it with her. But the details are unknown. It's strange, because his doctors keep meticulous medical records on every person they touch, yet there's no record of her."

Goosebumps blanketed Tate's arms. "Why did his men save her?"

"From what I've gathered, they happened to be in the area and pillaged the crash site for survivors. Easy targets for ransom. They found her and patched her up just enough to keep her alive, only to discover—"

"She has no living family." Tate's chest tightened. "No one to pay his ransom and compensate him for his trouble." His pulse sped up as everything clicked into place. "Instead of killing her, Badell made her work for him? Since he saved her life, does he think she owes him?"

"It's more complicated than that." Cole returned to the laptop. "Watch the video."

When he un-paused it, Lucia strolled across the screen and straddled the naked man's torso, facing his feet. The camera operator kept her face out of view, honing in on her hands as she wrapped them around the swollen erection.

A pained wailing sound came from the man, his body bucking beneath her. "No, please. I'm married. I don't want this."

She preceded to stroke him. No hesitation. No apparent prodding or force by the others in the room. It was as if she was orchestrating it.

The video panned to a black painted wall, where words had been scratched with chalk.

200,000 bolivars
72 hours
No money, he dies

"Ransom," Tate breathed, his stomach filled with lead. "This is a kidnapping."

Cole nodded. "The video was sent to the victim's wife with a bank account linked to it."

Tate was about to ask why Lucia was molesting the poor guy, but the camera angle returned to her. She stood over the man now, a pistol in her hand, aimed at his legs.

"No! No!" His high-pitched shouting crackled the speaker. "We'll pay. Please—"

She squeezed the trigger, and his knee exploded in a splatter of red. The camera jostled, lowering the view to focus on the pooling blood and gruesome injury.

No faces. No voices. Just the man's yowling screams. Then the video cut off.

"Christ." Tate leaned back, sick to his stomach.

His friends didn't move, their faces pale as they stared at the black screen.

"His wife wasn't able to collect the money in time," Cole said. "His body was dumped in an alley a mile away from the compound."

"Did Lucia kill him?" Liv closed a hand around Josh's bouncing knee, stilling him.

"No. She doesn't do the kidnapping or the

murdering. Her job is to inflict physical and emotional pain. Torture. Sometimes she rapes them. Sometimes she causes non-fatal injuries, like this." He gestured at the screen. "When the victim is female, Lucia operates the camera while one of the men puts on the grisly show."

"How did you get the footage?" Tate asked, his throat dry.

"I dropped a hack on her burner phone and—"

"Don't you have to have physical access to the device to do that?"

"Juice jacking." Cole's eyes lit up. "I tampered with her charging port, turned it into a data connection. When she charged her phone, I copied everything she had on it, including this video."

"Hang on." His neck went taut. "You were in her apartment? Why didn't you just take her?"

"Yes, I accessed her apartment." Cole scowled at him. "I didn't *just take her*, because I'm not in the business of kidnapping."

"It's not kidnapping if—"

"She's not being held against her will, Tate. She makes no attempt to flee, and there are plenty of opportunities. She knows the city, knows how to evade the gangs. In eleven years, she would've succeeded in an escape."

"Or died trying." He knew that denying the truth didn't make the facts go away, but maybe Cole had missed something. Something glaringly important. "The woman in the video… You're certain that's Lucia? There were dozens of women in that crash in Peru. What if you followed the wrong trail?"

Cole opened another photo on the laptop—a wide shot of a woman walking along an urban road in daylight. He maximized the view, bringing her face into beautiful clarity. Her hair hung like a shiny black curtain to her shoulders, emphasizing her delicate, ethereal features.

At first glance, she looked like Camila with short straight hair. Her huge brown eyes, warm complexion, stubborn chin—every familiar detail made his chest ache for the sister he'd spent the last six years with.

The woman in the photo had a narrower face and slimmer build. Too slim. Her bones jutted sharply, pressing against her skin. The smile he'd memorized from Lucia's childhood photos was missing, yet her beauty remained. A dangerous kind of beauty, like if he got too close, he would become hypnotized. Infatuated. Totally fucked.

"Still have doubts?" Cole asked.

"That's Lucia." Tate blinked, forcing himself to look away. "But the anonymous woman in the video—"

"Has the same scar." Cole re-centered the image, moving the focus from Lucia's face to the faded wound beneath the cropped shirt.

Identical scar. Same toned stomach and body shape. The evidence was there, undeniable. Lucia had aimed that gun and shot an innocent without flinching.

Ice filled his veins. He wasn't naive, and as much as he hated it, he could accept the fact she was a coldblooded criminal. The question was, what the fuck would he do about it?

"Can you still copy her phone?" he asked. "Wait. Do you have the number? I could call her."

What would he say to her? *Hey, you don't know me, but Camila escaped her kidnapper. She's alive and misses you. How about you come home, and we'll pretend you never tortured innocent people?*

"The phone was destroyed the day after the video was taken," Cole said. "As of yesterday, she still hadn't replaced it.

"The man she works for, this Badell guy... He must be blackmailing her. I mean, she's not working for money if she lives in a slum."

"They all live in the slum, outside of the law. It's their kingdom, where they make their own rules. She eats dinner with Badell every night. Goes in and out of his compound freely. She *is* watched and never leaves the city. I've seen his guards trailing her, but he puts guards on all his high-ranked officials."

She's a high-ranked official? For a street gang? Camila would be heartbroken if she knew this.

"What about the police?" Tate rose from the couch and paced through the room. "We could turn over the video and any evidence you have against him and shut down his entire operation."

"You're not getting it." Cole propped his elbows on his knees, pulling in a deep breath. "This is Caracas. The police are poorly trained, under-equipped, and aren't paid shit. They tip off the gangs when something isn't right, and the crime lords thank them for that service by giving them a cut of the profits."

Of fucking course. He dropped his head back and heaved a frustrated breath to the ceiling. He needed answers, and the only way he'd get them was to pay Lucia Dias a visit.

"Tate." Liv's melodic voice wove around him as she stood from Josh's lap and approached. "You need to call Camila."

"And say what? She breathes and bleeds a

passionate crusade against people like Tiago Badell. If she saw that video of her sister, it would hurt her irreparably. She thinks Lucia is dead and... Fuck, Liv, that's better than the truth, don't you think? I can't tell her. Not until I talk to Lucia."

"If you go to Caracas," Cole said, "you'll be kidnapped and killed inside of a week. You're untrained and unprepared. At a minimum, you need someone with you, preferably a security guard. Someone to watch your back."

"I'm not a security guard, but I'm good with a gun." Liv touched Tate's jaw, drawing his gaze to hers. "I'll go with you."

"The hell you will!" Josh leapt from the chair, eyes blazing.

"Josh," she snapped. "I'll do whatever—"

"No. End of discussion."

Josh glared at her, and she glared right back. Tension shivered between them, a silent battle of wills. Tate was certain Liv would win, but it wasn't up to her.

"Josh is right," he said. "You're not going. No—" He held up a hand when she tried to interrupt. "I'm not budging on this."

She sniffed, turned on her heel, and strode down the hallway, shutting the bedroom door behind her.

"Shit, man." Tate scrubbed a hand through his hair. "I didn't mean to cause problems. I'm sorry."

"Don't be. I'll enjoy the punishment later tonight." Josh's eyes gleamed, his smile twitching with mischief. Then he sobered, nodding at Cole. "Why can't he do it? He knows where Lucia lives and seems to have the *training* to move around the city without getting killed."

"Yeah, well..." Tate blew out a breath. "I can't

afford him."

"Even if I were to help you pro bono — which I won't." Cole gave him a hard look. "I don't extract people unless they're willing."

"I just want to talk to her." Tate studied him for a moment, an idea forming. "If I approached her, would she shoot me on the spot?"

"Her guards would." Cole shook his head. "You can't just walk in there, Tate. The gangs decide who enters the neighborhood."

"But you can. You rented an apartment across the street from hers. How'd you do it?"

"I know which palms to grease."

"Then get me in. I'll pay you to set me up in that apartment and tell me everything you know about Tiago Badell. I'll do the rest. Just name the price."

"It's a suicide mission. The price is your life."

"Train me." Tate paced through the room, fueled with determination. "Teach me whatever I need to know to make contact with her." He paused in front of Cole, hands flexing at his sides. "You know my account balance. Take it all."

Cole considered him for a nerve-wracking minute before lowering his head in his hands and exhaling. "Okay."

Hope surged. "Okay?"

"You're a stubborn asshole." Cole lifted his eyes. "If I don't help you, you'll go anyway, and I'll have your moronic death weighing on my conscience."

"Good man." Tate clapped him on the back and lowered onto the couch beside him. "For the record, I think she picked the wrong guy." He motioned toward the tattoo on Cole's arm.

Cole looked down, his eyes stark and unblinking as he traced the inked silhouette of the woman, his finger gliding with reverence and longing. He seemed to forget himself in that private moment, his gaze turning inward and the hard lines of his jaw softening.

Then, like a flip of a switch, he curled his hand into a fist and snapped his spine straight. "Do you think this thing with Lucia will give you what you need to finish *your* tattoo?"

Startled, Tate glanced at his own ink. How did Cole know it wasn't finished?

Roses of various sizes and blooms sleeved his arm in shades of black and gray. His mother's name had been Rose, but each flower on his skin represented the women who had helped raise him at The Velvet Den. They might've been whores, but they were also his friends. His only family.

The cluster of roses stretched above his elbow and faded away. The artwork was supposed to blur into another image across his bicep — the profile of a woman. He always imagined Camila's face would complete the design, but she didn't belong to him.

As he stared at the blank space on his bicep, he knew Josh and Kate were watching him, waiting for him to answer Cole's question. *Will I have what I need to finish it? Will I have someone to call my own?* He wanted Camila, and that dream was unattainable.

"No. The tattoo is finished."

Cole rubbed the stubble on his cheek, studying Tate with those perceptive eyes. Then he looked back at the laptop and sighed. "The apartment in Caracas is paid through the end of the month. I'll extend the lease for another month, get you into the neighborhood, train you on basic self-defense, and walk you through Lucia's patterns. After that, you're on your own."

"Thank you."

"I don't like this." Josh lowered into the chair, perching on the edge. "Can you hire a security guard to go with you?"

"Maybe." Tate didn't know how much money he'd have left after he paid Cole for the help, but he'd figure it out. He turned to Cole. "Do you have more photos of her?"

"Hundreds."

For the next hour, Tate scoured the images on Cole's laptop, memorizing every expression, gesture, and article of clothing that belonged to Lucia Dias. Cole showed him blueprints of Badell's compound, but other than the windowless concrete room in the video, there were no pictures of the interior. Cole hadn't tried to breach the iron gates because that level of intel hadn't been included in the finder fee.

As they ironed out an action plan, they decided to leave in a week. That would give Cole time to train Tate on basic weaponry and self-defense.

Liv eventually emerged from the bedroom, and about five minutes later, someone knocked on the door.

Tate pulled his attention from the laptop as Josh greeted whoever was on the porch.

"Hey." Confusion threaded through Josh's voice. "I didn't expect you guys tonight."

"I called him." Liv approached the door, opening it wider to reveal Van Quiso and his wife, Amber.

Kate, who had her nose in her phone for the last hour, shot from the couch. Shoulders hunching, she fumbled with her purse on the coffee table. "I need to..."

She made a beeline to the door. "I'm gonna go."

"Kate." Josh moved to chase her.

"Let her go." Tate cast a glare at Van. "She needs time."

"She's had four years." With a grip on Amber's hand, Van approached the couch with a casual gait, his gaze clapping onto Tate. "I don't think time is what she needs."

Probably not, but Van's dark baleful presence wasn't a cure for any of them.

Tate sent off a text to his roommates, letting them know Kate left Liv's house. They would find her if she didn't head home.

Cole stood from the couch and extended a hand to Van. "It's good to finally meet you in person."

"Same." Van shook his hand and introduced his wife.

Tate could guess why Liv called Van here, but before he asked, he had another question.

"How do you know each other?" He gestured between Van and Cole.

"Traquero." Van pulled a toothpick from his pocket and cut his eyes at Liv and Josh.

"What did you say?" Josh whispered, the blood draining from his face.

Traquero? The name was familiar, but Tate couldn't place it. "Is that...?"

"The misogynist prick who was supposed to buy Josh." Liv crossed the room, pausing in front of Van.

Right on her heels, Josh looped an arm around her waist, holding her against him as he spoke to Van. "Cole helped you find Traquero?"

With a nod, Van moved to the chair and settled

Amber on his thigh. The room fell still as everyone focused on the cozy position of the odd couple.

Amber curled against Van's chest, arms around his neck, clinging to him compulsively. It was one of her many tics that became acutely transparent whenever she left the safety of their house. All toned limbs and long brown hair, she had once been a renowned beauty pageant queen and fitness model. Something tragic had happened to her, ending her career and forcing her into isolation. Severe isolation. She didn't leave her house for years. Van said she was recovering from agoraphobia and OCD, but the rapid heave of her breaths and the way her fingers dug into Van's neck suggested she was still as nutty as ever.

Contrarily, Van reclined in the chair with a toothpick rolling between his lips. The six-inch scar on his cheek radiated intimidation and ice-cold confidence, as if to say, *Stare all you want. I'm a mean son of a bitch, and I won't apologize for it.*

Mean was an understatement, but since his days of human trafficking, he'd taken steps to make amends, like slaughtering the man who sodomized Liv.

Traquero.

Heavy silence clotted the room. No doubt everyone was thinking about that atrocious meeting when Josh's buyer raped Liv while Josh was forced to watch. When Van found out, he went ballistic and dismantled the whole sex slave operation. Shortly after, Traquero was murdered. *Passionately.* They all knew Van was responsible for that gruesome death. They just didn't know he'd hired Cole Hartman to hunt down the slave buyer. Until now.

"I always wondered how you found Traquero,"

Liv said quietly and turned her attention to Cole. "I guess I owe you my gratitude."

"I didn't kill him," Cole said. "I'm not in the business of murdering—"

"Or kidnapping. We know." Tate caught Liv's steady gaze. "Why did you call Van here?"

"You're going to the kidnap capital of the world. Who better to take as backup than—"

"The man who kidnapped me?" *The man who chained me in an attic and raped me for ten weeks?* He released a humorless laugh. "Are you serious?"

"He's not that man anymore." Amber straightened on Van's lap, her eyes alight with fire. "I know he hurt you, all of you, but he's driving himself into the grave to make it up to you!"

"Amber." Van rubbed his hands along her upper arms, the affection at odds with the chill in his voice. "Calm down."

"No, I won't calm down." She climbed off his lap and stepped into Tate's space, glaring up at him. "When Liv called tonight and told him what you're planning, he didn't hesitate." She pivoted and strode through the room, stopping to straighten a frame on the wall. "He's here, willing to risk his life to help you." She whipped around and thrust at finger at Tate. "So don't you dare judge him."

This, coming from the agoraphobic woman Van had abducted and raped because hey, she was a shiny new toy to play with. Yet she was still with him four years later. Married him, even.

A shudder rippled through her, and she clutched her hand, cracking her knuckles. *Pop-pop-pop-pop.* Another tic.

Van reached for her, but she sidestepped him and scanned the room wildly until her attention locked on the kitchen doorway. "Did you know there are dishes in the sink? Can I...?"

"Sure." Josh said. "Have at it."

When Amber left the room to feed her OCD, Liv arched a brow at Van, her voice low. "Did she stop going to therapy?"

"*I* am her therapy." Van bit down on the toothpick, flashing her a grin.

"That makes me feel so much better," she said dryly.

Cole remained quiet as his gaze pinged between Van and Liv. Did he know about the history they shared? That they had a daughter together? Livana technically lived with her adopted mother, but she spent most of her time either in this house or at Van and Amber's two-hundred-acre property. Because of this shared custody, Van and Liv had grown into an amicable, trusting partnership.

Tate shifted toward Van, hands resting on his hips. "Are you actually considering this? Do you understand the stakes?"

"Yes."

"What about Amber? You're willing to leave your wife for weeks, if not months?"

A dish clanked in the kitchen, and Amber poked her head through the doorway. "I'm not a helpless ninny, Tate!"

Van cracked a smile, straining the scar on his cheek. "Come here, baby."

"One minute." She slipped back into the kitchen, and the sound of running water drifted from the sink.

Tate moved to the couch and took the seat closest to Van, keeping his voice soft. "What happens to Amber and your daughter if you're captured or killed?"

"Liv explained the risks." Van sat back, legs sprawled wide, taking up too much space. "I'm not going to Caracas to die, Tate."

Bullheaded dumbass. He pinched the bridge of his nose, warring with the emotions that always accompanied interactions with Van Quiso. Tate forgave his former captor years ago, but had he ever admitted that aloud? Part of him wanted to hang onto the grudge, because what kind of man would he be if he made allowances for the monster who raped him?

The other part of him recognized this as what it was. An opportunity to wipe the slate clean. He wouldn't forget those weeks in Van's attic. He couldn't. But he could hold out an olive branch to the man.

"I forgive you." Tate lowered his hand and met Van's eyes. "For all of it. I mean it. You. Are. Forgiven. So take your wife home and sleep easier knowing one less person in the world wants to castrate you."

"Yeah? Well, here's the thing." Van plucked the toothpick from his mouth and pointed it at him. "I'm not doing this for forgiveness or preservation or whatever rose-colored reason you concocted in your head. I'm doing it because it's the right thing to do, and I have the *experience* to impact how this turns out." He turned his silver-bladed eyes to Cole. "When do we leave?"

CHAPTER 4

Deafening screams of agony chased Lucia out of the basement, sharpening the cramps that plagued her insides. She yanked off the balaclava face mask and dropped it in the hall.

Though she'd done nothing more than operate the camera this morning, she stayed long after the recording ended, ensuring she was the last one to leave the chamber. Tiago's stooges enjoyed forcing themselves on the female captives, but it was Lucia's ass on the line if the victim was too broken or lifeless to exchange for ransom.

The *click-click* of her heels along the spiral stone stairwell conjured power and confidence. She tried hard to exude that perception, even when she was alone, but she couldn't stop herself from gripping the handrail and using its support for the upward climb.

Fuck, it hurts.

It always started with a rush of saliva over her tongue. Nausea and excruciating stomach pain came next. Then the loss of coordination and the tingling sensation of impending paralysis, like now.

Her ankle twisted, and she righted it, dragging

herself around the final bend on the stairs. The doorway to the main floor came into view, and standing just beyond it was Tiago.

She breathed a sigh of relief.

His authoritative stance, hard lines of his lean body, unflinching intensity of his gaze—all of it embodied strength. Strength she so badly needed to scale those last few steps.

Her pulse weakened, and her legs wobbled as she struggled to close the distance. Tiago didn't move, didn't stretch out a hand to help her. He simply watched her, his disarmingly handsome features void of emotion.

When she finally reached him, she handed over the burner phone with the video footage from this morning. He turned, passing it off to one of his lackeys.

The video would be sent to the victim's father, who would watch a faceless man rape and kick his daughter repeatedly with steel-toed boots. The woman was an American college student, whose vacation was cut short when she stumbled into the wrong alley. If her father didn't pay the demand, her pretty face would be blown away by a shotgun.

"You look pale." Tiago brushed the backs of his fingers across Lucia's cheek with aching tenderness.

If he didn't have an armed guard standing beside him, she would've drawn one of the Berettas from her waistband and shot him in the face.

"I feel worse than usual today."

"I thought you might." He offered her a bent elbow and stroked the hand she curled around the crook of his arm. "I'll take care of you. I always do, don't I?"

"Yes." She canted against him as her abdomen clenched through a wave of pain. "Thank you."

He wrapped an arm around her waist and led her through the dank halls toward his bedroom. Two armed guards flanked them. Others loitered in the doorways, lounge areas, and dining hall. All men.

Tiago kept women in the compound to entertain his gang, but the girls weren't free to wander. Only she had that luxury. Because he knew she wouldn't flee.

She leaned against his side and did her best to match his long-legged gait. Raised by Colombian parents, she could speak Spanish, but Tiago always reverted to English with her. He did so now as he told her about the new recruitments he hired, the shipment of high-velocity weapons he acquired — *stole* — and the recent intel he gathered. He knew most of the local private bodyguards, and when they felt they were underpaid, they gave him the information needed to kidnap their employers. In return, they received a cut of the ransom.

She stopped flinching at these conversations years ago. Violence and corruption was the way of life here. Embracing it was a means of survival.

Thankfully, her hard-earned position in his gang allowed her to live outside of the compound. Tiago gave her an apartment within walking distance. A room with four mildewed walls and intermittent electricity and running water. She couldn't afford to furnish it or make it pretty, but it was a thousand times better than this crumbling dump.

Tiago's hideout had once been a popular hotel in Caracas. Like the rest of the city, it was abandoned during the country's economic crisis, and the squatters moved in. She didn't know when Tiago had chased them out and made it his primary residence, didn't know the locations of his other homes, but over the past eleven years, this was where he spent most of his time. And he'd done nothing to fix it up.

It smelled like smoke and death. Bullet holes riddled the concrete walls. Sheet metal covered every window. It was dark. So fucking dark and musty and packed with rotten, sweaty men. She didn't trust any of them, and she didn't think Tiago trusted them, either.

"With the new recruits," she said as they rounded a turn in the corridor, "how many men do you have now?"

"Why do you ask?" He stared straight ahead, his expression empty, except for the twitch in his clean-shaved cheek.

Shit. She'd angered him. The man was suspicious of everyone and everything. Though he seemed to confide in her the most, she often wondered if he kept her the closest because he trusted her the least.

As for the size of his gang, it was a number he never confirmed. She estimated it exceeded two-hundred men, which was larger than the local police force. He was physically unstoppable. Not that anyone ever tried. As King of the City, he had lackeys and informants positioned in every nook and alley, including in the military and police.

They strolled down a long hall. Or rather, *he* strolled. She was lucky to line up one heeled shoe in front of the other without face-planting. By the time they reached his bedroom door, a sheen of perspiration blanketed her skin. Agony coiled her guts, and bile rose in her chest.

Two more guards waited on either side of the steel door. The old-fashioned dead bolt required an old-fashioned key, one that Tiago kept on his person at all times.

He didn't move to unlock the door. She knew the drill. Clothes first.

The heels came off. Then she removed the handguns from her waistband, shimmied out of the jeans, the shirt, and unclasped the bra, setting everything on the wooden bench that existed only for this purpose. For *her*. As far as she knew, she was the only visitor he allowed in his room.

Clad in nothing but black panties, she rose to her full height, shoulders back, and waited for their inspection.

The two guards who had escorted them here remained at the entrance of the hall. The other two swept clinical hands over her butt and groin, digging fingers against the satin between her cheeks in search for weapons. She held still, muscles loose, and breathed.

Tiago watched with detachment until they finished. Then he stepped forward and combed his fingers through her hair, massaging her scalp. It wasn't out of affection. He was searching for weapons.

Knowing that didn't thwart a deep ache from swelling inside her. An ache for companionship. Desire. Love.

Oh, the hopeless dreams of a silly girl. She didn't know that girl anymore, but sometimes she entertained thoughts of her, imagined what life would be like if she hadn't been abducted from her beloved home in the citrus grove.

Satisfied with his search, Tiago unlocked the bedroom door, guided her inside, and bolted them in.

His living space was as spartan and crude as the rest of the compound. Deteriorated sheetrock peeled away from old stone walls. A small unmade bed was shoved into the corner. Two mismatched chairs sat in front of a fireplace filled with ash and cobwebs. A bare bulb glowed in the ceiling — the room's only source of light.

It was a sad space. Humble. But Tiago Badell's presence made it feel enigmatic, ominous, cloaked in secrets. He was one of the wealthiest men in the country, yet here he slept on a tiny old mattress in an abandoned hotel. Alone.

She stood near the chairs, as expected, while he opened a medium-size safe in the closet. The depth of the alcove prevented her from seeing the combination lock. She'd followed him to that side of the room once, hoping for a peek at the safe. But the punishment for doing so had been so grave she never did it again.

"Have you vomited this morning?" He removed her precious lifeline from the safe and relocked it.

"No. Just nauseous." She remained as immobile as possible beside the chair, refusing to give him any reason to send her away.

"Coughing blood?" Rolling up his sleeves, he approached her slowly, like a lazy lion with all the power and strength in the world.

"No blood since last time." Her attention fixated on the syringe cradled in his fingers. *Please hurry.*

He took his time walking toward her, knowing full well he held her life in his hands.

When he finally lowered in the chair and patted his thigh, she didn't hesitate to sit on his lap and recline back against his hard chest.

Her leg moved on its own, hooking over the armrest and bringing her thigh within his reach. A tremble shook through her and her hands flexed, joints cracking and tendons straining — the anticipation all-consuming.

He cleaned the injection area with the supplies on the side table and plunged the needle into the middle of her thigh. It was just a prick, nothing compared to the aches that endlessly tormented her.

"Shhh." He caressed her quivering abs, tracing the serrated scar from her breastbone to her hip. "It'll feel better soon."

"Thank you." She relaxed against him and waited for the relief to come.

It would take fifteen, maybe twenty minutes to saturate her system. In the meantime, he would hold her in this position, as he did every morning, and use his hands to fuck with her head.

When he set the syringe aside, he trailed fingertips around her breasts, ribs, hips, and the crotch of her panties.

"You're beautiful, Lucia." He found the seam of her pussy and slid his touch along the slit, up and down, keeping that small scrap of satin between his finger and her flesh. "You love to fuck, even though you pretend otherwise."

For as long as she could remember, she'd been a highly-sexual person. She gave her virginity to a Texan boy when she was fifteen and explored her sexuality with countless guys in high-school.

Then she was abducted, and all her choices were taken from her.

With her back against his chest and his hands roaming her body with distracting affection, it was easy to forget how cruel he was. When they were alone, he coddled her, cared for her, and whispered seductive compliments in her ear. But when they left the privacy of his room, his ruthlessness took center stage.

A numbing sensation trickled through her abdomen, and she inhaled deeply, relishing the initial effects of the injection. "Why do you make me fuck other men?"

His cock swelled against her backside, and he nuzzled his nose in her neck, his breaths growing heavier, faster. "It pleases me."

So vague. So damn mysterious. She knew nothing of his background or the thoughts that churned his mind. He had no family to speak of. No close friends. No wife or mistress. Yet the artwork that covered his arms meant something. It told a story. His story.

She lifted a hand and stroked the raised welts on his wrist. Scarification, he called it. She assumed he'd cut the images into his skin himself, only because she'd seen him do it to others. It was his preferred method of torture and the most barbaric thing she'd ever witnessed.

Suppressing a shudder, she traced the scarred outlines of animals and landscapes that marred his forearm. "Is this tribal-inspired?"

"You must be feeling better." Lifting her off his lap, he set her on her feet. "Leave."

A bout of dizziness made her sway, but the cramps in her stomach had faded to a dull ache.

With the flick of a finger at the door, he propped a foot on his knee and stared at the unused fireplace.

She lingered for a moment, willing him to look at her, to reveal something of himself. A twitch. A word. An emotion. Anything that might clue her in on what he was thinking. If he was angry, she wanted him to lash out, hit her if he had to. Then she would know.

Knowing was better than walking out of his room, wondering if a gun was trained on her back. Because he had no moral code. When he killed, his victims rarely saw him coming.

As she stepped toward the door, the space between her shoulders blades tingled and chilled. She didn't breathe until she entered the hall, grabbed her guns and clothes, and heard him turn the lock behind her.

CHAPTER 5

Tate leaned against the window of the second-floor apartment Cole had leased, growing more impatient by the second.

Come on, Lucia. Where are you?

The rustling of Cole's papers sounded behind him, followed by the clink of Van's tequila against the coffee table.

"Do you miss your wife yet?" Tate stared down at the grungy alley through a pair of high-powered binoculars.

"I missed her the instant I left the driveway," Van said from the couch.

They'd only been in Caracas for three hours, and in that time, Tate had watched a man drag a woman out of the apartment next door to Lucia's, punch her in the face, and stroll away. She called the police, and the five uniformed officers who showed up two hours later decided to rob her instead of helping her. They left with their arms loaded with shit, including a TV, a laptop, and her tiny dog. She'd crumpled on the sidewalk as they drove away and was still sitting there, head down, smoking a cigarette.

In the distance, the report of gunfire sounded. One shot. Then three more in rapid succession.

It wasn't the first time he'd heard that unnerving noise since he'd been here. He was already getting used to it.

"You should've stayed home." He glanced back at Van, who stared blankly at his empty glass.

"I have an idea." Van lifted his eyes, his smile clenched with straight white teeth. "Shut the fuck up."

"I didn't ask you to come." Tate sure as shit didn't want him here.

Forgiveness was one thing. Trusting Van to watch his back was a level of camaraderie they hadn't reached.

Beside Van, Cole bent over a spread of maps and circled all the danger zones. There were a lot of fucking circles.

They'd left their IDs and personal phones in a locker at the airport. Didn't bring photos of family members. No wedding ring on Van's finger. No calling home to check in on loved ones. No connection whatsoever to their lives in Texas. These were Cole's rules. *In the event one of them was kidnapped.*

Cole would only stay with them for a week. If something happened to Tate or Van after that, they were to give the kidnappers Cole's number. He promised to handle any potential ransoms as painlessly as possible.

"Technically, every alley in Caracas is a kidnap alley. But this is *the* Kidnap Alley." Cole circled another area on the map and looked up at Tate. "Give the window a rest and come here."

"But—"

"She eats dinner with Badell every night and isn't due back for another twenty minutes."

With reluctance, Tate left his vigilance and crouched beside him.

"See how winding this road is?" Cole traced a snaking street on the map. "It's a prime target for kidnappers. Lots of places for them to hide and trap motorists. And its proximity to the main motorway makes an easy escape." He cast Tate a flinty glare. "Stay the fuck away from this road."

"Got it."

"I'm going to make this clearer, just in case you don't." He pulled a document out of his backpack and set it on the coffee table.

The letter header was stamped with a United States seal, and beneath it was a long list of first and last names. At least a hundred names. Maybe more.

"There's a fuckton of competition in the Venezuelan kidnapping business. A lot of cops do it, too." Cole tapped the paper. "These are just the kidnappers the U.S. government watches."

A quick glance confirmed Tiago Badell was at the top of the list.

"Am I on any of those government watch lists?" Van arched a brow.

"I wouldn't know." Cole returned the document to his backpack.

"Bullshit." Digging in his pocket, Van removed a toothpick and popped it between his teeth. "I looked you up. Know what I found? Nothing. Nada. You might be able to cover your electronic tracks, but no one is that good. Unless you work for an entity like the United States. So what is it? FBI? CIA? Some kind of secret government agency?"

Tate wanted to know those answers, too, but it was

none of their business. "Van, don't be a dick."

"I work for myself." Cole straightened, meeting the challenge in Van's eyes.

"Guys in your line of work can't be married or committed. Gives your enemies a target. Makes you weak." Van lowered his gaze to the tattoo on Cole's arm. "Is that why you lost the girl?"

"You don't have to answer that." Tate shot Van a warning look.

Cole slowly rose from the couch and paced to the window. With his back to the room, he gripped the window ledge and said quietly, "I gave up that job for the girl."

And he lost her anyway. Tate felt bad for the guy and struggled for something to say to break up the thick silence. "I'm sorry, man."

"I'm not." Cole turned and rested his fingers in his front pockets. "She's happy. Happier than I've ever seen her. There isn't a single part of me that regrets that." He shrugged. "It's all I ever wanted for her."

Taking the high road. Good for him. But what about *his* happiness?

Tate wasn't in a position to preach. He'd walked into the innards of kidnapping hell to talk to a woman he'd never met. Why? Because he wanted to repay Camila for rescuing him? Wanted her to look at him the way she looked at Matias? Wanted to do something for her that Matias was unable to do? Yep. All those things. Fucked up or not, his ego demanded it.

"I thought I loved Liv."

The monotone declaration swung Tate's head in Van's direction, his eyebrows lifting in stunned silence. Van's obsession with Liv hadn't exactly been a secret, but it was in the past. No one discussed it. Especially not Van.

"Don't look at me like that." Van stretched his arms along the back of the couch, smiling at Tate. "You were there."

"Yeah, I had a front row seat to that madness. Thanks for the reminder."

Sitting on the floor, Tate reclined against the wall and lit a cigarette. During his captivity, the dynamic between Van and Liv had been the mindfuck of all mindfucks. Van's temper was unpredictable, and more often than not, he'd unleashed it on Liv — hitting her without warning, fucking her despite her protests — while Tate watched from his chains.

He shuddered.

"I only brought it up to make a point." The toothpick jogged in Van's mouth, and his gaze turned inward. "The thing with Liv is I never put her before myself. Fuck her happiness. I wanted her, and that was that. Then I met Amber." He shook his head and laughed to himself. "Setting her free was the bravest thing I ever did."

Amber's agoraphobia had been unmanageable back then, and Van realized he wasn't helping. It shocked the hell out of everyone when he returned her to her isolated life.

Tate dropped the cigarette in an empty beer bottle. "But you got her back."

"At the time, I was certain I wouldn't. And here's my point. When I lost Amber, I had a goddamn eye-opening epiphany, like a lightning bolt to the chest. I fucking love that woman so much it redefines the meaning of happiness. It's not a matter of putting her happiness before mine. When she smiles, I feel a peace unlike anything I've felt in my life. And if letting her go is the only way for her to keep that smile, I would do it again in a heartbeat."

"Poetic." Cole stared at the floor, his mouth twisting in a sad grin. "I mean it. Because I feel the exact same way."

"I know why you're telling me this," Tate said, "and let me remind you Camila is with Matias. I let her go."

"No, you didn't." Van leaned forward with elbows braced on his spread knees. "She was never yours. When she moved to Colombia, you didn't have a choice in the matter."

Not exactly true. Tate could've told her how he felt, fought for her, made her choose. He certainly didn't have to go along with Matias' plan to reunite them.

Matias would crap a cartel brick if he knew Tate was on a meet-and-greet mission with the man who abducted Camila eleven years ago. If Matias had it his way, Van would be dead, because he didn't just grow up with Camila. He grew up with Lucia, too. Loved her like a sister. He wouldn't want Van anywhere near her.

"Why are we here?" Van sat back, eyes glinting like razors.

Tate didn't owe anyone an explanation, so he decided to throw Van's words back at him. "It's the right thing to do."

"Good answer." With a wolfish smile, Van turned to Cole. "So tell me, hot shot secret agent, what happens if we leave the neighborhood?"

"Don't call me that." Cole pushed off the window ledge and knelt beside the map, pointing at an intersection of streets. "We entered the neighborhood here. Remember the men who approached the taxi?"

Tate nodded. The armed thugs had shared words with Cole through the open window. Since Tate didn't speak Spanish, the short conversation had been abstruse. But when Cole slapped some bills in their palms, the gist was clear. Cole had paid an entrance fee.

"When I came here six weeks ago," Cole said, "I made a deal with the gang that patrols that corner. Had to work my way up to the boss to negotiate safe passage. Which means that as long as I pay a toll each time I enter, they won't throw a grenade in my car window. But that only works for me. The gang boss doesn't know you."

"So what you're saying is, if we leave the neighborhood..."

"You won't be able to return. And one more thing..." Cole scratched his stubbled cheek. "Matias Restrepo doesn't have any sway here. Badell has more resources, more men, more guns, more everything. I'm not saying not to call him if you need help. Just don't expect a fast and successful rescue. It would take him weeks to get his men into this neighborhood, and coming here would be at a huge risk to his cartel."

Fucking great. Not that Tate intended to call him, but it had lingered at the back of his mind like a security blanket.

Cole glanced at his watch. "Lucia should be home any minute."

They moved to the window, and Tate trained the binoculars on the entrance of the alley, his entire body wound tight with nerves.

He'd only seen her in photos. *And that vile video.* How would his first encounter with her go? What if there was nothing more to her story? No redeemable reason for her involvement with Badell?

No matter what happened, he would have to tell Camila when it was over. Christ, he wanted more than anything to be the bearer of *good* news.

Dusk began to move in, making the gloomy street all the more gloomier. The woman who was robbed earlier was still sitting on the curb, hugging her knees to her chest.

Five minutes later, a feminine silhouette emerged in the alley. He didn't need the binoculars to see her, but he used them anyway, dialing in on her face.

The pale illumination of the moon haloed her head, giving her glossy raven hair an earthshine effect. The graceful curve of her neck, thinly arched brows, deep smoky eyes, and cheekbones so sharp they could draw blood — it was like staring into the face of Queen Nefertiti, one of the hottest women who ever lived.

Fuck him, but she was compelling. A living work of art. It wasn't just her beauty that arrested him. It was the way she moved, as if cutting through water with finesse and purpose. Not a single motion wasted.

Her black pants and sleeveless top looked painted on, her lips full and parted as she breathed through each seductive stride. Then her chin lifted, and her gaze scanned the top floor apartments, pausing on the one he was in.

Breathless, he lowered the binoculars and stepped back.

"She can't see us," Cole said beside him.

Tate pressed a hand against the glass. During Cole's previous stay here, he'd installed one-way window film. Even with the interior lights on at night, it was supposed to make the apartment look dark and vacant.

Sure enough, her attention quickly moved on.

"Let me see those." Van grabbed the binoculars and trained them on Lucia. "Not bad. Objectively attractive, in a male model sort of way. Looks like she skipped a few too many meals. I prefer women with more meat on their bones."

"You're so full of shit." Tate snatched the binoculars. "Your wife weighs a hundred pounds soaking wet."

"Amber's a fucking knockout, and if you mention her again, I'll chloroform you while you sleep and hang you by an ankle from the ceiling with a thirteen-inch dildo shoved up your ass."

Tate stared at him and blinked.

"Too soon?" Van asked.

"Yeah, Van. *Fuck.*"

"You two are giving me a headache." Cole leaned a shoulder against the glass, staring down at Lucia. "We all know she's a solid ten. Eloquent yet cute. She's…"

"One of the billions of women who wouldn't touch you with a fifty-foot pole?" Van grinned.

"I was going to say…" Cole squinted at him and returned to the window. "She's beautiful in an innocent, unintentional way, and she knows how to use that to her advantage. Something to think about when you make contact."

Tate raised the binoculars as she breezed past the sobbing woman on the street. The woman leapt up and said a string of words while chasing Lucia to her apartment door.

As the woman continued to speak, her body

language grew frantic in her efforts to get Lucia's attention. Without looking at her or acknowledging her in anyway, Lucia unlocked her apartment and shut the door in the woman's face.

"Cold," Tate muttered.

"Listen to me." Cole stabbed a finger at the window. "Out there, every single person is your enemy. Remember that."

"I get it, but that lady was just—"

"Trust. No one."

Tate touched his brow to the glass and exhaled. *Fuck this place.* What on earth would compel Lucia to live here?

The distraught neighbor finally went inside her apartment, and a few seconds later, Lucia's door opened. She stepped out and locked up again.

"Where's she going?" Tate asked.

"I don't know. She never deviates from her patterns." Cole took the binoculars from Tate and watched her stride down the alley in the direction she'd just come. "She changed her shoes."

"You sure?"

"Yeah. She always carries two compact 9mm Berettas in her waistband and *always* wears the same black heels. She had the heels on a second ago."

Tate hadn't noticed those details. *Because he'd been too enamored with the rest of her.*

"She's wearing flat-soled boots." Cole handed the binoculars to him. "The guns are still at her back, wedged in her waistband."

As Tate validated that, Van said, "Wherever she's going, it's too far to walk in heels."

"We need to follow her." Tate glanced at the door,

calculating the logistics of tailing her.

The main entrance to their apartment building opened on a different street, a block over from Lucia's alley. It made coming and going without her detection easier, but circling the exterior of the huge complex to catch up with her would take a few minutes.

"We're not going anywhere." Cole paced away from the window, headed toward the open kitchen. "You can't see them from the window, but her guards are watching. They'll see *us* coming from a mile away."

Hard to argue. They didn't exactly blend in. At Cole's suggestion, they'd packed plain clothes—jeans and t-shirts—and hadn't shaved in over a week. But the whiskers didn't hide their Caucasian complexions and pale eyes. The three of them didn't just look American. They looked like Marines on an undercover mission.

Given the total absence of body fat on their muscled frames, Cole and Van clearly shared Tate's dedication to working out. If they strolled down the street together, the locals would notice.

But Cole had a plan for everything. A local woman would deliver groceries and necessities at a scheduled time every week. Vetted and paid handsomely, she would guard her job with the utmost discretion. In the meantime, they would be cooped up in the tiny one-bedroom apartment until Cole gave them the green light to venture out.

In the kitchen, he lifted a long duffel bag from the table. When they'd arrived at the apartment, the first thing Cole did was pull the bag from one of the tiles in the drop ceiling in the bedroom.

He set it on the coffee table and unzipped it, revealing an arsenal of firearms, knives, and high-tech gadgets. "I collected this stuff during my previous visit here."

Made sense. It wasn't like he could sneak an assault rifle into his carry-on.

"When we eventually go out there," Cole said, "you'll be fully armed and *armored*." He held up a black t-shirt from the bag. "This is bullet-resistant."

"What?" Tate reached out and touched what appeared to be high-quality cotton. "No way."

"I was shot in the chest wearing something similar." Cole lifted the hem of his shirt, baring flawless skin over washboard abs and sculpted pecs. "The bullet broke skin. Fractured ribs."

"No scar." Tate couldn't believe it.

"The bullet didn't enter my body." Cole pulled another shirt from the bag and tossed at Van.

"Badass." Van held it up to his chest. "Machine-washable?"

"Good luck finding a washing machine." Cole laughed and nodded at the view beyond the window, where laundry hung from sagging balconies from one end of the alley to the other.

Who cared about laundry? Those shirts, though... If they could really bounce bullets, they were worth their weight in gold.

No wonder Cole's fees were so outrageous. He didn't just know what he was doing. He had the gear to stay alive. Tate couldn't imagine what this arsenal cost on the black market or wherever he'd acquired it. And he'd left it all behind after his last trip?

"You have to build a new stockpile of weapons on every job?" Tate asked.

"Yeah." Cole motioned at the duffel bag. "This was

included in your finder fee. Now you're going to learn how to use it."

Over the next hour, Cole instructed Van and Tate on the nuances of each firearm and how to conceal the pieces beneath their clothing. They couldn't hit the streets looking like avatars in a first-person shooter game. Discretion was paramount.

During the instruction, rain began to pelt the glass. By the time Tate made his way to the window, a tropical downpour was fully underway. The deluge of water fell from broken spouts and overfilled dumpsters, rushing a river of sewage through the alley.

Where was Lucia? Surely, she wasn't walking the steep, winding streets in this storm? After eleven years in this shanty town, she was probably used to it. But he didn't like it. Every instinct begged him to go out there, hunt her down, and drag her back to the States.

Instead, he stayed at the window, watching, waiting, and finally, she appeared.

"She's back," he said, drawing Cole and Van to his side.

Despite the torrential rain, her steps were unhurried, measured, as she navigated streams of rainwater. Her clothes stuck to her thin sodden body, her hair clinging to her face, and in her arms…

"What is she carrying?" He gave the binoculars to Cole, who shook his head and handed them back.

She strode toward her apartment, but before she got there, she stopped and knocked on the door next to hers.

"That's the apartment that was robbed earlier," Van said.

The woman poked her head out. Then she swung

the door open and grabbed whatever Lucia was holding.

Amid the blur of motion, Tate spotted a furry head. "Holy shit, she has the dog. How did she—?"

"Badell owns this neighborhood," Cole said. "She must've tracked down the officers and demanded Badell's cut of the loot."

"She could've taken the laptop or demanded money, right?" His chest filled with hope. "But she took the dog. That's—"

"Don't read too much into it. The most corrupt explanation is usually the right one. Lucia knows what the woman values most, and now she's in Lucia's debt."

"Christ, you're jaded."

"I'm realistic." Cole paced to the couch and packed away the weapons. "Lucia will stay in her apartment for the rest of the night. At dawn, she heads back to the compound."

"Every morning?"

"Without fail," Cole said behind him.

Tate remained at the window as she left the woman without saying a word and vanished inside her own apartment.

What's going on in your head, Lucia? Why are you here?

"You know why I abducted Camila." Van stepped beside him and stared out into the rain. "Why she was even on my radar."

"Yeah."

Van's father, Mr. E, had given him Camila's information and ordered him to take her. Her disappearance had been part of a revenge plan led by Matias' own brother.

"Two months after I took Camila," Van said,

"Lucia disappeared. It's related, isn't it? To Matias' cartel?"

"Yes, and Matias killed every person involved in the sisters' kidnappings."

Except Van. He had Tate to thank for that. Since Camila had made peace with her former captor, Tate had talked Matias out of retaliating.

"When Lucia was captured, Camila was presumed dead." Tate trained the binoculars on Lucia's apartment door, and an ache pinched his chest. "When Badell brought her here, he would've tried to collect a ransom from her parents, who were already dead." He met Van's eyes. "She believes she's alone."

He wanted so badly to storm into her apartment and tell her Camila was alive. But he couldn't. Not while she was being watched.

"I'm trying to be patient," he said, turning toward Cole, "but I need to know the plan."

"There's somewhere she goes twice a month." Cole lowered onto the couch. "Her guards don't follow her in."

"Twice a month?" His pulse raced. "When? Is it always the same days of the month?"

"Yes. Ten days from today, she'll be there."

Ten days? That's an eternity.

Tate paced the length of the room, agitated. "You're leaving in seven days."

"I have another job." Cole narrowed his eyes. "And I don't want to be a part of whatever you decide to do after you confront her."

"I'm not going to kidnap her."

Cole glanced between him and Van, eyebrows arched. "If you say so."

"Whatever. You already told us we'd be on our own." He continued to pace. "Where does she go twice a month?"

"A sex club. That's where you'll make contact with her."

"What?" Tate slammed to a stop.

"Don't look so offended. You should feel right at home there."

True, but... "What are you suggesting I do?"

"You'll go in there, and if she's willing, you'll fuck her until she loses all logic and paranoia. Then you'll put your mouth at her ear and say—"

"Thanks for the good time... Oh, and by the way, your sister's alive?"

"Exactly."

Tate closed his eyes and breathed, "That's a terrible idea."

CHAPTER 6

It was the worst idea ever. But as Tate walked to the X ten days later, he was all in. Shoulders back, weapons concealed, bullet-resistant shirt straining across his chest, he was battle ready.

Except the shirt wouldn't protect his head. Or his dick.

Christ. There it was. The X.

The sex club didn't have a name, but a huge black X marked the otherwise nondescript door — the only indication he'd arrived at the right place.

The temptation to glance back and scan the shadows for Van prickled his scalp, but he knew Van had followed him as planned, staying far enough back to not raise suspicion.

Cole left Caracas three days ago with the promise that he was only a phone call away. But who knew what part of the world he'd traveled to or how long it would take him to return?

Deep breath. Follow the plan. Don't look sketchy.

Hell, every person he'd passed on the short walk here looked sketchy as fuck. Thankfully, no one approached him. *Yet.* The locals were probably taking their time scoping him out and gathering their buddies so they could gang rush him.

He slid his hands into his pockets and approached the door all casual like. Nothing to see here. Just going to a sex club to get laid.

To fuck Camila's sister.

That was going to be hard to explain to Camila, but first things first. He needed to get inside, and once he walked through that door, he would truly be on his own.

Van was a lot of things, but he wasn't a cheater. His refusal to step foot in the sex club was as inconvenient as it was admirable. He was here to help Tate, but his wife was and always would be his number one priority. Tate respected that.

He knocked on the black *X* and removed a wad of bolivars from his pocket.

The door swung open, revealing a rangy Hispanic man with a cigarette protruding from the toothy gap in a scraggly beard. "*Sí?*"

Tate put the bills in the man's hand.

"*Sin armas.*" The man motioned at Tate's waistband, where his untucked shirt concealed a handgun.

Cole had warned him about the no weapons policy. There was also a no clothing policy, but the disrobing would take place inside.

He handed over the gun and pushed through the doorway until bony fingers circled his arm, stopping him.

"*Sin armas.*" The bearded man pointed his cigarette at Tate's boot.

Fuck. He relinquished the knife from under his pant leg, certain he'd never see either of those weapons again.

Then he was free to go in.

The only doorway up ahead led him into a dim locker room. The tiled space was vacant, except for a lone woman sitting on the floor in the corner. As he stripped his clothes, she was more absorbed by the syringe in her arm than his nudity.

There were no locks on the lockers. He had no choice but to stuff his belongings into one, loathing the idea of leaving the protective shirt. The material looked plain enough, nothing to indicate its worth. If someone robbed him, his biggest concern would be the naked walk back to the apartment.

Moving toward the exit, he grabbed a haphazardly folded robe from a pile, pulled it on, and tied the front closed.

Two baskets sat on a table by the door. He grabbed a fistful of condoms from one, shoving them into the pocket of the robe. The other was filled with silicon bracelets.

Cole's intel had been right. There were four different colored bracelets. No labels, but Cole said black specified a *straight* orientation. White was *gay*, and gray was *bisexual*. The red ones… Well, he said not to worry about those.

Choosing a color wasn't difficult. When Tate had unwillingly lost his virginity to a man at fourteen, it had emotionally and physically scarred him enough to *never* put himself in a situation like that again. And he'd succeeded.

Until Van.

With a bitter taste in his throat, he grabbed a black bracelet. Wrestled it onto his wrist. Left the locker room.

And walked into a setting unlike anything he'd ever seen.

Sex.

Everywhere he looked.

Piles of naked, writhing, sweaty bodies.

By his estimation, there were forty or fifty people with an even ratio of men to women. All naked and moaning, sucking and fucking, moving from partner to partner, and taking turns.

Group sex seemed to be the theme here — threesomes, foursomes, too-many-to-count-somes, gang bangs, daisy chains, double penetration, and the random circle jerk in the corner.

Holy.

Fuck.

Few things shocked him, and orgies were commonplace at the Velvet Den. But the similarities ended there.

A sticky smell clung to the air — a sour brew of smoke and body odor — made worse by the sweet aroma of a Febreze-type spray.

Scuffed furniture, cigarette burns, patched upholstery, dark stains — it was a germaphobe's worst nightmare. Not that he was obsessed with cleanliness, but some of these folks had clearly thrown hygiene to the wayside. At least they were using condoms. Most of them, anyway.

The seedy club consisted of one room, vast and dimly lit, with a plethora of shadowed alcoves hidden by half walls and equipment rigged for impact play and other fetishes.

Fully aware that several heads had turned his way, he clasped his hands behind him and stepped through

84

the room like he owned it. As his bare feet moved along the worn carpet, he tried not to think about the fluids that were transferring to his skin.

The mismatched couches and futons appeared to be surface-clean, but some of those stains should've been burned off. Like most clubs of this kind, the lights were kept low enough to hide stretch-marks and cellulite and just bright enough to ensure intended appendages were stuffing intended holes. Though there didn't seem to be a right or wrong hole here.

He checked his black bracelet and realized most of the club-goers wore gray or red ones.

The general male fantasy wasn't picky, but the majority of the men he knew preferred women.

Not the case here.

His aversion to having sex with men was deeply ingrained. Had his life taken a gentler path, maybe he wouldn't have so much damn dread building in his gut right now. But as he caught the interested stares of numerous men around the room, he couldn't stop a resentful scowl from thinning his lips.

One thing he hadn't counted on was his inability to get a hard-on. He was always ready to fuck, but as it stood — or didn't stand — he wasn't sure he'd be able to perform.

Then he saw her.

On the far side of the room, Lucia bent over a table, eyes closed and mouth parted, as a burly naked man beat her ass with a cane.

Every muscle in Tate's body tensed to go to her, but he forced himself to remain in place, to watch and evaluate.

The man's erection was as impressive as his strikes.

He was huge…everywhere, his swings powered by bricks of muscle. With each new stripe across her backside, she relaxed deeper onto the table. There were no creases of tension on her face. No restraints on her arms or legs. Nothing to hold her there but her own will.

She was enjoying the beating, and fuck if that didn't make Tate's dick swell with blood. He wasn't a sadist, but he loved it rough, loved the feel of a woman bending and sighing beneath the aggressive force of his unchecked desire.

He could approach her now, make his move, but that wasn't his style. When he wanted a woman's attention, he preferred a subtle approach.

He spotted an unoccupied couch and sat at the center of it, ensuring the robe protected his butt from whatever was breeding in the crusty cushion. The location put him in her direct line of sight. She only needed to open her eyes.

Goddamn, she was hot. Flirty shoulder-length hair. Creamy coffee skin. Thick dark eyelashes. A little on the thin side, but she had a great Latina ass.

He settled back on the couch. Then the piranhas closed in. He held his black bracelet in view, discouraging the men. But three women crept toward him with sex-induced oblivion written all over their faces.

One of them crawled on her knees from a nearby pile of men. Her Barbie-thin waist pinched in between an abundance of hips and tits. She was pretty enough, and as her hand slid up his leg and disappeared beneath his robe, he knew his concern about performance had been unwarranted.

He was as hard as a rock. It had nothing to do with

the fingers curling around his length and everything to do with the woman who had just opened her eyes.

Lucia stared at him from twenty-feet away, her cheek pressed against the table and her focus unwavering. She didn't blink, and neither did he. The cocky part of him exclaimed triumph, knowing he'd irrevocably seized her interest. He only needed to wait for her to come to him, and she would. They always did.

The other two women joined him on the couch. One on each side, they untied the knot on his robe, spreading it open.

He was prepared for this, had made the decision before coming here that he would allow touching and blowjobs from women. What straight man wouldn't? But the only woman he would fuck tonight was the raven-haired beauty watching him from the table.

The man behind her set aside the cane and gripped his latex-wrapped erection, stepping closer to her to line himself up.

Tate's jaw tightened, and he shot her a look she couldn't misinterpret. *No.*

It was an irrational demand, considering the three women who were currently exploring every inch of his body with hands, lips, and teeth. He was tempted to stop the girl between his legs from rolling a condom down his shaft, but he decided to let this play out, to see what Lucia would do.

He captured her gaze as warm lips stretched around his girth. Ahhh, fuck, that felt good. His skin heated, and his balls tightened, and the ungodly pleasure only intensified in the prison of Lucia's watchful stare.

He didn't lift his hands, didn't touch or look at the women grinding against him. He couldn't ignore the intoxicating desire they spread through his body, didn't want to. He felt like putty beneath their ministrations and melted into the couch.

His breathing accelerated, and his cock pulsed in the hot wet cavity of the woman's mouth. But his eyes were narrowed on Lucia and her alone.

She reached behind her, gripped the burly man's dick, and stroked it a few times before nudging him away. The man didn't look too put off by it as he moved to the next girl in line for a beating.

Then she stood and turned to face him fully.

Smallish tits, tight pink nipples, sharp collarbones — her delicate physique rounded into curvy hips and slender legs. The dark trimmed patch of hair between her thighs created a shadow over the part of her he so desperately wanted to see, to taste, to pound until they were both exhausted and sated.

Maybe she was a coldblooded bitch in a kidnapping gang, but unless she had a blade clenched between those tight ass cheeks, she didn't have the upper hand here.

He found her eyes and sharpened his in silent command. *Come here.*

Her chest hitched, an exquisite response. Then she slowly walked toward him.

CHAPTER 8

Sweet mother of God, he was beautiful. Easily the sexiest man in the room. Hell, in Lucia's thirty years, she'd never seen a man that jaw-droppingly stunning.

And that was the most crucial part. She'd never seen him before. Not in this sex club. Not in Caracas.

She would've remembered the intensity in those crystal blue eyes, the way they honed in on her, tracked her every move, and took her breath away.

She floated toward him, propelled by curiosity, desire, stupidity. He could've been any number of deadly traps—an enemy of Tiago, a Fed for the United States, a kidnapper or serial killer.

Her insides might've been damaged, but her gut was trustworthy, and it told her he was none of those things. Besides, it wasn't like she would leave with him or tell him anything incriminating. If he were simply here to fuck, she'd gladly take him for a ride.

While this was the only place she could have sex on her own terms, the pursuit of pleasure wasn't the reason she came. She had a job to do, a mandate from Tiago to visit twice a month. He didn't care who she fucked while she was here, as long as she cataloged the words exchanged around her. Some of Tiago's competitors frequented the club, and their tongues tended to loosen after an orgasm or two.

This moonlighting gig also aided her own agenda. An agenda Tiago could never, ever find out about.

Sliding one foot in front of the other, she approached the gorgeous stranger with deliberate slowness so that she could savor every glorious inch of him. Dark brows hooded those captivating eyes. Pillowy lips parted with his aroused breaths. Stubble shadowed his cheeks and jaw. And what a jawline. Even with the scruff, she could make out the chiseled angles.

His nose was perfect, no bumps or bends to suggest it'd ever been broken. *Unlike most of the brutes she kept company with.* His brown-blond hair was cut short. Neither buzzed nor long enough to style. *Low maintenance.*

For a white guy, his complexion had a remarkable glow, as if soaked with sunlight and lathered with oil. It was probably just the low lighting. But good lord, all that flawless tanned skin, the way it stretched over defined pecs and abs... No wonder every woman in the room was watching him, waiting for a turn to choke on his dick.

The one between his legs blocked Lucia's view of his package. The two on the couch looked like they were seconds from humping his face.

Time for them to go.

Lucia picked up her pace, suddenly very aware of her nudity. What a novel feeling. She'd thought the first couple of years with Tiago had broken her of all modesty. But now, goosebumps rose on her arms. Her nipples hardened in the stuffy air, and she fought the urge to hug

90

the scar on her abdomen.

The man didn't break eye contact, and as if held in hypnosis, she couldn't either. She paused within arm's reach, and without removing her gaze from his, she made a shooing motion.

At the edges of her periphery, the women skulked away, knowing better than to challenge Tiago Badell's favorite confidant.

Her eyes stayed on his as he lowered his hand and removed the condom. Then he sat back and rested his arms along the back of the couch, unabashedly nude with the robe open, as if inviting her to look.

She meant to take a leisurely stroll down the length of his body, but she only made it to the thick column of his neck before skipping straight to his cock.

Her breath caught, and heat flushed between her legs. God almighty, the man was blessed in both length and girth. So hard and thick. Beautifully shaped. A vein pulsed along the fat shaft. The wide, suckable crown and silky skin pulled taut—

Wait. He was circumcised? It'd been so long since she'd seen a cut penis. It wasn't a common practice in South America. Or Europe.

But it was prevalent in the United States.

Her gaze lifted to the blue of his, which hadn't moved from her face. "You're American."

He glanced at his erection, a frown piercing his forehead. Then he returned to her eyes. "So are you."

Her Colombian heritage made it easy to blend in here, but her American accent always gave her away.

For the first time since she spotted him, he released her gaze, lowering his down her body, inspecting her mouth, throat, chest, and lower. He gave her ugly scar a cursory glance and paused on her pussy.

The brazen way he examined that part of her made her inner muscles spasm. Could he see the throbbing? The desire dripping onto her thighs?

She endured his predatory stare for long seconds before lowering to her knees and settling between his spread legs. Her hands itched to wrap around his swollen length, but she wouldn't. Not until he was feverish and ready to crawl out of his skin with need.

She started with his ankles, trailing feather-light caresses up the backs of his calves. The dusting of coarse hair tickled her fingers, and his muscles bounced against her touch. She gave the fronts of his legs the same attention and moved above his knees, inching her body closer and relishing the feel of his powerful thighs around her.

When she reached his heavy sac, she let her fingernails graze the skin but otherwise neglected the neediest part of him.

His arms lowered from the back of the couch to his sides, and his breathing deepened, his lips separating to accommodate the pull and release of air.

He looked ravenous, and she fed off it, her hands traveling over his torso, exploring every brawny bump and carved furrow. She kept the motion unhurried, rhythmic, seductive. Then she added her mouth, licking and nibbling his velvety skin.

God help her, he smelled heavenly. Clean and pure, without a hint of cologne or aftershave. He smelled natural, fresh, like a man who took care of himself. His pubic hair was trimmed. His teeth were white, and his physique was a powerhouse of sculpted muscle. The perfect example of a healthy male.

The sounds of slapping flesh and hoarse groans saturated the room, spurring her on. She worshiped his body with her hands and mouth, delighting in every twitch, every moan. His erection pressed like a hot iron against her belly, and his lashes fell half-mast over sexy bedroom eyes as he teasingly caught the edge of his bottom lip between his teeth.

Oh, how she wanted to taste the hunger on that sinful mouth. Which was crazy. She couldn't remember the last time she'd kissed someone, the last time she'd been kissed. It was before Venezuela. Before she was taken.

It wasn't like she avoided it. She just didn't have access to the kind of sex that invited intimacy. But as his tongue darted out to wet his lips, she knew she would kiss him. She just wished she remembered how to do it well.

Peering up through her lashes, she fell into his vivid stare and waited for him to get bossy. He would. She knew his type. She just had to be patient. Or maybe give him a little push.

Sliding her fingers over his hard nipple, she pinched it, twisted it hard.

He groaned and rocked his hips. Then he gripped the base of his cock and met her eyes. "Put your mouth on me."

"Hmm. I don't know." She fought a smile.

He held out a foil packet from the pocket of his robe. "I'm not asking."

There he is. Demanding. Coarse. So fucking sexy.

She plucked the condom from his fingers and rolled it on, fighting to stretch it into position. One-size-fits-all didn't quite cover the full length of him. *Poor guy.*

A chuckle escaped her lips.

"Stop laughing at it," he said, gripping the hair at her nape, "and work it into your mouth."

Her thighs clenched, and she lowered her head, keeping her gaze locked with his. Then she stopped.

She never gave blowjobs without a condom protecting her mouth from disease. But she didn't want to taste the latex on him. She wanted his flavor on her tongue and the warmth of his skin sliding against her lips.

He looked and smelled like the kind of man who kept himself clean and safe.

Fuck it.

She unrolled the condom, tossed it aside, and brought her face close, inhaling the salty, masculine scent of his cock. Her mouth watered.

The first brush of the broad tip against her lips produced a tremble across his thighs and a rumbling groan in his chest.

He adjusted the fist in her hair, tightening the hold to guide her mouth, closer, deeper, forcing her to swallow him. And she did, as much of him as she could, flattening her tongue and measuring her breaths.

Jesus, he was long. And unbelievably hard and hot. If he kicked his hips, she'd feel the bruise in her throat for days.

But he didn't. He used his hand instead, guiding her head up and down at the pace and rhythm he wanted. She might've been the initiator, but she wasn't the one in control.

Dominance encapsulated every bone, muscle, and breath in his body, and he knew it. Owned it. It was right there — the glare of masculine confidence in those brilliant blue eyes. He stared her down as if to illustrate that very point, to make her squirm.

She wasn't the squirmy type, but he did affect her — the erratic pulse in her throat, the clenching heat between her legs, the impulse to submit to him on a fundamental level — if only for one night.

Her instincts said he wouldn't abuse the gift. He wasn't Tiago. Wasn't any of the other selfish, corrupt men she'd encountered over the past eleven years. He reminded her of Matias. Even as a young man, Camila's boyfriend had that persuasive *something* in his bearing, in his eye contact, and in the way he handled her sister.

Camila...

Her heart gave a heavy pang, and she quickly shoved those thoughts away.

Re-doubling her efforts, she tongued and sucked the beautiful cock in her mouth.

Blood pulsed along the length, beating strong and hot beneath his velvety skin. He was close, his breathing labored and muscles taut.

But she didn't want him to come. Not until he was impaled deep inside her pussy.

His cock slid from her mouth, and she crawled up his body, the welts on her ass pulsing deliciously with each movement. She kissed a path from his sternum to his neck and lingered on his whiskered jawline.

Then she felt it — the excess of saliva in her mouth, the flare of nausea in her gut, and the sudden sweep of vertigo.

No, please. Not now.

She held still, blanking her expression to hide the stabbing pain.

It'll pass. It'll pass.

"Hey."

His lips moved, his voice raspy. She focused on that, on his mouth and how badly she wanted to feel it against hers.

CHAPTER 8

A strange look crossed Lucia's face. It was such a fleeting twitch Tate wondered if he'd imagined it.

"Are you okay?" He cupped her cheek, searching her beautiful brown eyes.

She stared at him, stared at his lips. Then she attacked his mouth in a bruising kiss.

Fuck, he was primed for it, had spent the last few minutes warring between blowing his load in her throat and pounding her into the filthy carpet.

Either way, the onset of orgasm pushed against the edges of his tenuous control. He needed to calm the fuck down and remember why he was here.

Hard to do with her sweet tongue working against his with diabolical skill. The tongue that had just ruined him for all other blowjobs.

Commanding her to suck him had been gratuitous and narcissistic. He only needed to get her alone to tell her about Camila. But he couldn't bring himself to regret the ungodly pleasure her mouth had given him.

Just like he couldn't stop his hands from learning every dip and curve of her shape. She was so damn small, all delicate bones and compact muscle. He could snap her in half. But it wasn't just her fragile size that turned him on. It was the compliant way she responded to him, the ease in which she knelt and bent to his will.

He let her lead the kiss as he stroked her from tits to ass and back again. Then he took over, chasing her tongue and setting the tempo. Her palms pressed against his chest, her fingers curling in as she met him bite for bite, opening as he deepened the kiss, and sighing as they unraveled into groping, rubbing, heedless hands and grinding hips.

Heat panted through him as he lowered his touch to her cunt and stroked the soft flesh, sliding through the wetness and pressing inside. The clasp of her body sucked him, clenching and pulsing and scrambling his brain.

Goddamn, she was tight. Swollen and slick and so fucking hot. He ached to be inside her. Felt rabid with the need to spear her with his cock. But he was too big. He'd hurt her if he didn't start slow and gentle.

When she reached between them and gripped his length, he nudged her arm away. She'd removed the condom, which he greatly appreciated during the blowjob, but he never had unprotected sex.

Quickly rolling on another rubber, he positioned himself. His other hand caught her waist, stilling her, making her wait for it.

The elegant column of her neck filled his view, the vein in her throat pulsing wildly. The tips of her stick-straight black hair brushed against the sharp lines of her shoulders. As her greedy hands prowled his body, her thick lashes lowered, partially concealing the lust in her eyes.

She was, without question, the sexiest, most

striking woman he'd ever seen. But it changed nothing. She was still a gang member, and he still loved her sister.

This was just sex. An exchange of pleasure and, by the end of the night, information.

She squeezed her thighs around his hips, leaking honey all over his shaft.

"Your impatience only makes me hungrier, sweetheart." He licked the seam of her lips.

"Take what you need, American." She licked him back.

Christ, she couldn't say shit like that to him. As it was, he struggled to keep himself from tearing into her with unrestrained barbarity. And she would let him. Maybe she was masking her expressions, but her body's responses were honest and real. She'd let him use her savagely and selfishly, let him bite her nipples, bruise her skin, and welt her ass. It was incredibly erotic to know he could fuck this woman any way he desired, and she would allow it.

Because it pleased him.

Because she was submissive to her core.

She's also Camila's sister.

The inconvenient reminder gave him pause.

When the time came to talk to Camila, he wouldn't provide details of this encounter. Wouldn't tell her how fucking perfect her sister's pussy felt sliding against his dick, pulsing and dripping and begging to be stuffed.

Fingernails bit into his arms, narrowing his focus on the sexy woman on his lap. She'd waited long enough.

Clutching her waist with both hands, he sank her onto his cock with excruciating slowness. As the suction of her body stretched and clamped around him, he released a low, long groan.

His cock strained so hard and full inside her it was agonizing. He wasn't even buried yet. Could she take him to the hilt?

The question was answered as she slammed downward and ground her clit against his pelvis. He grunted, and she moaned, scratching her nails down his chest.

Then he fucked her, lifting her up and down, pushing into her, and riding the intoxicating waves of bliss. There were no traces of pain in her body's reactions, nothing to dissuade him from deepening his thrusts. His balls tightened, and his hips flexed as he devoured the view of her bouncing, perky tits.

He wasn't a fan of this position, preferred to be on top, but he allowed it for a moment because it gave him unrestricted access to her body. And he took advantage, gliding his hands from her waist to roam her feminine peaks and valleys, plucking at her nipples, and caressing the velvety smoothness of her neck.

The fissured scar across her midsection glowed white against her caramel skin. He traced it, just a steady slide of reverent fingers, but didn't linger. He would demand the full story from her...later.

It was remarkable how well they moved together—the synchronization of their rolling grinds, the give of her body with the force of his thrusts, and the stretch of her pussy as he pounded her inner muscles. It felt as though they'd been lovers for years, like there was a familiarity between them, a uniquely matched closeness he'd never experienced with another woman.

The reason was simple. She yielded to him in a way no one ever had, craved the freedom in relinquishing control. And it was in his nature to take the reins.

With his hands on her hips, he drove inside her, feeding her every ruthless inch and unleashing the last of his restraint. The tip of him hit her so deeply he felt the back of her narrow cunt, groaned, and hammered her again.

Driven by primal instinct and the urge to punish her for making him want her so goddamn badly, he fucked her viciously, mercilessly, gasping and plunging, his fingers digging into bone.

With a whimper, she fell against his chest, pressing her mouth into the bend of his neck, kissing, licking, and panting noisily. Then she leaned up and nibbled his earlobe.

"You feel incredible, American." She nipped and teased the sensitive skin beneath his ear before whispering again, "Are you a doctor?"

"What?" He slowed his thrusts and nudged her back to see her face. "No. Why?"

"Oh, I…" She returned to his neck, distracting him with those soft, hot lips. "I thought I saw you at the hospital."

She was lying. The hospital was miles away, outside of a neighborhood she never left.

"Why are you looking for a doctor?" *In a sex club of all places?* He clutched her shoulder and pushed her up, studying the vastness of her deep brown eyes.

"I'm not—"

He gripped her throat to silence another lie. But something else happened. She didn't struggle, didn't claw at the collar of his unyielding fist, didn't show any of the fight-or-flight responses expected from a woman being choked by a stranger.

Instead, she *melted* into the restraint. Lips parted, eyes dilated, she squeezed her pussy so tightly around him he saw stars. Shudders exploded through his body, and his dick throbbed and swelled so hard it was the only heartbeat he felt.

He couldn't hold back. The robe came off in a frenzy, tossed on the couch at the last second to protect her from the cushion, before he flipped her onto her back and plowed his way inside her.

Goddamn, he was stark raving mad with need and couldn't fuck her hard enough, deep enough. It was raw and beautiful, not just where they were joined or the urgency they shared, but the way she stared up at him, her eyes glazed with desire, awe, and *trust*. She stared at him like she wanted to give him everything, like she wanted him to take it, to liberate her.

He wrapped his fingers around her fragile throat, taking more care this time with her windpipe. Just the right amount of pressure, the illusion of strangulation, and...

There she goes.

Her mouth gaped in a silent scream as she detonated around the stabbing drives of his cock. He swooped in and feasted on the curves of her lips, the warm hidden caverns around her tongue, and the clean wet flavor of her frantic breaths.

She tasted like sin and paradise, a sweet combination that would never tire, never completely sate, because he would always want more. More of her mouth. More of her pussy. More of *this*.

But he'd reached the limit of his self-discipline, his entire body trembling and overdosed on pleasure chemicals. He needed to come.

He released her throat and braced his arms on the cushion to buffer the force of his thrusts. A few more deliriously brutal strokes and he fell still, staring into her dazed eyes as he filled the condom with his spent enthusiasm.

The eruption of orgasm throbbed for long seconds through his cock, attacking every nerve-ending with delicious sparks of electricity. Had he ever come that hard? No way. He felt like he was going to pass out.

But he couldn't. He had to finish this, say what he needed to say, and get this gorgeous, unexpectedly perfect woman reunited with her sister.

Piloting his movements with deliberate care, he peppered her neck with kisses as his fingers moved along her arms to hold her hands against the cushion above her head. Just a light hold, not enough pressure to cause alarm.

Then he leaned back and watched her face. "Listen carefully, Lucia Dias."

Her eyes widened at her name, and he tightened his hold on her wrists.

"Shh. I won't hurt you." He kissed her slack lips. "Ten years ago, your sister escaped her kidnapper. Camila's alive and well and living with Matias in Colombia." He pressed another kiss to her mouth. "She misses you."

She stopped breathing, didn't blink. He released her hands and gave her room. There was no emotion in her expression. Was she in shock?

He removed the condom and sat back on his heels, letting her see the honesty in his eyes as she processed his words.

She lay there for a moment, breathless, unmoving.

Then she pushed off the cushion, limbs loose and face relaxed. Her hands slid up his chest, and her body followed. It was strangely sensual and totally not the reaction he expected.

Curling her fingers through his hair, she kissed a path from his mouth to his ear and whispered, "If you want to live, do *not* follow me."

With that, she rose from the couch and strode out of the room.

CHAPTER 9

Lucia leaned over the toilet in her dark apartment and spit the last of the bile into the bowl. There were traces of blood in her vomit, but it wasn't uncommon. At least tonight's sick spell hadn't been debilitating. Now that her stomach was empty, she felt almost healthy. *Almost.* It would take a while before her heart slowed down. It'd been hammering uncontrollably since she sneaked out of the sex club two hours ago.

Camila's alive and well and living with Matias.

Was it possible? Yes. But not likely. If her sister lived, Tiago would've found her. Because above all, he loved collecting ransoms and had searched long and hard to find someone willing to cough up money for Lucia.

The fact that he hadn't killed Lucia was a mystery that tormented her daily. She was the only exception he'd ever made, which was why she didn't take risks, didn't do anything that would give him a reason to end her life.

Until tonight.

The first thing she did when she exited the club was slip past her guards. They didn't see her leave through the back door, didn't know she hid in a nearby building, waiting for the American.

When he'd finally emerged, she'd tracked him to his apartment. Not just him. Another man had trailed the American, keeping a block of distance between them. They were smart to not walk together — made it easier for them to protect each another. But they weren't smart enough to sense they had a tail.

Once she'd learned where they were staying, she returned to the club, sneaked back in, and walked out the front where her guards expected her.

Then she had no choice but to go home. Any diversion from her routine would've been reported to Tiago. Under no circumstances could he find out Camila might be alive. Even if her sister had the funds to pay a ransom, it would only end in devastation.

Camila's alive and well.

Why would the American lie about that? Was he in contact with Camila? Did her sister know she was alive? If not, she had to stop that man from telling her, whoever the hell he was.

Kissable, commanding, well-endowed, insanely, wildly attractive — he was all those things. Good God, she'd never been fucked like that. The power he'd wielded, the gravelly rumble in his voice, and the poise in which he'd seduced her had turned her into a carnal creature intent on wringing every last drop of seed from his body.

She wasn't even close to being done with him.

The next few minutes was a whirlwind of determination. She flushed the toilet. Brushed her teeth. Kicked off her heels. Pulled on the boots. The Berettas sat snugly between her tailbone and the waistband of her jeans. She would definitely need those.

There were no windows in her apartment. No

other doors. Just a mattress, open bathroom and kitchenette, and a closet.

The closet. As quietly as possible, she removed her meager belongings from within it.

It'd been a couple years since she'd slipped her guards, and she was about to do it for the second time tonight.

God help me.

The closet now empty, she stepped inside and dragged her fingers down the back corner, prying at the hidden seam.

Years ago, she cut a narrow passage in the wall and used it to sneak out. She was more tenacious then. Braver. But that was before the gruesome incident with that poor doctor. Her chest tightened.

She wouldn't make the same mistakes. Wouldn't leave the neighborhood. Wouldn't try to make contact with the outside world. She was just going to pay the American a visit, threaten him at gunpoint, and would be home by dawn.

The wood paneling creaked as she slid it open. The worried whine of a dog sounded on the other side, and she hurried through, squeezing between the gap in the vertical wall supports and stepping into her neighbor's closet.

Franchesca didn't own much before she was robbed, but as Lucia crept into the dark one-room unit, the space looked cruelly bare.

A furry ball on short legs scurried toward her. She scooped up the dog before it started barking and patted its head.

"Franchesca?" she whispered, approaching the sleeping silhouette on the mattress.

When her neighbor popped her head up, Lucia handed over the dog and held a finger against her lips, demanding silence.

They had a long-standing agreement. Lucia would protect Franchesca when she could, and Franchesca wouldn't ask questions when Lucia came and went through the hidden passage.

Her neighbor was a passive woman and didn't have enemies — except for a dirtbag father, who came around every couple months to beat her. While Lucia did favors for her, like getting the dog back tonight, it didn't mean she trusted Franchesca. If the price was right, Franchesca would sell Lucia down the river.

With a steadying breath, she left the woman in bed and strode toward the rear of the room.

Lucia's apartment sat at the intersecting point of a T-shaped complex, surrounded by other units on three sides. But Franchesca's apartment didn't, and she had a back door. Lucky for Lucia, her guards didn't watch the rear alley.

She slipped out the back, and fifteen minutes later, stood in front of another apartment door in an unlit corridor. This was where her plan met its first obstacle.

The apartment building was a shit hole, much like the rest of the slum. She'd expected a flimsy lock, one she could pick without making a sound.

This lock had been upgraded with a heavy-duty, electronic-looking thing. *Goddammit!*

It'd been added recently, given the shiny steel casing. Definitely not the kind of hardware one would find in a shanty town.

Her pulse sped up. Who the fuck were these guys? *Deep breath.*

She could shoot off the deadbolt, rush in, and take them by surprise. Gunshots rang out all night long, so the neighbors wouldn't bat an eye at the racket.

Or, since there wasn't a peep hole, she could knock and let one of them open it to the barrel of her 9mm.

Option two was less dramatic, so she drew one of the Berettas from her waistband and rapped on the door with her knuckles.

She expected to wait a while or maybe hear an apprehensive *Who's there?* on the other side. But the lock turned within seconds.

Were they stupid?

Then she saw it. Wedged in a crack high on the door frame was a tiny black disk.

A camera.

The door opened, and with a racing heart, she trained the gun on a chiseled bare chest. Shifting her gaze, she followed the stretch of tight boxer briefs to carved packs of muscle and inched upward to a dark trimmed beard, a toothpick lolling from smirking lips, a mean-looking facial scar, and finally, the sharpened slits of silver eyes.

So this was the American's companion. Despite the welted laceration across his cheek, his smile was arresting, and he ranked pretty high up there on the handsome scale. But there was an echo of something in his eyes, something chilling and fractured, like a frozen scream in a haunted basement.

"Don't make a sound." She locked her outstretched arm and rested a finger against the trigger of the gun. "Do exactly what I say."

"I appreciate the spirit in that," he drawled with an American accent. "But when it comes to orders, I'm a giver, not a taker."

He motioned for her to enter the unlit apartment. She didn't move.

"I can see how that's worked out for you." She flicked her gaze between his scars — a bullet wound on his shoulder and a knife wound across his cheek. "I won't hesitate to put another bullet in you."

"Suit yourself." With a shrug, he retreated into the apartment and flipped a light switch. "I'm Van, by the way."

The fluorescents flickered on, illuminating a sleeper sofa converted into a bed, an open kitchen, a bedroom door, and leaning against the frame of that door was the man who had fucked her so soundly she still felt him in her teeth and her legs and everywhere in between.

Head tipped down, he stared at her from beneath heavy brows. His arms folded across his chest, with one sleeved in tattoos. Like his friend, he was clad only in fitted boxer briefs, his short hair disheveled and eyes sleepy.

She must've woken them. Neither man was armed, and the weapons they carried earlier were out of reach on the kitchen table. There were probably more firearms, but hers was out and ready.

Drawing the second Beretta from her back, she trained a gun on each of them, stepped into the apartment, and kicked the door shut behind her.

The one with the toothpick — *Van* — tilted his head as he watched her approach. "I expected you to walk funny. With more of a limp." At her confused look, he said, "As small as you are, it wouldn't have been easy to take Tate's beast of a cock."

Tate. The name fit him, and his cock… Her inner

muscles clenched in memory, reawakening the delicious soreness there.

"How was it?" Van asked. "Did he ram it inside you with all the ferocity and pain it deserves?"

"Boundaries," Tate growled. "Heed them."

"Did the ol' dog at least make you come?" Van asked conversationally, as if she weren't aiming a bullet at his chest.

"That's enough." Tate lifted his chin in her direction. "Lucia, lower the weapons."

"Who are you?" She steadied both guns, ticking her gaze between them.

Tate straightened from the doorframe and slowly closed the distance. His strides were slow but long, eating up the floor with muscled nonchalance. But there was nothing casual in the way he looked at her, those blue eyes seeking her most intimate places and setting her on fire from the inside out. He looked at her as though he were recalling the feel of being sheathed inside her, like he wanted to feel her again.

She took great pleasure in the knowledge that such a ridiculously handsome man was attracted to her. But the stupid, girly, instantaneous attachment she felt for him was an embarrassing sentiment, so very un-Lucia-like. What was her deal with this guy?

It had just been sex, really fucking good sex, with a beautiful stranger. She wasn't here for a repeat.

She was here to save her sister from more heartache.

"Who are you?" she asked again.

Two feet away, Tate pressed his chiseled chest against the barrel of the gun. "I'm Camila's best friend."

He could've been lying, but there wasn't a trace of

deceit on his stunning face.

Everything inside her cried with joy. Not only was Camila alive, she had a strong, protective friend who cared for her enough to track down her only family.

It was more than Lucia could've ever wanted for Camila, and she felt the sudden need to sit down. Hard. But her arms and legs remained stubbornly locked.

"What about him?" She gestured at Van with the gun she trained on him.

"He's...uh..." Tate gripped his nape, stalling, holding something back.

"He's what?" Her stomach tightened.

Van lifted his chin, giving her the full force of his icy eyes. "I'm the one who kidnapped your sister."

CHAPTER 10

Confusion spiked through Lucia, followed by furious understanding. This scary-looking, scarface motherfucker abducted her sweet, innocent, seventeen-year-old sister.

"What did you do to her?" She directed eleven years of pain into the scalding glare she aimed at Van.

A day hadn't passed without the loss, the torment, and the dire unknowns that surrounded Camila's disappearance. She hadn't saved Camila from being taken, but dammit, she could avenge her, right now, with the squeeze of a trigger.

"You won't shoot him," Tate said quietly, his chest pushing against the other gun barrel. "Think about it. He captured Camila and me with the intent to sell us into slavery. Yet I'm here. Camila's with Matias, and Van's still alive. There's a good reason for that."

"He captured *you*?"

Tate nodded, his eyes growing heavy and dark. "Six years ago."

"Put down the guns, little girl," Van said, "and I'll confess all my sins."

She held her ground, seething with venom. "How dare you?"

"The weapons, Lucia." Tate held out a palm. "Now."

The command in his deep voice was meant to subdue her, but it was the compassion softening his eyes that urged her rage to creep back into the darkness and go dormant once again.

It took longer to lower the guns, but after a few calming breaths, she placed them in his huge hand. "Don't make me regret this." *Please don't abuse my trust.*

He set the weapons aside and twined his fingers around hers. Then he steered her toward the bedroom. "Give us a minute, Van."

In the bedroom, he left the door open and directed her to sit on the foot of the bed, out of view from the main room.

"We'll tell you everything you want to know. Every secret. Every crime." He pulled on a pair of jeans, zipped, and left the button undone. "But first, I want to make something clear."

She stared at him, mesmerized. How could she not be? It wasn't just his sculpted perfection. There was something extraordinary beneath the physical strength. Something in the tenderness of his touch, the vigilant way he watched her, the gentle inflections he wove into his commands. As if no matter how damaged or sick she was, he would still hold her hand, hold her close, and let her lean on him as hard and as long as she needed. He was that person.

She never had a person and didn't know what to do with the warm feelings it soaked into her bones.

He perched on the mattress beside her and touched her face, studying her eyes.

"Tonight was..." He rested his forehead against

hers and inhaled deeply. "I'm not going to label it. Just know that I didn't fuck you as part of some scheme. I went to the club, willing to do exactly that to get you alone. To talk to you. But once I had you..."

He edged closer and dragged his nose along her neck, sniffing her. It was such a primal gesture, animalistic, and the reverberating groan in his throat produced a groan of her own.

Sliding her cheek against his, she indulged in the scratch of his whiskers. His proximity instilled her with an addictive sense of security—something she didn't even know she craved until now.

"When I was inside you," he breathed against her ear, "it was real and natural and just us. Understand?"

She nodded, her throat too tight for sound as she floated to an imaginary hinterland where *everythings* and *forevermores* glittered like stars in the sky.

"Sex between us... That was a straightforward thing. But everything else..." He leaned back and rubbed the crease between his eyebrows. "There are complications, histories."

"My sister?"

"Yes. And Tiago Badell, the work you do for him. We have a lot to discuss."

The mention of Tiago made her wonder how Tate found her, but more importantly... "Does Camila know I'm alive?"

"No. We need to talk about that, too." He clasped her hand and stood, leading her to the sitting room. "Did you run into trouble on your way back?"

"My way back...?" She stopped and released his hand, her mind spinning to understand his meaning. "Wait. You knew I followed you earlier?"

"Of course. And I knew you had to return to the club where your guards were waiting. How did you dodge them again to get back here?"

She could tell him. She could lay bare all her secrets and ugly truths and hope she was right about his compassion. But that required trust—something he had to earn.

She left the question adrift and stepped along the window in the main room. Below, two of Tiago's guards stood across the street from her apartment door, smoking cigarettes and shooting the shit.

Could they not see her up here? She flattened a hand against the window, studying the glass.

"There's a film on it." Tate stood so close to her back his breath stirred her hair. "It makes the apartment look dark from the outside."

No wonder she hadn't noticed movement in the window when she came and went in the alley. "How long have you been watching me?"

"Ten days. The man I hired to find you watched you for weeks."

"Tell me about that, about your relationship with Camila, all of it." Shifting away from his intoxicating presence, she sat on the unfolded sleeper sofa and settled in. "Start at the beginning."

"It started with me." Van, now dressed in athletic pants and a shirt, brought her a glass of tequila, which she refused. "My father was the Police Chief of Austin. But in the criminal underground, he was known as Mr. E." He swallowed the tequila and set the glass on the coffee table. "He trafficked sex slaves, and I was the kidnapper and trainer for the operation."

She sat motionless and silent as he outlined seven

116

DEVASTATE

years of blackmail, kidnapping, submission training, and rape. He explained how Liv Reed shot him the same night she killed Mr. E, how the slaves escaped over the years, and the roles Camila, Tate, and Matias played in that.

It was agonizing to hear how her sister had been forced to kneel, beg beneath a whip, and suck his dick. But when he confirmed he never raped her, Lucia sagged with relief. Then he spoke about the ten weeks he imprisoned Tate.

"I'm attracted to submissives. Women *and* men." Van stood with his back to the window, moving only his lips around an ever-present toothpick. "As you already know, Tate is neither gay nor submissive. I preyed on that. Used it to humiliate him, hurt him, and yes, I fucked him countless times while he fought uselessly in his restraints."

As Van delivered his monotone confession, Tate smoked one cigarette after another without interjecting a word. She peeked at him, expecting to see fury in his eyes. There were remnants of that in the blue depths, but there were so many other emotions twisting and turning at the forefront. Unease, turmoil, distrust... But she might've glimpsed forgiveness there, too.

He'd had six years to come to terms with what Van had done to him. There must've been some level of resolution, because here they were, together. During Van's account of the events, he admitted he wanted to help Tate and Camila any way he could. Even so, the unfinished tension between him and Tate electrocuted the air.

Another thing she noticed... If Van was bisexual, why didn't he look at Tate with sexual interest? Tate was so damn eye-catching even a straight man would give him a second glance.

Though now that she thought about it, Van didn't look at her with desire, either. Maybe he had a partner or spouse he was faithful to? If so, he didn't mention it. Not that she blamed him, given her connection to Tiago.

At some point during the conversation, nausea and muscle aches crept in. Her earlier bout of vomiting had given her a momentary reprieve, but it didn't always keep the symptoms at bay.

Come what may, she hid the pain and turned to Tate. "If my sister helped rescue all the slaves, does that mean she saved you, too?"

"Yes." His eyes caught fire. "She's fucking fierce, Lucia. Brave and beautiful and determined. You would be so proud of her."

As he outlined the four years that followed Mr. E's death, his expression grew brighter and more alert. His entire existence seemed to be centered on Camila and her vigilante group, the Freedom Fighters. He'd lived with her, protected her, and even helped Matias reunite with her.

With restless strides, he paced through the room, expounding on Camila's fight against slavery and the sacrifices she made. After all these years, she and Lucia were still considered missing persons. But Camila had the impenetrable shield of a cartel in front of her, keeping her safe from enemies and invisible to the law.

That explained why Tiago never found her.

And holy shit, Matias was the capo of the Restrepo cartel? He was such a good-looking man in his teens. And one-hundred-percent, head-over-heels in love with Camila. Add to that his powerful position and Lucia couldn't be happier they were together.

Then Tate told her about her own abduction — how and why Matias' brother orchestrated it, her parents' involvement, and their ultimate death at Matias' hand.

She waited for the tears to come, but she'd cried enough for them when she was taken. They'd sold both of their daughters into slavery. She would mourn them no more.

"You okay?" Tate asked.

"Yeah. How did you find me?"

He detailed the efforts Matias had made to track her to the crash in Peru, the investigators he himself had hired, and finally Cole Hartman, the man who located her here.

When all the hard questions were answered, she asked him easy things — *Is Camila happy? Healthy? Still as ornery as ever?* — and he was all too eager to answer. The adoration he felt for Camila was as clear as his crystal blue eyes. He spoke of her as if he were eternally bound to her and wouldn't want it any other way. They shared a connection that had nothing to do with Lucia. He was here, doing what he thought was right, not for Lucia, but for Camila.

Realization gut-punched her. "You love her."

"I do."

It stung. Like a thousand angry bees stung. Even though she'd only just met him and her jealousy didn't make a lick of sense, she felt what she felt and there wasn't a damn thing she could do about it.

Still, she couldn't stop herself from pointing out, "She loves Matias. Always has." She gentled her voice. "That's not going to change, Tate."

"I know." His tone matched hers despite the flare

of persistence in his eyes.

Her stomach chose that moment to cramp painfully, but she didn't let the illness reveal itself, didn't show a hint of discomfort on her face. "Do you intend to win her heart with news of my survival?"

"No. And let's talk about that—*your survival*. I know Tiago's men pulled you from the crash and brought you here. You're not locked up, and you've already demonstrated your ability to evade his guards. Why are you still in this godforsaken place?"

Her defenses bristled. "Venezuela is a beautiful country. The landscapes alone… Have you even seen the forests and the mountains and the beaches? What about the birds? There's like fourteen-hundred bird species here. Oh, and the dolphins. Have you seen the Amazon river dolphins?"

She hadn't seen any of those things, but often when she sat alone in her apartment at night, she imagined what it would be like to leave the slum and become an explorer. Or maybe go to a university and become one of those scientists who discovered new plants that cured diseases.

"You're not here for the damn dolphins." He prowled toward her and leaned down, bracing his hands on the couch bed and caging her in. "You're going to leave with us. I'll take you straight to Camila and—"

"No." Panic rose, and she pushed at his chest, unable to move him. "I can't."

"Why the hell not?"

"If Camila thinks I'm dead…" Anguish swelled against the backs of her eyes, magnified by a blooming migraine. "It needs to stay that way."

"That's not gonna happen." He straightened,

scanning the room until his gaze landed on a burner phone. "I'll call her right now so you can tell her yourself."

"Listen to me, goddammit." She leapt from the couch and grabbed his arm, digging her nails into muscle. "She already mourned my death once. Please, if you love her, you won't put her through that again."

"What are you saying?" His voice took on a lethal bite, making her shiver.

"You can't tell her I'm alive." She strode toward her weapons on the kitchen table.

With a disbelieving laugh, he stayed on her heels, breathing down her neck. "You need to give me a lot more than that, sweetheart."

"I'm living on borrowed time." She reached for her guns.

He knocked her hand away, and in the next breath, he had her pinned against the wall with a fist wrapped around her windpipe.

"You answer to me now. You're under *my* protection." He put his face in hers, his lips so close she smelled toothpaste on his breath. "You will leave with us — gagged, blindfolded, shackled, whatever it takes." He glanced at Van. "You good with that?"

"Sure." Van reclined on the couch bed, with an arm bent behind his head.

"What's it going to be, Lucia? The easy way? Or..." He tightened his fingers against her throat, cutting her airflow. "The hard way?"

She couldn't breathe, couldn't pry his grip away. The urgent need for oxygen grew stronger and more desperate, but did it really matter? She was alone in the darkness save for the strong grip around her throat. She couldn't think of a better way to die than fading beneath his beautifully ferocious eyes. But those eyes were traps, the possessive gleam in them compelling her mouth to soundlessly form two words she'd held back.

"What?" He yanked his hand away, freeing her. "Say that again."

"I'm dying." She wheezed, clutching her throat as her attention snagged on the paling sky beyond the window. "Shit, I have to go."

"Dying?" He exchanged a startled look with Van then scanned her up and down, pausing on her midsection. "How? Is it your injury from the crash in Peru?"

"I don't know." It was a terrible truth, one she should've figured out by now. "But if I'm not where I'm supposed to be by dawn, I won't get my medicine. And if I don't get that injection, I'll be in respiratory failure by lunchtime."

He went still. So still the air around him thinned and charged, sweeping over her like a blanket of static and raising the hairs on her arms. He looked floored, volatile, teetering on the brink of eruption.

"Tate—"

"You're telling me you're terminally ill." Denial flexed at the edge of his voice.

"Yes."

"But you don't know what's wrong with you?"

"No, I... I don't know the medical diagnosis."

"How can you not—?" He swiped a hand down his face and glared at her. "Tell me the symptoms."

"I don't have time for this."

His eyes were as deep and turbulent as the ocean, his lips perfectly arched despite the pressed line of

122

disapproval. Muscles twitched across his bare chest and broadcasted his impatience. But it was his demeanor that demanded her attention.

He rendered her immobile simply by standing there, looking utterly self-possessed and cavalier, like a saintly king or a gallant warrior. Or a sociopath. Whatever it was that made him so damn compelling seemed to glow like a backdrop for his powerful legs, broad chest, and brutally gorgeous features.

He was strong enough, assertive enough to take her burdens so she wouldn't have to carry them by herself. It was his presence that spoke to her, commanded her at a cellular level, and she obeyed.

"The symptoms vary, but what I experience most is chronic nausea, abdominal pain, hematemesis, migraines, bradycardia, tremors, ataxia, seizures, muscle paralysis…" She released a breath of exhausted pain.

"Fucking Christ." He lowered his head and squeezed the bridge of his nose. Then he was staring at her again, his expression dangerous. "Are you experiencing any of that tonight?"

"Some, yeah."

"Told you she was too thin," Van said from the couch.

Tate tossed him a warning glare and softened his eyes as he looked back at her. "Badell gives you medicine? It helps?"

"His doctors developed a treatment. The injection is the only thing keeping me alive."

"Did *he* tell you that?"

"Yes, and I know what you're thinking." With trembling hands, she snatched her guns from the table and holstered them in her waistband. "Sometimes he lets me see just how close to death I can get. I've tasted it, Tate. Felt its icy breath suck the life from my body. Have you ever experienced that? The abject, black void of extinction? The dismal nothingness? There's no bright light at the end of the tunnel. There's no fucking tunnel. When your heart stops, there's *nothing*."

"You're leaving with me, Lucia. Right now. We'll go directly to the hospital."

"I'll be dead within hours. Long before they can diagnose me."

His nostrils flared. "Badell knows what's wrong with you?"

"Of course. As long as he keeps my condition a secret and the antidote locked in his safe, I can't leave."

"Have you tried to find —?" He swore under his breath. "That's why you asked me if I was a doctor."

Tiago owned every medical practitioner in the neighborhood. Moonlighting at the sex club twice a month was her only opportunity to furtively search for visiting doctors. She just hadn't had any luck.

"If I had more time…" She glanced at the window, where the graying sky signaled the coming of dawn. "I'd tell you all about my attempts to escape, my failed visit with a doctor, and the bloodshed that followed."

She strode toward the door, opened it, and wobbled on the threshold.

"You can't fix this, Tate. Go home. And tell my sister…" Keeping her back to the room, she swallowed the heartache shredding her voice. "Tell her I'm already dead."

Forcing one foot in front of the other, she walked out and closed the door behind her.

CHAPTER 11

The door shut, slamming Tate's pulse into overdrive.

"Goddammit." He spun, searching for shoes, a gun, his phone… "She's not walking away from me again."

"She just did." Van threw a bullet-resistant shirt at him and shoved on his own shoes.

"I need you to stay here." He dressed at breakneck speeds and grabbed a burner phone. "Watch the guards from the window and call me if there's trouble."

"You're going to get yourself killed." Van gripped the back of Tate's waistband and wedged a gun against his butt crack.

"Dude, get your dick beaters away from me." Twisting away, he moved the weapon from his ass to the front of his jeans.

"Dick beaters?"

"Your fucking hands, man. We're gonna talk about boundaries when I get back."

"Are you sure you want to put the gun there?" With the arch of an impish brow, Van stared at Tate's groin. "It would be a shame if you shoot your dick off."

The thought made his balls shrivel, but it was a

helluva lot quicker to draw a gun from the front than to reach around the back.

"My dick isn't your concern." He crouched to lace his boots. "I'm going to follow her, find out how she enters her apartment, and come right back."

Cole had said there was only one way in and out of her unit, but that couldn't be right. How did she slip past the guards at her door?

She had too many secrets, but he'd find a way to unwrap her, crack her open, and expose all her mysteries.

I'm dying.

That one had hit him sideways, and he still felt off-balance and outraged from the blow. And doubtful. She seemed pretty fucking resigned to die, but he wanted proof, validation from a professional, someone *not* connected to Badell. There were ways to go about that, but the logistics would be tricky and could put her at risk.

"Now we know why Cole couldn't find medical records on her." He tied the second boot and stood.

"Badell figured out how to hold her captive," Van said, his voice eerily calm, "without locks or shackles."

"Doesn't mean I can't get her out."

Maybe he could get a blood sample and ship it to a lab? Could it be that easy? *Not likely.*

Gun, phone, armored shirt... He had everything he needed and raced to the door, pausing with his hand on the knob. "Did you record her symptoms?"

"I captured the entire conversation." Van held up a small recording device. "What about you? Any luck with the tracker?"

"I stuck one on each of her Berettas when she handed them to me." He opened the door and scanned the vacant hall.

The trackers — courtesy of Cole — were also listening devices. A spy camera on her body would've been ideal, especially since Tate had no choice but to let her return to Badell this morning, but wearable cameras were bulky, and the battery life was shit.

Putting audio transmitters on her weapons was risky enough. If someone discovered them, Lucia would pay the price.

"Try not to die," Van called after him as he closed the door.

Down the stairs, out the main entrance, and along the empty street, he sprinted to catch up with her. The half-light minutes just before dawn was the sleepiest time in Caracas. There were fewer gunshots. No passing motorists. No people anywhere. Just the pound of his boots hitting concrete and the heave of his lungs.

He rounded the first corner of his building, ran a block toward her apartment, and slowed at the next bend. If he turned right, he'd walk into her alley and the guards who waited for her.

Removing his phone, he pulled up the tracking program and pinpointed her location. She'd gone around the block? Why? Maybe to circle the rear of her apartment complex to enter a side door? But how would she get in from there? He'd seen the blueprints of the building and her one-room unit. The front door was the only way into her living quarters.

He followed her moving location, veered left, and ran two blocks out of the way, which spit him out at the rear of her T-shaped building. Sticking to the shadows, he kept his senses sharp and aware. But he couldn't watch his back while sweeping the shadows in front of him.

And that was how he ended up with the unmistakable press of a gun against the back of his head.

He froze, spine twitching and pulse thrashing in his ears. For a hopeful second, he thought Lucia was behind him, aiming a Beretta with irritation twisting her gorgeous face.

Couldn't be her, though. This gunslinger was a mouth-breather, hacking air with a scratchy throat and reeking of cigarettes.

The string of words that followed were spat in Spanish. A man's voice. A tall man, given the height and direction of sound. His impatience was evident in the jab of the gun against Tate's head.

Each shout and jab made his muscles tense to react, to knock the man on his ass. But he forced himself to remain still and think through the best course of action.

He'd practiced this exact scenario with Cole before they left the States. A little movement to the side, just a quick-second shift would remove his head from the path of the bullet. But he wouldn't have time to pause after that. It had to be a single flow of motion. Shift to the side, reach back for the gun while dropping, turning, drawing his own gun, and firing without hesitation.

Christ, it was a shot in the dark. Literally. The odds of turning before he ate a bullet weren't in his favor, but it was the only shot he had.

Breathe in. Breathe out.

Then he moved.

A gunshot rang out—a single jarring bang that resounded in his chest, disorientating him. He blinked at the gun in his hand, at the finger that never made it to the trigger.

The scent of blood clotted the air, so sharp and

acrid he could taste it. Was it coming from him? His stomach turned to ice as he ran a numb hand over his head, seeking a wound.

It took him a second to register the overweight man at his feet, sprawled in a dark puddle of gore and leaking from a hole in his temple.

Whoever fired that shot had impeccable aim and could've just as easily hit Tate.

A chill swept over him, and he quickly put his back against the building, surveying the perimeter. No movement. No apparent witnesses. The shooter had to have been Van or Lucia.

Another minute passed before the slender form of a woman emerged from behind a car across the street. *Lucia.*

With a heavy exhale, he seated the gun in the front of his jeans, right next to the delicious ache clenching in his groin. Because fuck him, she was all legs, perky tits, and fearless beauty charging toward him like a warrior princess.

There was nothing sexier than a woman with a gun. But Lucia was more than that. Strong, stunning, and gutsy as all hell, she was badass personified. And to think, she was sick. *Dying.* She didn't let it show in the square of her shoulders or the jut of her chin. She looked for all the world like she was bulletproof. Impenetrable.

Except he'd penetrated her, impaled her deeply and thoroughly, and fuck if he didn't want to do it again.

By the time she reached him, he was so goddamn hard he had to step back and fold his arms across his chest to stop himself from falling on her like a rabid animal.

"Are you pissed?" She crouched beside the body

and rifled through the pockets.

"Pissed?" He lowered his arms, dumbfounded. "You saved my life."

"No, I didn't." Pocketing the dead man's money, she tossed the empty wallet on the ground. "You moved your head. His bullet would've missed you. With your gun out and the way you turned so fast, you had the shot." She glared at the corpse. "Sorry I took that from you. I've wanted this kill for years."

"Why? Who was he?"

"One of Tiago's stooges." She rose to her full height and spat on the body. "A serial rapist."

The pain simmering beneath her voice triggered his protective instincts.

"He hurt you?" He gripped her arm.

"Not anymore." Pulling away from him, she strode down the alley behind her apartment building.

He wished he would've been the one to shoot the fucker. He'd killed before, right alongside Lucia's sister, and enjoyed every second of it. Evidently, he had an unquenchable thirst for the blood of the guilty.

"What about the body?" he asked her retreating back.

"Leave it."

He trailed after her, lengthening his strides to catch up. "The police—"

"They can't touch me." She set a moderate pace, her steps even and eyes straight ahead. "Tiago, on the other hand, would punish me for killing one of his men."

His jaw clenched. "Punish you how?"

"Death." She lifted a shoulder and veered around a dumpster in the narrow alley. "But hey, I didn't do it, right? I mean, I've been in my apartment all night with guards on my door."

"Jesus, Lucia." He tipped his head up, probing the dark second-floor windows. "Someone might've seen you."

"Maybe, but it's their word against that of his two best guards and his favorite girl."

His favorite girl?

What kind of relationship did she have with Badell? When he gave her medicine, what did she have to do in return? The only information Tate had was the video of her at the compound and Cole's words.

Her job is to inflict physical and emotional pain. Torture. Sometimes she rapes them.

If she raped the victims, why did she have such a grudging reaction to the rapist she just killed? It didn't make sense, and he desperately needed to understand.

It would be daybreak in about ten minutes, and they'd reached a bend in the alley where the three arms of her building came together. Her apartment would be right there.

He didn't know how she would get in from back here, but first, he needed to settle this one thing.

Grabbing her waist mid-stride, he swung her around and held her against him, chest to chest. "How are you his favorite girl?"

She stared into his eyes for a span of several heartbeats, her face an emotionless mask.

"Does he fuck you? Or force you?" He wrapped his fingers around her neck and forged his voice with steel. He wasn't angry with her. He was angry *for* her. "Answer me."

A muscle bounced in her cheek. Then slowly, reluctantly, her aloofness shuddered and broke away.

Uncertainty creased her forehead. Disquiet twitched her lashes. Concession sighed from her parted lips.

"You're possessive." She raised a tentative hand and traced the corner of his mouth.

His lips felt a little weak and a lot hungry. "I told you you're under my protection—"

"I don't mean *me* specifically. You're possessive as a general rule." She moved her finger along the seam of his mouth, exploring with achingly sweet curiosity. "It's a quality I've never given much thought to…until now. It looks good on you. Like really fucking good."

Her breath whispered against his face, weaving with the flutters of her featherlight touch. A touch he felt all the way down to his balls.

She caressed a path across his cheek and slid her fingers through his hair, all the while inching closer. Hovering her lips just out of reach. Leaving a hairbreadth between *stay* and *go*. A sliver between *yes* and *no*.

It all blurred together as he leaned in with single-minded focus. Maybe it was just the perfect combination of feminine seduction—the sultry look in her eyes, the drugging feel of her touch, the warm scent of her skin—but he felt buzzed, utterly drunk on this woman, and he needed to kiss her like he needed air.

Only she shifted back. He chased her mouth, and she evaded again, blocking the next advance with a finger against his lips.

He reached up to remove her hand, but her words stopped him.

"I've never had sex with Tiago Badell." She didn't give him time to respond as she lifted on tiptoes and pressed her lips next to the finger she held against his mouth.

Then she stepped back, pushing against his chest until he released her waist. "Goodbye, Tate."

Oh, fuck that. He gave a humorless chuckle. "Can't get rid of me that easily. I'm walking you home—"

"And you did. Thank you." She turned to the nearest apartment door and removed a key from her pocket.

Given the vicinity of the door and his recollection of the building's blueprints, she was accessing her next-door neighbor's unit.

She unlocked the door, and the yap of a tiny dog on the other side confirmed it. There must've been a hidden cut through between the two apartments?

He moved to follow her in, but she flattened a hand against his chest.

"I really love how protective you are." Her voice was gentle, but it felt like she was fighting tooth and nail to hold herself together. "Camila's lucky to have you."

Her face was ghastly pale, and her legs trembled to keep her upright. Christ, she didn't look well at all. It killed him to let her out of his sight, but he didn't have the medicine she needed. She had to go to Badell.

"I'll be here when you get back."

"No. You need to go." She met and held his eyes as the first light of dawn reflected in hers. "Take care of Camila. Please."

Then she shut the door in his face.

CHAPTER 12

Lucia must've looked like death by the time she arrived at the compound, because Tiago gave her a narrowed glance and immediately led her to his room.

The short walk wasn't short enough. She kept her expression impassive while dragging her listless feet and fighting the urge to retch. She hadn't eaten since Tiago's dinner last night, but her stomach buckled anyway, trying to empty its emptiness.

Her misery had long ago passed the point where she thought she couldn't endure more. Knowing her days were numbered broke her even further. With each staggering step, she heard the distant beat of her dying heart, felt it weakening, fading, taking her with it. Then she blacked out.

When she came to, she was being carried, undressed, and separated from her weapons, her consciousness flickering in and out through it all.

She stirred at the familiar prick of a needle. As the medicine trickled warmth through her thigh, she knew she'd live to loathe another day.

Tiago was there, holding her on his lap and stroking the edges of her panties — the only thing she was permitted to wear in his room. It was always the same. Injection in the morning. Dinner with Tiago at night. Torture, ransom, and debilitating pain scattered throughout the day.

"Why are you keeping me alive?" she murmured.

He set the syringe aside and smoothed his hands along her body. "I enjoy you."

The erection swelling against her backside said his enjoyment was sexual. *Without sex.*

"I don't have much time left." She rested her head back against his shoulder and closed her eyes. "What's wrong with me, Tiago?"

He cupped one of her bare breasts and rolled the nipple between his fingers. "You're perfect."

Over the course of a thousand mornings, in his room, on his lap, she'd grown indifferent to his touch. The caress of his hands, the absence of her clothes, the arousal in his voice—it was all just part of her daily medicine.

But this morning was different.

The feel of his fingers sliding across her skin set her teeth on edge. She didn't want him touching her, resting his gaze on her nudity, or telling her she was perfect.

What she wanted was Tate. Him on top of her, around her, locking her in the circle of his arms, and keeping everyone else out. Just him and her and the heady glide of their lips.

She'd said goodbye to him, but he wasn't going anywhere. She was certain he wouldn't leave until he got what he came for.

Her.

Not a future with her. No, his dream of the future was Camila.

Lucia just wanted a future. Period.

They were both fucked.

"Tiago?"

"Hm?" He nuzzled her neck.

"What if there's a cure your doctors aren't aware of? If you'd let me see another physician—"

"Did you know seventy percent of plants with anticancer properties exist only in the Amazon?"

Her blood turned to ice. "Cancer?"

"You don't have cancer." He slid a hand to her collarbone and traced the shape of it. "I'm feeling generous this morning. Would you like to hear a story?"

She doubted anything he told her would bring her comfort, but information was a weapon. "Yes. Please."

"My father was a pharmacist and an expert in medicinal botany. When he died, I brought his medical team here, to work for me."

Why would his doctors go from saving people to assisting him with kidnappings and torture? Maybe they were never the *saving* kind of doctors.

Except they'd saved *her*.

"The rainforest," Tiago said, "produces thousands of variations of seeds, berries, roots, leaves, bark, and flowers that have healing attributes. Only a small percentage have been discovered by modern man. But as you know, my doctors aren't modern."

The medical team of four men were in their sixties and seventies, with thick indigenous accents native to a land she couldn't place. Their skin, the darkest pigmentation she'd ever seen, bore picturesque scarification—different designs and words than that of Tiago's, but the welts appeared to have been cut with the same brutality. They reminded her of an ancient civilization, rich in culture and ceremony.

"My doctors know what ails you." He dragged the backs of his fingers across her abdomen. "And they've developed the only known antidote for it. Keep that in mind next time you try to seek a second opinion."

She already assumed he had the only antidote and often wondered if her illness was a byproduct of the crash in Peru. While chained in the back of a truck with a dozen other slaves, she'd felt the jolting, crashing fall as they tumbled off a cliff, heard the twisting of metal and agonized screams, and smelled the blood. After that, she remembered nothing.

The year that followed had been a drug-induced haze of surgeries and coma-like sleep. She had a scar across her abdomen but didn't know what damage lay beneath the marred skin.

The strange part was that her illness didn't surface until three years ago — seven years *after* the last surgery. Maybe the fix Tiago's doctors put in her was failing? The medicine erased the pain, but she couldn't go longer than twenty-four hours without another injection.

"What did you learn at the sex club?" Tiago asked.

"It was a quiet night." She'd been too busy riding a blue-eyed god to overhear the conversations around her.

"Tell me about the men you were with."

"There was just one. One of my usuals." The lie floated effortlessly off her tongue.

"Did he fuck you here?" He feathered his touch across her lips.

"Yes."

"And here?" His hand spread over the front of her panties, his fingers pressing against the satin crotch.

She nodded.

"I envy him." His voice, scratchy with desire, rasped at her ear.

Such an odd thing to say, since he didn't do more than touch her. Did he ever have sex? She never saw him with a lover and knew he didn't allow anyone else in his room. Yet he was so easily aroused and constantly hard.

He was also distrustful and paranoid and never took unnecessary risk. Maybe he thought sex was too risky. It was, in a way. At the peak of climax, when the body let go and the mind lost all reason, a man was at his most vulnerable.

If she could lure him to the edge of orgasm, she'd use his distraction to stab her thumbs into his eyes and crush the sockets. It was a plausible way to kill a man, right?

Problem was, after spending eleven years with him, he hadn't shown a single moment of weakness.

Twenty minutes had passed since she received the injection, and the pain had retreated into the sickly place inside her. Her heart rate found a normal tempo, and feeling returned to her legs.

Tiago, who was always attuned to her state of health, nudged her off his lap. "Let's go see to our newest victim."

Her insides twisted anew.

He led her to the hall and waited as she dressed. When she tucked the Berettas in her jeans, she let her hands linger on the grips.

She could shoot him. His guards would fire immediately, probably before she even squeezed the trigger. But maybe, just maybe she could get a shot off before she died.

It was a hopeless paradox. On one hand, she

wanted to die, ached to end the endless misery. On the other, if one of his guards aimed a gun at him, she wouldn't hesitate to shoot the traitor to protect Tiago.

If Tiago died, she couldn't access his safe, didn't know how to locate his doctors, and wouldn't be able to find a cure before her organs failed. His death would bring the onset of hers, and as much as she wanted that, there was a brighter, stronger yearning inside her.

She wanted to live.

Her contradictory train of thought circled back to the armed guards. If she were willing to shoot his men to save Tiago's life, the same must've been true for them. This wasn't an operation rooted in loyalty. She suspected Tiago's men were indebted to him somehow, and like her, it was in their best interest to keep him alive.

Tiago's gaze fell to the vicinity of her hands on the Berettas at her back, and she tensed.

A ghost of a smile, deprived of amusement, touched his lips. "Try it, Lucia."

"I'm not stupid." She lowered her arms to her sides and stood taller.

"No, you're not that." Offering his arm, he escorted her to the basement and the kidnapped victim who waited.

CHAPTER 13

Two hours later, Lucia left the sobbing victim chained to the floor in the chamber. As she stepped into the hall and tossed the condom in the trash, she tried to embody the cold precision of a blade, sharpening her expression and steeling her posture. But despair swelled an unwieldy pressure behind her eyes, and every breath was a fight to keep the tears away.

Armando had been the cameraman, and as he followed her out, his probing, over-staring eyes produced a stampede of goosebumps across her nude skin.

"When are you going to milk my nuts?" he asked in Spanish.

The gun was already in her hand, so it only took a fraction of a second to aim at the nuts in question.

"Another time then." With a grin, he lumbered toward the stairs.

She waited until he was out of sight before lowering the Beretta and pulling on her clothes.

Today's victim was a middle-aged married man and father of five, who had come to Venezuela on a religious mission.

And she'd just raped him.

If she had any humanity left before she'd stepped into that room, she didn't now. But despite the man's wretched crying, he wasn't broken. If his wife paid the ransom within three days, he'd live.

Lucia dragged the balaclava off her head and let it fall to the floor. She was the one who was broken, and if she lived three more days, she wouldn't deserve it.

Footsteps approached from the stairs. She holstered both guns in her jeans and turned to find Tiago strolling toward her, flanked by two guards.

He gave her a cursory once-over. "Was it convincing?"

The victim had wept prayers to his god, begged for his virtue, cried for his wife to forgive him, and in the end, ejaculated in the condom, inside her, with a self-loathing howl. As far as torture went, he was emotionally wounded, and the camera caught every second of it.

"Yes." She breezed past Tiago, anxious to escape the basement. "If his wife has the money, she'll pay it."

"I know why you did it."

Her breath caught. Did what? Rape that man? Or did he know about the one she killed this morning? Oh God, did he find out about Tate?

She slowed her steps, arranged her features into a detached visage, and pivoted to face him. "What do you mean?"

"Leave us." He swept a hand at the guards without looking at them.

The two armed men retreated to the stairs and closed the door, leaving her alone in the dark hall with Tiago.

The guns at her back suddenly felt heavy and threatening, like foreboding shadows looming behind her. There wasn't a single time in eleven years when she was permitted to keep her weapons in Tiago's presence without his guards. If this was a test, she was guaranteed to fail.

"Come here." He snapped a finger at the space before him.

Heart hammering, she held her arms at her sides and closed the distance. When she reached him, he slid his hands around her waist and rested his fingers on the grips of her guns.

She closed her eyes as everything inside her froze. This was it. He was going to shoot her with the guns she'd earned in his employ.

"I know why you petitioned me to use your method of torture," he said at her ear.

Oh. A ragged breath fled her lungs.

When she was initiated into this job, her role had been to hold the camera as Tiago exacted ungodly pain from the skin of his victims. She'd been weaker then, her stomach unbearably sensitive to the sight of blood and sounds of anguish.

She'd also been naive enough to believe rape was a mercy over the flesh-cutting cruelty Tiago inflicted.

The victims only needed to look distressed for the video, mistreated just enough to convince a family member to send money without hesitation. Rape had been her solution.

And that was the flaw in her logic. When was rape ever a solution?

But in her idiocy, she'd persuaded Tiago to use her vile approach instead of his. Not only had he agreed, he'd designated *her* as the resident torturer of the male victims.

It was on the tip of her tongue to tell him she'd been wrong, that her way wasn't as effective. But could she really go back to watching him carve up the bodies of innocent men? *Men.* He never tortured women in that way. She didn't think it was out of chivalry. Quite the opposite. He'd told her once that his art of mutilation was a *man*'s rite of passage.

"You're trying to make a difference in the kidnapping world." His mouth hovered over hers, his breaths warming her lips. "And you're doing it with sex."

"Rape." She ground her molars.

"Whatever you want to call it, Lucia. You could've begged me to abandon my ruthless line of work."

"You would've killed me."

"That's right, and you can't make a difference if you're dead, yeah? So instead, you suggested what you believed was a gentler method of torture. A suggestion that didn't make you appear weak to me or my men."

Her method was psychological and emasculating. His was physical, gruesome, and barbarous. Whether one was better than the other was debatable.

"I feel nothing in particular for the victims." He squeezed the grips of her guns, pressing them against the rise of her backside. "Except maybe pity. It's their own stupidity that brings them into my kingdom. But that wasn't the case with you. Taken from your home, left to die in a fatal crash… None of your choices led you to me. Do you know why I kept you imprisoned all those years? Why I didn't just kill you then?"

She tried not to think about her first eight years in his compound — locked in a room on the upper floor, the unbearable isolation and fear, the news of her parents' deaths, Camila already gone. In those darkest years of her life, she lost parts of herself she would never recover.

Her illness developed over that time. When she became too sick to go without daily injections, Tiago had a new way to cage and torment her.

"No." She met his heartless eyes. "I don't pretend to know why you do anything you do."

"I hope you never give me a reason to kill you." He slid the Berettas out of her waistband and glided the metal frames along the outsides of her arms. "No matter how ill you are or how intolerable I make your life, you manage to keep something in your possession, something I lost long ago." Lifting one of the guns, he trailed the barrel across her cheek. "You still have compassion."

Her throat tightened. It was the closest he'd ever come to saying anything sentimental without making it feel sexual.

It was also possible that he said shit like this just to fuck with her head.

"I live in an ugly world," he went on, "and you're… You're a pretty little flicker of compassion, begging to be extinguished. Sometimes I'm tempted to do just that. But I like you like this. You remind me how weak and foolish it is to cling to humanity."

Her nostrils flared.

"You can retrieve your guns from my guards." Without a backward glance, he ambled toward the stairs with her weapons. "You're free until dinner."

Free.

She wished for nothing, prayed to no one, and had zilch to lose. If freedom was a state of mind, she was hopelessly liberated.

CHAPTER 14

"She's leaving the compound." Tate paced through the apartment, his pulse wound up and nerves shot to hell.

The tiny microphones on Lucia's weapons broadcasted to a receiver on his phone. He'd listened to her activities all morning while burning through a pack of cigarettes and seething every shade of rage.

Without visual confirmation, it was difficult to understand exactly what was happening. But from the sounds and conversations, he knew she'd passed out, was separated from her weapons for a while, then used a stairwell to the lower levels of the compound. That was when he'd sent his fist through the wall.

"You're gonna give yourself a coronary." Van reclined on the couch, tracking his movements with a narrowed glare.

Van was notorious for his explosive temper, yet he'd remained chillingly calm when they'd listened to her rape a sobbing, pleading man. Maybe it was because Van had been in a similar situation and was the one person who could empathize with her.

Tate, on the other hand, had gone ballistic when she was in that basement chamber. His imagination had created all kinds of graphic images to fill in what he couldn't see. It wasn't until he'd heard the pain in her voice during her conversation with Badell that his vision cleared, and his head stopped pounding.

She was stuck in a living nightmare, and there was fuck all he could do about it when he couldn't get to her.

But she was on the move now, stepping onto the street outside of the compound and turning...

"She's not heading toward her apartment." He strode toward the door, phone in hand and weapons concealed beneath his clothes.

Without a word, Van followed him out of the building and trailed a safe distance behind.

The tracking signal led Tate to a street market fifteen minutes away on foot. Although the tents were crowded with people, it didn't take long to spot her raven-black hair amid the throng.

A thin shirt hung from her shoulders, the wide neckline clinging to the delicate peaks of her tits. Flat stomach and toned legs encased in denim, she had the body of a young girl, but she wore it like a woman. A woman who would fuck rigorously, unapologetically, in every position and manner he wanted.

And he wanted.

He wanted to feel her fall apart on his cock, hear her cry in relief, and see a glimmer of happiness on her face. But more than that, he wanted her safe and healthy and out of this city.

Her guards wouldn't be far, so he kept his distance, marking her as she moved from stall to stall, touching the produce and staring at the meats. Jesus, she looked hungry, her gaze crawling over the food with ravenous longing, yet she didn't buy anything.

148

Watching her poke through the market empty-handed produced a protective twinge in his chest. She was too thin, too alone, and given the dark circles around her eyes and the sag of her shoulders, too goddamn sad. Every bone in his body thrummed to take care of her.

As he slipped deeper into the market area, the sweet smell of slow-cooked meat and fried dough saturated the air. He paused within a few paces of her and directed his eyes on the hanging rope of bananas she'd caressed.

She must've sensed him, because she turned at the edge of his vision, and that deep brown gaze warmed the side of his face.

Knowing her guards were watching, he held out some bills to purchase a few bananas and gave her no reaction.

With a casual twist of her neck, she scanned the perimeter, likely searching for his backup.

Van stood at his nine o'clock across the street, and the moment she spotted him, her chest hitched with a sigh. Then she continued to the next stall.

From there, they eased into a wordless interplay. She touched or glanced at the foods she liked, and he bought them—bread, pork, strawberries, coconut cookies. When she reached the last tent, she selected a paper bag of tea and handed it to the merchant.

Tate sidled in behind her, fighting the impulse to rest a hand against the small of her back. He couldn't touch her, but she was close enough to infuse his senses with hints of citrus and gun oil, sunshine and city air.

He didn't look at her as he paid for the tea and whispered against her hair, "You're not alone."

Before she could respond, he left the bag of food on

the table in front of her and strolled out of the market.

For the rest of the day, he sat in his apartment, listening to the receiver. The silence on her end stretched for miles while she sat by herself across the street. Hopefully, she was sleeping since she hadn't slept at all last night.

He took a short nap, but it was restless, as his hearing was constantly tuned into the receiver. So he gave up and used the time to research her symptoms, leave messages for doctors in the States, and order the most comprehensive home blood test kit he could find online.

"Is that your plan?" Van gnawed on a toothpick, scrutinizing him. "An online blood test?"

"Got a better idea?"

"No. I just want to make sure you're not planning to storm the compound and steal the medicine."

He laughed, because dammit, it'd crossed his mind. "I'm not that reckless."

"I don't know. You have a crazy look in your eyes."

"I'm going to start staying with her at night." He paced to the window and surveyed the alley until he located her guards. "I need to learn everything she knows about her illness, the injections, the doctors, her injury... There's so much she hasn't told me. Maybe the solution isn't as hopeless as it seems."

"And if it is? Hopeless?"

"I'll draw her blood and send it off to a lab. Maybe figure out a way to bring a doctor here to her."

"If she has a terminal illness, Tate, there's little you can do."

"I know." He pivoted away from the window and

dragged his hands down his face. "I know."

They'd been in Caracas for eleven days. The trip could extend twice that or longer. Van never mentioned his wife, but he was so damn smitten with her the distance must've been eating at him something fierce.

"I could be here another month." Tate crossed his arms and met Van's eyes.

"I know. I'm with you till the end." Van gave him a soft, genuine smile.

The human side of Van was an anomaly. Witnessing its rare appearance wedged something deep inside Tate, crowding out some of the cynical, mistrustful feelings he'd harbored for so long.

"I'm sorry I haven't said it before, but thank you." He released a slow breath. "I'm glad you're here."

"I know." Another smile from Van, this one twisting with his standard wickedness. "Wanna mess around? This dry spell is brutal."

He closed his eyes and pressed his fingers against his brow. "And there you go, ruining it."

"You make it too damn easy." Erasing the few feet between them, Van stepped into his space. "Just so you know, I'm going to rid you of your homophobia."

His hackles went up. "I'm not homophobic."

"You have a problem with men fucking men."

"No, Van. I have a problem with *you* fucking *me*."

"Well, then let me clear that up." Van braced a hand on the window behind Tate and pressed close enough to exchange breaths. "I love my wife, and I'd cut my dick off before I cheated on her. I like to fuck *with* you, but I don't want to *fuck* you. Feel me?"

He'd rather not feel Van's breath on his face, but... "Yeah, I feel you."

"Good boy." Van patted his cheek and held the touch there, cupping his jaw for a defining moment before strolling away.

The familiar touch paired with the murmured words should've triggered a flashback of those agonizing weeks in the attic. But as Tate tempered his breathing, he felt strangely...peaceful.

"All teasing aside, you seem more comfortable around me." Van lowered onto the couch, his expression serious. "You're healing."

Tate nodded absently, thinking. Being cooped up with Van in a small apartment and depending on him for protection might've been a much-needed catharsis. He could honestly say he trusted the perverted psychopath. He might even like him, but he wouldn't admit that out loud. So he left it at a nod.

"Good." Van grabbed a bottle of tequila and poured two glasses. "Let's drink to that."

A few hours and shots of tequila later, Tate watched from the window as Lucia left her apartment to meet Badell for dinner.

Armed and ready to go, he left Van behind to keep a lookout on the alley.

When he hit the street, the sky was dark enough to cloak the buildings in shadows. He kept his head down, gait swift, and managed to arrive at the rear of her building unmolested. After a quick *I'm here* call to Van, he knocked on the neighbor's back door.

The middle-aged woman looked as harmless as her little dog when she answered, but she refused to open the door farther than a crack. When he slipped a few bolivars through the opening and said, "I'm Lucia's *amigo*," she was more than happy to escort him in and show him the hidden cut through in the closet.

It was too easy. Giving up Lucia's hidden door to a total stranger meant she'd do it for anyone willing to bribe her.

"What's your name?" he asked.

She stared at him blankly.

Well, shit. He'd only picked up a few Spanish words. "Uh...*nome?*" No, that wasn't right. "*Nombre?*"

"Franchesca."

"Franchesca, don't let..." *Damn language barrier.* He needed a translator. "Hang on."

He dialed Van, who had grown up in a border town and spoke fairly decent Spanish.

"Miss me already?" Van rumbled through the phone.

"Nope. I need you to translate. Tell Lucia's neighbor to never let anyone in the back door. Never show anyone the passage through the closet. Never, no one, under no circumstances. You get the idea. Use your threatening tone."

"I have a threatening tone?"

The innocent act was bullshit, so he decided to poke the sleeping bear. "You used to, but you've grown soft. And gay. So gay your pretty wife is at home right now bouncing on a harder, straighter dick."

"What the fuck did you just say to me? You're going to find out exactly how gay I am when I fuck your skull through your asshole, motherfucker. You're fucking dead."

"Yeah, *that* tone. Here she is." He handed the phone to Franchesca.

As she listened, her breath wheezed, and her eyes grew wide. When she handed the phone back, he disconnected and placed a larger bill in her trembling hand. No translation needed for *hush money*. It was a universal language in this town.

He left her staring at the money and slipped into Lucia's unit through the closet.

Other than the muted glow from a night light in the wall, her windowless space was dark. He did his best to seal up the passageway. She needed a lock or something to brace against it. Something to keep trespassers like himself from breaking in.

At least, she wouldn't be sleeping here alone anymore, and when he left Caracas, she would be with him.

Switching on the ceiling light, he scanned the barren room, which entailed a single-person mattress, mini fridge, sink, toilet, and shower head that aimed at an open tiled space.

Her boots and a small stack of clothes sat in the corner. On the counter was the bag of tea, a toothbrush, toothpaste, and a generic bottle of hair and body wash.

That was it? A lump formed in his throat. Everything she owned would fit in one small bag.

There were no cabinets or pantries, so where was her food? Her dishes and cookware? Hell, she didn't even have a stove.

His attention zeroed in on the fridge, and he yanked it open. The scanty contents wobbled on a single shelf—a sandwich of bread and pork, strawberries, bananas, and coconut cookies. The only food in her possession was what he'd bought her.

She has nothing.

No one should live like this.

A restless pang clenched behind his sternum, and

his muscles burned to do something, anything, to fix this.

But he couldn't fix it. Not without risking her life.

Phone in hand, he paced the room, back and forth, back and forth, staring at the screen.

It was time to call Matias. The cartel capo could find the best doctors and bring them here. According to Cole, it would take weeks, but Tate could at least get that ball rolling.

Drawing a calming breath, he dialed the number by memory and hovered his thumb over the button that would connect the call. And he hesitated.

I'll be dead within hours. Long before they can diagnose me.

Lucia knew how resourceful Matias was, yet she'd begged Tate not to call him or Camila. She was fucking stubborn in her conviction that Badell held the only antidote.

Then there was Cole's warning that Matias wouldn't have enough men and sway here to fight Badell.

Fuck! He erased the number on the phone and slumped against the wall. He needed to talk to Lucia first. Then he'd call Matias.

Over the next hour, he listened to her dinner conversation with Badell. Strange how she was allowed to keep her guns in his presence. Though there was a span of time this morning when it sounded like they'd been taken from her. Was it when she received her injection? If she was given medicine, Tate didn't hear it happen.

As long as he keeps my condition a secret and the antidote locked in his safe, I can't leave.

Where was the safe? Did she have access to its

location? Were guards posted in every room?

There might've been guards where she met Badell for dinner, but it was just the two of them talking and eating. The discussion focused on business—police activities, competitor secrets, and weapons suppliers. If Tate were a government spy, the information would've been gold. But he didn't give a shit about Tiago Badell's dirty affairs.

The entirety of his concern focused on the brown-eyed beauty who was sitting with a man who could kill her on a whim. Meanwhile, Tate paced her apartment with knots the size of Texas tying up his insides.

When she finally left the compound, he turned off the light, stood behind the front door, and listened to her footsteps through the receiver. When Van called to tell him she was in the alley, he silenced the phone and waited.

The seconds felt like a marathon—sprinting pulse, labored breaths, the urgent need to cross the finish line.

She was his finish line, and when she opened the door, it took every ounce of his self-control to remain silent and still.

Close the door, Lucia.

The instant she did, he launched...right into the barrel of a gun in his face.

"It's me," he whispered into the darkness.

"What are you—?"

Without warning, she dropped the Beretta in his hands and covered her mouth. Then she ran through the unlit room, falling with a thump near the toilet.

"Lucia?" He holstered the gun and searched for the light switch.

DEVASTATE

When he found it, the sound of retching shuddered the air.

CHAPTER 15

"Shit." A surge of panic sent Tate racing toward Lucia's doubled-over body as she emptied her dinner into the toilet.

The guards would be outside on the street, probably out of hearing range. But just in case, he would have to keep his voice soft.

"Did you get your medicine this morning?" He dropped to his knees beside her and gathered her hair.

"Yeah." She moaned weakly with her head in her hands and elbows wobbling on the seat. "Nighttime is always the worst."

He stroked her back, vibrating with anger at his own helplessness. "What can I do?"

She vomited again, and tears streaked down her pallid face. "I'm sorry."

His chest caved in. Why the fuck was she apologizing?

Her arms dropped, and her head hung over the toilet, swinging back and forth and plopping tears into the bowl. "I raped a man this morning."

Fucking Christ. This was wrong. Wrong timing. Wrong place. Wrong everything. As each wrongful second passed, he felt more and more useless.

"You just puked the only thing you've eaten today." He hit the toilet lever and glimpsed specks of blood before it flushed away. "Goddammit!"

There was no drug store. No urgent care. Nothing in this apartment to help her. There wasn't a goddamn thing he could do. *Nothing!*

"Please, don't be mad," she whispered.

"I'm not mad." He was so fucking livid he couldn't think straight. "What hurts?"

She sat back on her heels and wiped her mouth. "I probably look like the living dead, but I feel better."

Her complexion was ghost-white, her eyes sunken and bruised, and she appeared to have lost ten pounds she didn't have to lose. But despite it all...

"You're beautiful." He touched a knuckle to her chin.

Her pretty, pixie-like features contorted in misery, and her chest heaved in sudden bursts, as if she were swallowing down a sob. "You're lying."

"Lucia—"

"Don't." She made a wretched sound and pushed him away.

He wouldn't budge and instead reached for her.

"I don't want you to see me like this." She twisted, giving him her back. "Please, Tate. Just go. Go back to Texas."

"You're fucking crazy if you think I'll leave you." He shifted around her and got in her face. "We're doing this. Together. *Us.* Get that through your stubborn head."

She laughed, a painfully broken sound that sent more tears skipping down her hollow cheeks.

"What?" he asked softly.

"*Us?* What does that even mean?"

"It means I'm staying—"

"For how long?"

He wanted to sling her over his shoulder like a damn caveman and take off tonight, right fucking now.

She must've read it in his eyes, because she heaved a frustrated breath. "Let's say I left with you. *Hypothetically.* What happens next?"

"I'll take you wherever you want to go." His pulse accelerated as he edged closer and brushed the hair out of her face. "We can stay with your sister in Colombia or go home to Texas. We'll get you healthy and safe."

"Then what?" More tears brimmed her eyes.

"Then we can…I don't know…get a Netflix subscription, rescue a dog, take a road trip to wine country, whatever people do. I don't give a fuck as long as you're well and we're far away from here."

"You talk about *us* and *we* in terms of a relationship. In terms of always."

Goddamn, woman. He wasn't prepared for this conversation.

"You're in love with Camila," she said.

"This isn't…" Jesus fuck, he wasn't pursuing a relationship with anyone. His focus was on here and now and keeping Lucia alive.

"It's not what?" she asked.

"We're not doing this right now." He gripped her elbow. "Can you stand?"

"You just said we're doing this. Together." She stared at the floor and didn't move. "I want to understand."

"You're right." He closed his eyes and gave himself a second to calm down. "We can talk about the future, but right now, I'm focused on your health and the danger you're in. You're hurting, and it's..." Helpless rage locked up his fists, and he breathed through it. "It's not in my DNA to sit back and let you dictate how this will go."

"Okay," she said numbly.

"Tell me what you need." He bent down to capture her gaze.

Her chin trembled, and she hugged her waist, shaking her head. "Why do you have to be so nice?"

It looked like she needed a hug more than anything else.

He pulled her onto his lap and embraced her tightly. "You're about to spend some time with me, and you'll find out just how *not* nice I am."

"You might be crazier than I am." She looped her arms around his neck and buried her nose against his throat. "Thank you for the food."

It was comforting, in an unfamiliar way, to hold her like this. It was also exactly what he needed, and he hadn't even realized it. She had the ability to hurt his heart and put it at ease all at once.

"I'll bring you more to eat," he said. "I'm also going to install slide bolts on both of those doors."

"You don't need to—"

"I'm sleeping here from now on. Until we leave."

Her muscles tensed, as if she were bracing to argue. Then she seemed to deflate with her next exhale. "I need to brush my teeth and take a shower."

He carried her to the sink and prepared her toothbrush. "Did you sleep today?"

"Yeah. How did you know I was at the market?"

"I'm watching you, Lucia. Get used to it."

She surprised him with a simple nod and turned

her attention to the toothbrush.

As she cleaned her teeth, he slid the heels off her feet, removed the gun from her waistband, and grabbed the second Beretta from his. Then he set everything beside her clothes in the corner.

The bugs on her guns were too conspicuous. It was only a matter of time before she or someone else noticed them. They also had a limited battery life and would need to be recharged every few days.

A glance over his shoulder confirmed she was bent at the sink with her back to him. He removed the bugs, pulled a fully charged one from his pocket, and adhered it to the arched underside of her heeled shoe.

The location was less noticeable, and since the audio quality was so good, he could adjust the receiver to tune out the tread of her footfalls.

If he told her about the listening devices, it would add another burden on her shoulders. He didn't want her walking into Badell's domain every day worrying about being wired. He also didn't want her filtering her conversations.

With the new bug on the sole of her shoe, he moved the mattress to butt up against the front door, checked the lock, and set his gun and knife beside the bed where he would sleep.

"The guards never come inside," she said from the sink. "They don't even stand near the door."

After watching the alley from his apartment window, he knew the guards usually hung out down the street. But he wasn't taking chances. If someone tried to push their way in, the door would bump the mattress and wake him. He would also make sure they kept their voices at a whisper.

Moving to the shower, he turned it on and adjusted the water temperature.

There was no curtain, no privacy whatsoever, but did she need that with him? She'd had her mouth on his cock, his cock in her pussy, his hands and lips all over her body.

"Has the nausea passed?" he asked.

"Yes."

"I'll help you with the shower."

"I'd rather you didn't."

Dignity. Despite her frailness, she glowed with it.

"I'm not leaving." He stared into her honey-brown eyes.

"I know." She stared right back.

Gripping the hem of her shirt, she pulled it over her head. The bra and jeans went next. Then she hooked her thumbs under the elastic of her black panties, slid them off, and carried them under the spray of the shower.

He meant to turn away and give her space, but he couldn't unglue his shoes from the floor, couldn't avert his greedy gaze from her body.

Bones protruded along her ribs and hips, but toned layers of muscles flexed in her arms, abs, and legs as she washed her panties.

She's washing her underwear in the shower?

"Is that the only pair you own?" He glanced at her skimpy stack of clothes and didn't see undergarments.

"The other pair ripped, so..." She stared at the worn scrap of satin and shrugged. "This is it."

"Give them to me."

When she handed them over, he scrubbed them in the sink, taking care with the delicate, thinning fabric.

Then he hung them on the doorknob to dry. "Anything else need washing?"

"Not tonight." She lathered bubbles through her hair and over her fragile curves, spreading the small dollop of soap impossibly far.

The impoverished way she lived seemed so disturbingly normal to her, but she hadn't been raised this way. Her parents had been successful citrus farmers and had given her a comfortable upbringing. *Until they sold her into slavery.*

It infuriated him to think that over the past eleven years, she'd adapted to hardship to the point that it didn't even faze her.

As she continued her shower, watching him watch her, a fog of complicated questions hung between them. Questions he wasn't ready to answer.

Did he want to get to know her romantically?

Could he be with her without thinking about her sister?

Would she resent his feelings for Camila?

Was it wrong to want her on such a carnal, animalistic level?

He couldn't stop thinking about fucking her again. Her gorgeous tits looked so damn appetizing. Round and firm with stiff pink nipples, they were perfect for biting and pinching and bruising.

His mouth watered, and blood surged to his cock, swelling his length at a painful angle behind the zipper.

"You're staring," she said.

He snapped his gaze to hers and glared unapologetically.

"What are you thinking about?" She ran her hands through her hair, rinsing the soap.

"You don't want to know."

"I can guess." She gave his erection a pointed look. "Tell me."

A conversation about her and him and Camila was a minefield he didn't want to tread, but sex was different. Lust was simple and clear-cut.

He clasped his hands behind him and gave her an honest answer. "You have great tits."

She glanced down and made a face. "I imagine they're a lot smaller than Camila's."

Well, that fucking backfired.

"They fill my hands," he said. "What more do I need?"

"Camila's?"

He pulled in a long breath. She wasn't going to let this go. If it made her happy, she could ask her questions, and he'd answer them. But first, he wanted her comfortable and fed.

"Time's up." He shut off the water and searched the room for a towel. "What do you dry off with?"

"Air dry." She squeezed out her hair and swiped the water off her arms.

Swallowing a string of explicits, he yanked off his shirt and used it to dry her shivering body. "You can't live like this."

"I get by."

With his hands grazing across her soft skin and her pussy inches from his face, he would've been wildly turned on under other circumstances. And he was. But his mind was stuck in a whirlwind.

She had a partial roll of toilet paper, toothpaste, soap, and a razor for shaving. She needed shampoo, underwear, basic pain medication, a fucking towel, and... What about feminine products?

"Where are your tampons? Pads?" he asked.

Her hand flew to his, where he wiped the wadded shirt across her stomach.

"I don't..." She made a sound in her throat and stepped out of his reach. "I don't need that."

A fist of dread clamped his insides. "Why not?"

"I haven't had a period since the accident." She grabbed a t-shirt from the pile of clothes and pulled it on.

No period in eleven years? Were her female organs damaged? Removed? Or was it stress? Malnutrition? An IUD? Having been raised in a brothel, he had an in-depth knowledge of monthly cycles, hormones...all the female stuff. If she couldn't conceive, the destruction would reach far beyond a physical injury.

Everything inside him thrashed to demand answers, but he remained silent, motionless. It was one of those instincts he depended on, and it was telling him not to push her on this.

She seemed to have shut down, moving robotically through the apartment, straightening and organizing with no purpose. Pausing at the sink, she ran hot water until steam floated into her face. Her hand trembled as she reached for a paper cup and tried to unwrap a pouch of tea.

He went to her, taking over the task. The water wasn't hot enough to steep the leaves, but it was the only option. Once the tea was prepared, he lifted her onto the counter, set the cup in her hand, and molded her fingers around it. Then he fixed her something to eat.

Her silence pressed against him, but at least she was drinking. Dehydration was one thing he could control in this fucked-up situation.

There were no plates, so he arranged the sandwich

and strawberries on the counter beside her. Then he crowded into her space, pushing against her knees until she spread them.

Wedged between her legs, he lightly stroked her damp hair and waited.

She drank half of the tea before she set it aside and closed her eyes. "I remember the crash in Peru. The falling sensation as we rolled. The bodies slamming against me. Bones being crushed. The sharp scent of blood." Her fingers skated over her midsection, shaking as she traced the scar. "And the pain..."

He felt it, the terrible hurt in her voice, as if he were living in the memory with her. It hit him right in the chest, and he clenched his jaw until his molars protested.

"I blacked out before I saw what impaled me." Her tone flattened, becoming detached. "I don't remember much of the next year with all the surgeries and sleep-inducing drugs. After that, Tiago kept me locked in a room. A suite in the old hotel. He didn't let me out for eight years."

"He what?" Fury hit him like a thunderbolt, ringing his ears and scattering his breaths.

"I was a prisoner." She lifted a shoulder. "He could've killed me. God knows why he didn't."

The impulse to hit something simmered beneath his skin. The next best thing would've been a cigarette, but he couldn't smoke here and risk the smell alerting the guards.

He pulled away from her and paced.

"He visited me every day," she said. "Always ate with me. Dinner was our thing. Still is. It's like he doesn't have anyone to talk to, no one he trusts anyway, and I was a safe ear since I was locked in a room with no contact with the outside world."

"When did you get sick?"

"During my isolation in that room. After the accident, the abdominal pain never went away. Then it spread, and new symptoms emerged. The headaches, nausea, muscle paralysis... It started happening about once a month. Increased to once a week. Then daily. Some days were better than others. It took his doctors months to diagnose me and develop a treatment. When Tiago eventually freed me from that room, I was sick every day and... Well, I was never free. Not with the guards." She gestured at the door. "I've made several attempts to escape, only to get hauled back and deprived of medicine until the only thing that could save me was a ventilator."

His nostrils widened with the force of his seething breaths. "Lucia..."

"I made contact with a doctor once, someone who didn't have his hands in Tiago's pockets. I met him at his house outside of the neighborhood. A gentle, kind man — he was willing to help me for free. But we didn't get past the medical questions before Tiago's men showed up and..." She clutched the hem of her shirt and stretched it to her knees, covering her thighs. "They cut off his arms and made me watch as he bled to death."

His heart ached for her. She'd endured so much and had done it alone. How could she not be defeated and despondent and at the end of her limit? Her luck was in the red, her strife ceaseless. She had a never-ending shortage of anything good in her life.

Yet here she was, asking him about *us* and the future. She hadn't given up, and it left him awestruck and overwrought with admiration.

"I think the antidote is derived from Amazon plants." She told him Badell's father had been a pharmacist and what little she knew about the team of indigenous doctors. "They're experts in medicinal botany."

"They're also surgeons?" He stepped toward her and touched her shirt over the scar.

"Yes. Tiago won't tell me what organs were damaged or removed, or how the sickness is related to the injury, or if—" She sucked in a hard breath, her expression blank. "Or if I can bear children. But hey, at least I don't have periods."

Her smile was hapless and heartbreaking, so utterly void of humor it tore him apart.

"I want you to do something for me." He held her face in his hands and forced her to look at him.

She sawed her teeth together, and a glimmer of fight lit her eyes.

"Tonight," he said, "I want you to not be so damn tough. Let it go. Give it to me. Let me be your strength."

"Tate—"

"One night, Lucia. Everyone needs someone. Even me. Tonight, I'm yours. Your someone."

"My person?" she whispered.

"Yeah."

It was a sluggish, circumspect unraveling, her entire body shuddering, fighting the turmoil that rose behind her eyes. She visibly wrestled with it, battling an inner storm he couldn't comprehend. But when she finally gave in, he was there, his arms around her, his lips in her hair, and his whispered words swaddling her in truths. *You're resilient and brave. I respect you. You're not alone. I'm here for you.*

She wept quietly, gracefully, and with every tear, he felt her muscles loosen and her joints give until she was pliable and spent and maybe even relieved.

As her tears slowed, he chased them with his lips, kissing them away one by one. He'd never been so moved, so absorbed in the emotions of a woman. He loved Camila, but she didn't need him. She'd never needed him. Not like this.

And that wasn't all. The taste of Lucia's tears, the provocative scent of her skin, the directness in her questions, the glimpse of vulnerability beneath her strong exterior — it turned him on like nothing else. This woman was everything he never knew he was attracted to.

When her eyes dried, he leaned back and inspected her exquisite face for signs of pain. "How do you feel?"

"Better." She placed a hand on his bare chest and idly stroked the muscle there. "Thank you."

"Your stomach?"

"Settled."

"Eat." He placed the sandwich in her hand and stepped back.

She nibbled on the bread, ate a strawberry, and after a few more bites, she tore into the pork with voracity.

Satisfied, he rested his fingers in his pockets and caught her gaze. "You have questions about Camila and me. Ask them."

CHAPTER 16

The last bite of the sandwich stuck in Lucia's throat under the force of Tate's stare. The intensity in his ice blue eyes, assertive growl in his voice, stillness in his confident posture — everything about his pushy, take-charge style made her blood throb and heat in places that had no business reacting at all.

He towered over her, a head taller and shoulders twice as wide. His expression was that of a man restraining his need, one who seemed to have everlasting patience. He adjusted his fingers in his pockets, shifting the front of his jeans to accommodate that huge, relentless erection — an erection that had been tenting his zipper since she removed her clothes.

Chemistry was an effortless thing between them. Last night at the club left no doubt in her mind about that. But this was more than sex.

He'd washed her panties.

Kissed her tears.

Held her as she'd cried.

Offered to be her person for one night.

And he loved her sister.

Her gaze faltered, bouncing around the room until

it collided with his once again.

You have questions about Camila and me. Ask them.

"Does Matias know?" She swallowed down the last of the tea and slid off the counter.

"Know what?" He caught her arm, steadying her.

"That you love her?"

"Yes."

And Tate was still alive? Maybe Matias wasn't threatened by him, though that seemed impossible. Tate would have a shameless effect on any woman he set his sights on, including her lovesick sister.

Lucia was thoroughly intimidated in the shadow of his powerful body and plundering gaze, but she also felt protected. And lucky. Without him here, she would've spent tonight like every other night — starving, homesick, heartsick, *sick* sick, and so terribly alone.

His hair was a sexy mess of short blond spikes. Black roses tattooed one muscled arm, the rest of his upper body a landscape of unmarked skin and ripples of definition. Though he wore a deep scowl and seemed to enjoy staring her down in a condescending way, he was also tender and possessive.

He was a man to love. If Camila hadn't already belonged to Matias, she would've given her heart to Tate without hesitation.

"Was it hard to...?" Did she want to ask this? She sat on the mattress on the floor and pulled the shirt down to cover her thighs. "Was it hard to have sex with Camila then let her go?"

"I wouldn't know."

"You mean...?" Her heart thundered. "You haven't...?"

"I've never so much as kissed her." With a sigh, he

sat beside her and stretched his legs along the floor in front of them. "When I met your sister, I'd just spent ten weeks with Van. I wanted her instantly, but I was..." He wiped a hand down his mouth, his fingers lingering on his barely-there beard, his expression pensive. "I needed time to come to terms with what happened in that attic. We both did. I lived like a monk for the next two years, waiting for her and... Maybe I was waiting for myself. To feel worthy of her. To feel like a man again." He dropped his hand on his lap. "When I was finished waiting, the very night I decided to go after her, Matias showed up." He laughed a sharp sound that wasn't a laugh at all. "I knew then that I didn't have a chance in hell with her."

He must've had superhuman staying power. To wait for Camila like that only to lose her in the end? Lucia commended his patience.

"You haven't tried to move on?" she asked. "With another woman?"

"For the last four years, I've fucked everything that moved."

An ice-cold jolt knifed straight through her chest. Is that what she was to him? Something that moved? "How's that working for you?"

"It's..." He stared at his dusty brown boots, his brows knitting. Then he huffed another non-laugh. "It's been utterly joyless." He turned toward her, head cocked and eyes squinting. "You asked if it was hard to have sex then let her go. Are you worried about that? With us?"

Us.

She looked away, an involuntary reflex she immediately regretted and forced her gaze back to his. "Am I worried because we had sex? Because I might not want to let go of something you found *utterly joyless*?"

175

"We didn't just have sex. We had great fucking sex." His perfect lips formed the words with natural seduction, making her shiver all over. "You enjoyed it as much as I did."

Her nipples hardened beneath the shirt. He zeroed in on her chest, and something flickered in his eyes.

"If I could make you happy..." He unlaced his boots and pulled them off. Then his socks. "Even if it's just a fleeting happiness..." His hands went to his jeans, unzipping and shucking them off. "I'll do whatever it takes."

"A pity fuck won't make me—"

She was pinned beneath him on the mattress before her next breath. He was so heavy and solidly built his weight was alarming.

"Does this feel like pity?" He grabbed her hand and shoved it between them, molding her fingers around his cock.

Trapped in his tight briefs, his swollen length angled toward his hip, so damn thick and long the cotton barely contained it. It definitely didn't feel like pity. He felt ruthless.

"Don't ever mistake my desire for you as a mercy." He ground himself against her hand. "I don't care if you're sick, sweetheart. I intend to exhaust my need for you until you forget where you are and how many breaths you have left. How's that for a nice guy?"

It was arousing, electrifying, stimulating and lubricating the deepest, hungriest part of her.

"I've never come as hard as I did when I was inside you." His breathing sped up, his lips parting and brushing against hers as he rocked his hips in the V of her thighs. "I know you felt it—the crazy consuming shock of it. I'm going to take you there again and again, until you never want to let go."

"Never let go of you?"

"If that makes you happy."

His response confused her, and given the creases on his forehead, it confused him, as well.

"Be careful, Tate." She stroked the line of his sculpted jaw. "It's just sex, remember? We'll have to let go eventually."

Considering the state of her health, it would be sooner rather than later. But for now, she wrapped her arms around him and held tight.

"We'll see about that." He took her mouth in a kiss that stole her thoughts and bowed her spine.

The instant his tongue met hers, sparks of energy flashed through her body. He must've felt something similar, because he gasped against her lips and leaned back. His eye contact was brief yet poignant before he tangled a fist in her hair and returned to her mouth with an explosion of passion.

It was a full-body fusion—legs entwining, hips grinding, chests heaving, and hands groping and clutching. He shaped her to him, like heat melting glass, and she softened, liquefied, inhaling when he exhaled, moaning when he groaned. It was the best kiss she'd ever experienced, and he kept it going for a lifetime, letting her feast, savor, and soar.

When he pulled back, she blinked at him, dizzy with hunger.

His lips were wet and swollen, his pupils huge and breaths careening out of control. Knowing he was as affected as she was only made her want him more.

"Arms up." He shoved her shirt toward her head

and yanked it off.

Then he was on the move, his chiseled torso and hard cock shifting out of reach as he settled his shoulders between her legs.

"I fucking love your cunt." His fingers slipped through her wet heat and circled her opening. "You're dripping."

"Tate..." She wriggled beneath him, hating and loving the way he spread her flesh open and bared her to his eyes.

"God, I can smell you." He buried his nose in her pussy and inhaled. "The sweetness of your skin mixed with your arousal... You're a goddamn sinful temptation."

He pushed a finger inside her and turned his head to nip at her inner thigh. His strokes kissed along her inner walls, rubbing with wicked precision and setting her on fire. Her hand fisted the blanket, the other flying to the silken strands of his hair.

As he fingered her cunt and licked along her thigh, his thumb danced over her clit, swiveling and whisking and making it hum.

With his long digit curling inside her, he rested his lips against her mound and captured her gaze. "Did you use a condom this morning?"

Shame punched her in the gut. During her delirious puking episode, she'd told him she raped a man. *I've raped so many innocent, married men.*

The reminder swelled a sob in her throat and sent her scrambling to get away from him. She was humiliated, so fucking disgusted with herself, she couldn't bear his touch or whatever look was on his face.

"Stop." He caught her swinging arms and

restrained them above her head.

She fought him for a useless moment before falling still. The struggle had shifted her fully beneath him with his legs straddling her hips and his huge body bent over her.

"Why are you doing this?" She glared up at him through a sheen of tears. "You can have your pick of untainted, *clean* women."

"I'm not asking for me." Holding her wrists in one hand, he removed three condoms from the jeans on the floor and tossed them on the mattress. "I need to know if you're protecting yourself."

"When I can." Her voice broke into a flat, dead sound. "Sometimes I'm not given a choice."

His eyes clouded, darkening with understanding. Like her, he'd been forced by a man. He didn't just grasp the ruin. He'd lived it. But unlike her, he'd never inflicted that ugliness on another. Her crimes were hypocritical and heinous.

"How can you stand to look at me?" she asked. "Let alone touch me?"

"Do you enjoy raping them?"

"No!" A flood of misery crumpled her face. "I'm hurting them, and I don't want to. I thought..." Guilt spilled from her eyes and down her temples, tickling along the curves of her ears. "I thought it would be better this way, but it's not. It's insidious, disgusting abuse, and when they..." She gulped down a sob and evened her voice. "When they come, I see the destruction in their eyes. They hate themselves as much as they hate me. I'm doing that. I'm—"

"Listen to me." He gripped her chin and held her head immobile. "You didn't do it for yourself. You did it for them, and doing so hurt *you*. Dammit, Lucia. I know you know that."

"I'm not a martyr." She clenched her teeth. "Not even close."

"Doesn't matter. It stops now."

Her breath hitched. "What? I can't—"

"You're dying, right? So be sick. Fake the symptoms if you have to. Vomit. Pass out. Do whatever you need to do to avoid that torture room."

"He'll hurt them! He has this…this razor thing he puts on his finger, and he…" Her stomach rolled with nausea, thickening her words. "He cuts and mutilates their bodies."

"We can't save them." His fingers tightened against her jaw. "But I can save *you*. You're my only concern, and I want you out of that room. Understand?"

She swallowed, and swallowed again. "Yes."

"I'm waiting on a medical test kit. It should be here in a couple days." He released her and propped his elbows on either side of her shoulders. "I'll draw your blood and test for STDs."

"I'm clean." She averted her eyes. "No STDs. Tiago's doctors test me regularly."

"Okay. Good." He lifted up and gazed down the length of her nude body, chewing on his lip. "I don't know if the blood test will tell us anything. But while we wait for the results, no more torturing. And I'll be here every night…"

He dragged a knuckle over her breast and down her trembling stomach, pausing on the short hairs above her pussy. He had that look in his eyes, the prowling predator look that told her in no uncertain terms that he wasn't finished with her.

But the conversation they'd just had left her feeling raw and loathsome. She killed a rapist today only to turn around and inflict the same evil on someone else. Yet Tate stared at her as if she were the loveliest woman he'd ever seen. It was appalling.

"I can't do this." She shoved at his chest with enough force to knock him off balance.

Then she fled. Off the mattress, across the floor, she didn't make it to her feet before he seized her ankle and yanked her back to the bed.

"You're a fighter." He shackled her wrists in the unbending clamps of his fingers, holding her down on the mattress. "But you want me to fight back. You want me to punish you and use your body to get myself off. Because that's what gets you off."

"That's not—"

"I saw you with that man at the club last night. The pleasure on your face while he caned you was undeniable." He spread her legs wider with his knees and brought his mouth to her ear. "You're a dirty, kinky girl. Tell me I'm wrong."

The protest stuck in her throat. He wasn't wrong. Punishment and capitulation balanced her horribly unstable world, and she needed that now — the liberation that came with pain and pleasure and willing surrender.

"You're right," she whispered.

He hauled in a rough breath and blew out slowly.

"If you move your arms," he said, pressing her wrists to the mattress above her head, "I'll flip you over and fuck your ass."

CHAPTER 17

I'll flip you over and fuck your ass.

Heat flushed through Lucia's core, and her legs fell open, unbidden.

"Ah, fuck, baby." Tate's hand shot to her pussy, stroking the soaked flesh. "You like that, don't you? You want me inside your ass."

She'd never had a pleasant experience with anal. It had always been forced and blindingly painful. But she ached to feel him there, knew he would do it with care, and nodded her consent.

"You're killing me." He stole a deep, heart-pumping kiss. Then he gathered the condoms and lined up the three foil wrappers along her breastbone. "I'm going to use all of these tonight and wish I'd brought more."

Instead of sheathing his cock, he slid his hands beneath her butt and lifted her pussy to his mouth.

The first lick followed her seam from bottom to top. She throbbed against the hot greeting of his tongue, fighting to keep her arms above her head. He buried his face, and she moaned, jerked, and choked on her own breath.

As he sucked and licked with ferocity, his scratchy jaw burned a trail of fire along her thighs. His lips covered every thrumming nerve between her legs as he gripped her ass cheeks and spread them so he could roll his tongue around her rim. She bucked against his unyielding mouth, drenching his whiskers with her arousal.

At some point, the condoms tumbled away, and her hands moved on their own, pulling at his hair and clawing his scalp.

He knocked her fingers away. "Your ass is mine."

Tossing her to the side, he flipped her to her stomach and covered her back with his body.

She panted in response, wanting him to fuck her there but also scared shitless. "It's going to hurt."

"Probably." His mouth teased her ear, his breaths hot and shallow. "If it's not the good kind of hurt, I'll stop. Trust me to take care of you."

Trust. That was a thing she gave no one. But as he tore open a foil packet with his teeth, she found herself relaxing beneath him, savoring the heat of his body on her back and the flex of his hand rolling on the condom.

"Breathe." He notched himself against her pussy.

Not her ass?

When she exhaled, he clamped a hand over her mouth and thrust.

Everything inside her stretched as he slammed against the back of her cunt. She screamed against his palm, sucking hard through her nose and writhing against the invasion. His cock was impossibly huge and vicious and *oh my fucking fuck fuck fuck*, he pounded her into the mattress, breaking her open and stabbing her darkest depths.

He grunted with the exertion of his hammering hips, his fingers digging into her cheek and his other hand chasing the lines of her body, squeezing and kneading and scratching her skin.

But there was pleasure amid the savagery, an unlocking sensation that set her breaths free and her skin ablaze. When her cries turned to moans, his hand slid from her mouth to her throat, pressing lightly and turning her neck. His lips were there, feeding from hers, licking and biting with the voracious tempo of his breaths.

She was so turned on she felt it in her veins — that wild, erratic, reckless thrill she hadn't experienced since she was a teenager. She'd forgotten what that was like, to just live and play and love. Tate had returned that feeling to her. With his cock ramming brutally, powerfully inside her, he treated her like a desirable woman instead of a dying invalid. He reminded her how to be herself again.

"Is that all you got?" She arched her back and wriggled her ass against him.

He let go of what little restraint he'd held back, thrusting harder, deeper, faster, as if trying to drive himself right into her heart. With the hug of his arms around her and the caress of his lips on her neck, maybe he'd already buried himself deep within her existence and left his mark. Fuck it, she didn't care. He felt too damn good, too perfect.

He fucked without mercy, working himself in and out with brute force. But the caress of his hands on her body was an intimate communication. Each touch made her feel sexy and loved. Every stroke thrummed with appreciation.

It didn't take long for her to shoot off with a

gasping, electrifying, body-tingling release that fired her nerve-endings from her hair to her toes. She was still groaning when he pulled out, and she missed the stretch of him instantly.

He slid his fingers inside her, lubing them up before slipping them out and back, right into her forbidden hole.

"Christ, you're horny." His breathing was tight, bursting sharp gasps past his lips. "You're opening right up for me."

She didn't feel the usual pain. Not even a pinch. Just a tingling swirl of desire and warmth. She was so sated and drugged on pleasure maybe she didn't have the wherewithal to tense. "Can't believe how good that feels."

"You're nice and relaxed." He thrust his fingers in and out of her ass.

"Only with you."

His touch vanished. "When you say things like that..." He leaned down and spit on her clenching ring of muscle. Then he pressed the wide flare of his cock against the moisture. "Makes me really fucking possessive, Lucia."

"You're already possessive."

"Not like this." He pushed, just enough to stimulate her nerves. "Can you keep quiet?"

"Yeah." She breathed deeply. "Fuck me, Tate."

He grabbed her waist with both hands and kicked his hips, tunneling his massive shaft straight through her.

She choked on the sudden burn, but it only lasted a second. The incredible fullness that followed was unlike anything she'd ever felt. Intense. Consuming. It stunned her how much she welcomed the dark thrilling feel of him inside her like this.

A groan vibrated in his chest as he buried his length and thrust slowly. Bending over her, he trailed a shaky hand up her spine and rubbed her back. If he was trying to soothe her, she didn't need it. Maybe he was calming himself.

His hands roamed, teasing every exposed inch of her before clutching a fistful of her hair.

"I'm not going to last long." Using that grip, he yanked her up until her back hit his chest.

On their knees with him seated fully in her ass, he wrapped a hand around her throat while the other slid up her thigh and sank three fingers in her pussy.

Then he fucked her, plunging and retreating with the speed and stamina of a machine. He held her tight to his body and pumped his fingers as his cock drove viciously, greedily in her ass.

His grunting, erotic breaths revved her up and made her insane with need. He was a beast, untamed and wild, as he shoved himself deeper and deeper. She felt every ridge and bump of his cock, and his muscled physique generated so much heat she was certain he would reduce her to ashes.

She couldn't move or meet his thrusts, but she could put her hands on him. As he slammed into her tirelessly, she reached back and palmed the flexing brawn of his butt. He continued to thrust, burning red-hot aftershocks through her body, and she held on, moaning, panting, and taking exquisite pleasure in the ride.

When his fingers slipped from her pussy to work her clit, she knew she would climax like this. And she did moments later, anchored by his cock and the hand around her throat. Her eyes rolled back in her head, and she came and came until white flashes blotted her vision. It was ecstasy. Nirvana. Total attainment of everything right in the world.

"Fuck, Lucia. I'm coming." He jerked his hips and released a long, deep groan that penetrated her chest. "Oh goddamn, fuck!"

His hand slipped from her neck, and his head dropped to her back. He stayed that way for several heaving breaths before smacking a stinging palm against her ass.

"You wore me out." He fell to his back and gasped at the ceiling. "Go drink some water and eat more of that fruit."

"Bossy." With a grin, she removed the rubber from his softening cock and obeyed his orders.

A few minutes later, she stood at the counter, eating strawberries and tingling all over with a rhapsody of sensations. She felt full and glowy and utterly ravished.

His footsteps approached from behind, stretching her mouth into a smile. Then his hands were on her, cruising her hips, slinking around to her abs and cupping her breasts.

"Still hungry?" He kissed a trail of electricity from her shoulder to her neck.

"Not for food." Molten heat curled through her belly, burning hotter with each stroke of his hand and brush of his lips.

The sound of a foil packet caught her ear — the only warning she got before he pushed himself inside her from behind.

"I can't get enough of you." He rocked into her and

nibbled on her neck.

"We have all night."

"I need more than a night, baby."

He fucked her against the counter. Then the wall, the floor, in the shower, and back on the bed. Over the next few hours, he made good on his promise to use all three condoms before collapsing on top of her, winded and spent.

"I think you broke my dick." He pressed his face into the crook of her neck, his chest rising and falling, and his cock softening inside her.

When he lifted to move away, she hugged him to her.

"Don't pull out."

"I'd stay here forever if the damn rubber wasn't strangling me." He kissed her lips and left the bed to dispose of the condom.

"Those things don't fit you."

"It's fine." He strode back to the mattress, unabashed with his nudity.

Even flaccid, he hung longer and thicker than the average erection. God, he had a glorious cock. It should never be covered in latex.

"Feels like I'm chapped." He stood above her and ran a hand along the length, glancing at it.

"Maybe I can help." She lifted onto her knees and gently kissed along the soft, warm skin of his thick shaft.

"I wasn't complaining, but..." He released a happy breath and twitched against her lips. "That's nice."

His hand went to her hair, sliding through the strands from the roots to the tips. His cock filled with blood, but he seemed content to just let her nuzzle and tease with chaste kisses.

Without an inch of fat on his body, every sinew and vein stood out in stark relief beneath his taut skin. She traced the lines of his narrow hips and the sexy cuts and ridges that formed the *V* of his abs. He was beautifully formed. So powerful and manly, and if she touched him much more she might beg him to fuck her without a condom.

She sat on her heels, and he knelt beside her, nudging her to her back.

"How are you feeling?" He guided her legs apart and probed his thumbs around her swollen tissues. "Sore?"

"I'm good."

She brushed his hands away, but he was relentless, inspecting and touching and shifting down to examine her rectum.

"Tate, stop." She twisted away from him. "I'm better than good, okay? Better than I've been in years."

"Yeah?" He flashed her a grin.

"Yeah."

He reached up and flicked off the light switch, leaving the dim illumination of the night light in the wall outlet. Then he prowled toward her on hands and knees, his blue eyes glinting. Unsure of his intent, she didn't know whether to sigh or tense up.

His arm caught her waist, and he dragged her against him. She clung to his shoulders as he rolled and adjusted until they were on their sides, chest to chest, snug under the blanket.

"We're going to sleep?" She slid her fingers through his hair, stroking.

"Yep."

He was so close she smelled all his distinctive

aromas — salty skin and warm sex and musky masculinity.

She felt high on his scent, the deep sounds of his breaths, and the euphoric heat of his body tucked against hers. "Are you still awake?"

He laughed, a rumbling delightful sound. "I doubt I'll sleep tonight."

"Why?"

"I want to enjoy this." He twined his legs around hers and rubbed her back. "Feels too good."

Her chest fluttered and stretched with his words. "Tell me about you. Your full name. Age. Childhood. Anything."

"Tate Anthony Vades. Twenty-five. I grew up in a whorehouse."

"No way."

"Yes way."

His gravelly voice drifted around her as he told her about The Velvet Den, the traumatic way he lost his virginity, and his admiration for the woman who raised him.

She talked about the citrus grove and her favorite memories of Matias and Camila.

He spoke about the roses inked on his arm and the whores he spent his childhood with.

Then she explained how Tiago administered her injections — in his room, without her clothes and weapons, with the safe only a few feet away. Locked. Inaccessible. She'd never seen inside it.

As the night crept by, they got to know each other through words. And kissing. He kissed her often. Lazy, unassuming kisses without urgency or intention. Kissing for the sole purpose of expressing affection.

He told her about his house and his roommates — four men and a woman. Then he kissed her again, his hands never leaving her body and his arms tightly wound around her back.

"I want to call Matias," he breathed against her lips.

She knew why. In just a couple short hours, she would be back with Tiago where Tate couldn't protect her, couldn't control what happened to her, and that didn't sit well with a man like him. But if he made that call, Matias would come to Caracas and risk his life and that of his men to extract her from Tiago's world. And for what purpose? To free a dying woman?

She couldn't even consider threatening Camila's happiness until she knew there was a chance of survival.

"Wait for the blood test," she said. "If it reveals a diagnosis and treatment, I'll go wherever you tell me to go. How long will it take to get the results back?"

"Several days." His jaw flexed against hers. "I don't like this."

"I know." She snuggled closer, burrowing against his chest. "But I like *this*. I've never slept in a bed with a man."

He hummed a growly sigh and squeezed her butt. "I'll be your first and your last."

What did that mean? She lifted her head. "Why?"

"As long as I'm alive, I'll be the only man in your bed."

She stared at him, lips parting, and blinked.

"Close your mouth and go to sleep." He gripped her neck and pressed her cheek to his chest.

"You're a Neanderthal."

"I've been called worse. Now sleep."

And she did. It was the best sleep she'd ever had, and so was the next night, and the next.

For the next five nights, it was just him and her and the protective bubble he built around them.

She went to the compound for her injections in the mornings and the mandatory dinners in the evenings. While in Tiago's presence, she exaggerated her illness, moaning and stumbling and feigning vertigo until he sent her home.

And Tate was always there, waiting for her.

He stocked her apartment with food and necessities, added discreet bolts on the insides of the doors, and drew her blood when the test kit arrived.

Now it was a waiting game, a delay of action until the results came back. They bided their time in her tiny windowless space, talking, eating, sleeping, and exploring each other emotionally and physically.

His hunger for her was insatiable. They fucked daily and nightly, in every manner of motion, mood, and position. And holy hell, the man loved to kiss. She was kissed more in those five days than in the previous thirty years of her life.

It was five days of intoxicating, Tate-induced bliss. She never wanted it to end.

But like all good things...

The old adage got it right.

Except her good thing didn't just come to an end. It ripped open and bled out in a devastation of pain.

CHAPTER 18

"Feeling better tonight?" Tiago studied Lucia from across the table in his private dining room.

She let him see the trembling in her hand as she pushed away her empty plate. "No."

It was the truth. Tonight was going to be a bad night. She felt it simmering inside her — the queasiness, the tremors, and the pinpricks numbing her lower body.

The last time she lost mobility, he left her on the floor in the common area of the compound, paralyzed, vulnerable, unable to move her legs to walk home.

"I don't feel well at all." She shifted to the edge of the seat and craned her neck for a better view of the hall outside the dining room. "I'm ready to go home."

Armed guards lined the corridor. Three times more men than usual. Restless energy buzzed through them as they fidgeted and whispered to one another. Something was wrong.

"Did something happen?" Dread curled in her gut, aggravating the nausea.

"There's a spy in my neighborhood." Tiago set his utensils down, casually dabbed his mouth with a napkin, and imprisoned her gaze. "Do you know anything about that?"

"No."

It took every ounce of discipline she could muster to moderate her expression. Meanwhile, her heart clambered the rungs of her ribs and pounded a terrified howl in her throat.

Did he capture Tate? Was he holding him in the basement chamber to await an unspeakable night of torture?

Saliva rushed over her tongue, bringing with it the urgent need to throw up. Her sickness, nerves, fear — all of it rose up and contorted her face.

But Tiago didn't notice, his attention locked on the man striding into the room.

Armando, her fellow torturer, paused beside Tiago's chair and said in Spanish, "We have him."

Her stomach bottomed out, and her blood turned to ice.

No, please, God. This can't be happening.

The guns holstered in her waistband grew hot and heavy, begging her to reach for them. But a guard stood at her back, and two more bracketed the door.

"Muy bien." Tiago stood and offered her his hand. "Shall we?"

Terror held her frozen in the chair. She could fight, but they were physically stronger. She had weapons, but they had more. If she died in this room, Tate would die, too.

He's dead no matter what.

She needed to get the fuck out of there and alert Van. He could contact that Cole Hartman guy and… She didn't know, but it was the only option she had, and Tiago was waiting.

She made her legs work, putting her weight on the heels as she hoisted herself from the chair. Her knees locked, and she took a wobbly step.

"Tiago... I think I'm..." Dizziness swept her into a spinning fog.

She clutched the table, careening sideways and catching herself before she hit the floor.

Fucking hell, she was going downhill quick. Her abdomen spasmed and clenched, and her head pounded. Her throat was so tight she couldn't swallow. It felt like her insides were being wrung out and tied up. Everything hurt.

Tiago stared at her from a foot away, his bored expression growing blurrier with each heavy blink of her eyes.

Fuck him. I can do this.

Resisting the urge to puke, she pushed through the pain, straightened to her full height, and stepped toward him.

Only her legs didn't move. She couldn't feel them. Couldn't feel her hands or her heartbeat. She swayed in the whirling room, battling to stay upright, and willing her body to cooperate.

Don't give up on me. Please, not now. I can't —

The floor fell out beneath her, and she plummeted into the black void of nothingness.

CHAPTER 19

Lucia woke to the sound of bloodcurdling screams. The strident howling echoed at a distance, but she knew it was coming from only feet away. Garbled and frothing with spit, it sounded like a dying animal. But as her senses focused and disorientation burned away, she realized it was a man in unfathomable pain.

Tate.

Fury snarled though her veins, surging her upright. The sudden motion knocked her off-balance, and she teetered, falling with the hard smack of her cheek against the concrete floor.

Pain burst behind her eyes. Overhead lights burned into her skull, and the scuff of rubber soles sounded near her head. She recognized the floor, the unforgiving glare of the fluorescents, and the reek of death that lived in the walls.

She couldn't let the basement chamber claim its next victim.

Must get up. Protect him. Save him.

Rolling to her back, she immediately noticed her guns were missing. She tried to move her legs and couldn't. Tried to focus her eyes and couldn't. Tried to sit up and only made it to her elbows. The room was empty before her. All the activity was at her back — the guttural screams, the scrapes of multiple shoes, and the rattle of chains.

Swimming in a thick soup of lethargy, vertigo, and nausea, she mentally prepared herself. Given the rawness in his voice and the scent of blood and urine, the torture had been going on for a while.

"Welcome back." Tiago stood behind her, bending over her head so he could smile at her upside down. "Still can't move your legs?"

She couldn't fucking feel her legs, and she was two seconds from retching all over his shoes.

He prowled into her line of sight, his shirt smeared with crimson stains and his index finger tipped with a razored claw.

The claw he used to carve pictures into flesh and muscle.

She despised him with such deep, searing, vile hatred it vibrated her bones and popped blood vessels behind her eyes.

"What have you done?" She choked on the bile rising in her throat, blinking back tears as she fumbled to shift her useless body toward the scene behind her.

Blood. It was everywhere, dripping from deep cuts in the hanging slab of breathing meat. The dissection was gruesome, and though she'd seen his macabre handiwork before, she still went into shock. Her nervous system shut down. Her lungs froze up, and her mind struggled to process the rivers of red and the stench of carnage.

She looked away and forced herself to move. Crawling on her belly, she dragged her legs behind her and lost a heeled shoe in the process. Desperate to get to him, she couldn't stall the burning tears, the wretched sobs, and the violent shaking in her arms as she inched forward with strenuously slow movements.

Too much blood. I'm too late.

When she reached the sticky dark pool at his feet, she angled her neck to look up, up, up and…

She stopped breathing.

The slaughtered body was too thin, the hair too long and black, and the trousers too baggy and unfamiliar.

Not Tate.

Not Tate.

That man isn't Tate.

Her relief was so profound and overwhelming she lost control of her stomach and vomited across the floor.

"You never appreciate my artwork." Tiago stepped around her, easing her away from the puke and onto her back. "You look like hell."

"Fuck you."

His chuckle was worse than any response he could've given. She was here for a reason, and like all the other times she'd been in this room, she wouldn't leave unscathed.

The man's wails weakened, ebbing into silence. He must've passed out. Or died. With his back to the wall, his head hung toward his chest, eyes closed. Chains wrapped his wrists and suspended him from the ceiling, and his chest… She was certain if she looked close enough she'd see bone in the trenches of some of those cuts.

She glared up at Tiago. "You're a monster. A butcher."

"You're a whore. Now that we got that out of the

way..." He gestured toward the door. "Armando is waiting."

Horror spiked through her heart as she followed his gaze.

Tall and pear-shaped with an overhanging belly, Armando caught and held her glare. He smoothed a hand over his greasy hair, his grin a rictus of yellow teeth.

"Waiting for what?" Her question didn't need an answer. She knew. Deep in the pith of her miserable existence, she knew.

"He discovered the spy." Tiago approached the mutilated man and inspected the carved designs. "This was one of my new recruits. Turns out, he works for the competition. Came here to steal from me."

He pulled a gun from his pants, aimed it at the man's bowed head, and fired.

She averted her gaze as the bang reverberated through her chest, making her shoulders twitch.

"To reward Armando for bringing him in," Tiago said, holstering the gun, "I told him he could have anything of mine for one night. Guess what he chose?"

Me.

She closed her eyes and tried to temper her runaway breaths. Spasms ignited in parts of her butt and midsection, but feeling still hadn't returned to her legs. There would be no running. She wouldn't even be able to kick in defense or clench her thighs together.

She calmed herself with the reminder that it could've been worse. It could've been Tate hanging there, carved up and dead. She wouldn't have survived that.

But she could survive this. *Just like all the times before.*

"I know you're sick." He crouched in front of her and slid the other heeled shoe off her paralyzed foot. "But you're a trooper, Lucia. Spread those pretty legs and show him a good time."

She didn't have use of her legs, but she had a wealth of aggression in her bones. Her body was dying, but her spirit sang with life. Her muscles would give, but her mind would not.

Armando would rape her while Tiago watched. She would spit and punch and cry until Armando hit her hard enough to knock the wind from her.

Then they would do it all again.

No matter how hard she fought — and she would — the result would be the same.

This was happening.

Because that was the way of things.

CHAPTER 20

Hours later, Lucia hung upside down with a shoulder jabbing her unbearably sore stomach. Her body was too broken to obey her commands, so one of the guards had to carry her to the apartment.

She'd been punched in the gut so many times the nausea had gone silently numb. Every bone, tissue, and tendon throbbed with fire. Her legs were heavy dead things attached to joints made of sand and dust. Her skull pounded rhythmically. Her swallows felt like serrated blades, and molten lava tunneled between her thighs and buttocks.

Armando had brutally violated every hole in her body. He'd bitten her breasts and thighs, kicked her ribs and face, and repeated the torment until she lay curled in the fetal position with her arms around her head.

His cruelty had been so severe Tiago had to interfere several times to stop him from crossing the line.

But lines had been crossed. All of them. The wreckage was so complete, so excruciating, her body didn't feel like it belonged to her. It'd become a burdensome, pulsating prison of pain. It had failed her. Over and over again.

Her arms dangled toward the oily pavement, and

the shadows of surrounding buildings rocked with the guard's heavy-booted steps.

Then those boots paused, and an impatient hand dug through her pockets and found her key.

The scraping sound of her door urged her to move her limbs, but she couldn't. She'd left the last of her strength on the floor in that basement chamber.

But it'll be okay now. Tate would be waiting for her inside, like he did every night.

At that thought, her traumatized heart stirred to life, beating with urgency. She needed Tate so badly. Needed the protection of his arms, the comfort of his voice, and the affection in his kisses.

He was smart enough to stay hidden until she was inside with the door shut. So she didn't worry when the guard stepped in, dumped her on the mattress, and set her guns and shoes out of reach on the floor.

When the door clicked shut behind him, she released a shredded breath and listened.

Silence.

"Are you there?" She didn't hear Tate's footsteps, didn't feel his touch, didn't sense his imposing presence in the dark.

"Tate?" she whispered, rolling to her stomach with a painful heave.

The continued silence closed in around her, swelling her throat and heating her eyes. "Tate... Please, I need you."

She knew he wasn't here, but she kept calling for him, kept hoping.

Where was he? Was he safe? What if he'd left town? Maybe her test results had come back and there was nothing he could do for her. Would he return to

Texas without saying goodbye?

He wouldn't do that. It was just the voice of misery inside her, taunting her while she was down.

And she was down, face in the mattress, trapped in a dying, throbbing body. Everything burned and trembled as her injuries set in. There would be bruises, swelling, and possible scars around her rectum, but the surface stuff was negligible compared to the damage wrought inside.

"Tate... Tate, where are you?" She lay immobile, lifeless, as the tears welled up. She didn't bother blinking or rubbing them away. There was no one here, nothing to see.

She was alone.

Alone was her normal. She learned long ago how to fend for herself, fight for herself, and endure by herself. But she didn't want to be alone anymore. She was exhausted, hurting, and...done. She was so fucking done.

So she let the tears fall until she was emotionally bankrupt. Until all that remained was the hollow husk of a battered body.

Eventually, her eyes dried, and her vision cleared, bringing her guns into focus on the floor across the room.

One bullet. It was all she needed.

It would erase the pain. Eradicate the illness. End the loneliness.

Her arms moved without hesitation, elbows grinding against the hard floor as she hauled her body toward the end.

She was afraid to die, afraid of the terrible nothingness that awaited. But more than that, she was terrified to live, to endure another day of this vicious circle. She didn't want to fight anymore.

As she lugged her body toward the guns, her mind traveled to a better place. She smelled the citrus grove, the sunshine, and the fertile soil. She felt the warm breeze in her hair and the tickle of long grass on her legs. She saw her sister—her beautiful, laughing, vibrant baby sister. Camila and Matias would have such adorable, brown-eyed children. Their love for each other was so strong it would carry through generations.

Then she heard Tate's voice, his breathy whispers at her ear. A tearful sigh billowed past her bloodied, cracked lips. She ached. God help her, she ached to see him one more time.

He had a magic about him, an allurement that went beyond his model-perfect looks. He'd experienced the kind of brutality that would destroy a man, but he'd ridden it out and stood taller, stronger, despite it.

She felt the strength of his fingers around her throat. Smelled the clean scent of his breath on her face. Tasted his possessiveness on her lips.

For a moment, she thought he was actually here, but there was only the empty room and the gun that was now within her reach.

Her hand shook as she lifted the metal frame, her entire body screaming in agony from the effort it'd taken to crawl there. It was a heavy trigger, but she would have just enough determination left to pull it.

With her cheek on the floor, she positioned the gun in front of her face and stared into the barrel.

It would bring her peace.
It would bring the end.
She wanted it to end.
She needed the end.
End it.

DEVASTATE

End it.
End it.

CHAPTER 21

A stinging slap across Tate's face woke him from a violent dream and shoved him into a goddamn nightmare.

"Wake up."

The heartless voice magnified the ringing in his ears, and a furious roar burst from his throat. Except the sound was deadened, muffled by the wad of cloth in his mouth.

That motherfucking, psycho, bastard fuck!

He jerked forward, vibrating with rage and out for blood. And he went nowhere. Because he was fucking duct taped to a kitchen chair.

He glared at the man who had bound him there. *I'm going to kill you.*

"You made me knock you out." Van sat in front of him on the couch, all casual and calm, despite the bloody, swollen mess of his face.

Tate's cheekbone pulsed with its own swelling pain, his knuckles split and sore. He and Van had beaten the shit out of each other, and he seethed to do it again.

After Lucia is safe.

He hadn't heard everything that had been

transmitted from the bug on her shoe, but he'd heard enough. The dinner, the torture, and *Armando's reward.*

Listening to her being assaulted, violated, and forced by that man had been a horrifying, inconsolable hell. In a fog of murderous wrath, he'd holstered his guns and stormed toward the door intent on raining death and destruction on the compound in his effort to save her.

But Van had stopped him with a fist. Then they fought with more fists, putting holes in walls and breaking furniture. Until one of Van's swings caught him on the temple and *lights out.*

How long had he been unconscious? He tried to bellow the question, but the gag garbled his words.

"She's in her apartment." Van lifted a phone and held it near Tate's face. "Alone and quiet."

He strained his hearing until he caught the distant sound of her raspy, wheezing breaths.

His blood boiled anew, steaming through his veins and clouding his vision. He thrashed against the tape across his chest, desperate to get to her.

Let me go! Let me go! Fucking release me!

"Calm down." Van stood and paced through the room, picking up broken pieces of the coffee table. "I saved your life."

Fuck off. He growled low and deep in his chest, heaving against the gag.

"You're here for her. I know that." Van dropped the splintered wood in a pile and stepped toward the window to peer down at the alley. "But I'm here for *you.* To protect you. To keep your stupid ass alive."

Tate closed his eyes and drew a sharp breath through his nose. Maybe Van had saved him from a bloody, unproductive death. And maybe he would thank

Van later. But only if Lucia was still alive.

He still didn't have the blood results back, and the lab wasn't returning his calls. He'd talked to Cole Hartman earlier today and explained Lucia's situation. Cole could bring a doctor to her, but it was going to take two weeks.

She didn't have two fucking weeks.

"What's it going to be, Tate?" Van prowled toward him and gripped his jaw, forcing his head up. "Are you going to be smart? Or dead?"

CHAPTER 22

Something soft and warm whispered across Lucia's lips, rousing her. Arms slipped beneath her body and lifted her from the floor, jostling swollen joints and pushing against bruises. Pain blasted through her bones, and she cried out.

"Shh." The satiny sensation returned to her lips, making gentle sounds and infusing her inhales with a clean, minty, familiar scent.

"Tate?" She opened her eyes to a crystal blue dream.

"I'm so sorry." He brushed his mouth against hers again, lingering over the cuts on her lip. "I would've been here, but…"

He raised his head and glared at something across the room. The glow of the night light illuminated a crisscross of gashes on his cheek and around his eye.

"What happened?" Her pulse kicked up, and holy fuck, it hurt.

Her heart, her head, her stomach, everything hurt so badly. She still couldn't move her legs, but she summoned the strength to turn her neck and follow his gaze.

Van. He folded his arms across his chest and leaned his butt against the counter, his scowl as puffy and battered as Tate's.

"We had a disagreement." Van narrowed his eyes. "Why were you sleeping with a gun pointed at your mouth? With your finger on the trigger?"

Her thoughts imploded with painful sparks. Flashes of the Beretta in her hand. Echoes of her dismal hesitation. She'd wanted to die, had even tried to squeeze the trigger. But she hadn't tried hard enough. Hadn't wanted it bad enough. She must've passed out.

She focused on Tate, on the swirling depths of his vigilant gaze. "I couldn't do it."

Now would be a good time to tell him what happened with Armando. But as his entire body shook against her, vibrating with barely-contained fury, she decided not to throw salt in the wound.

"If I'd been here, I wouldn't have allowed you to even consider it." Another death glare at Van. Then he lowered her to the mattress and stretched out beside her, cradling her against his chest.

He was so close his short beard tickled her chin. His fingers combed through her hair with agonizing tenderness, and his exhales incited her to breathe.

He was here. This was real. She was *breathing.*

Those merciful thoughts swarmed in with the ugly ones—her abused body, her necessary return to the compound in the morning, and the inevitable fate that awaited her at the end of this.

But for now, she had him, his arms around her, his hand stroking her hair, and his unspoken intent to take care of her.

Tears leaked from her eyes and dripped into the

cuts on her lips. It was neither sadness nor contentment, but rather the overwhelming weight of the past eleven years finally catching up with her.

He kissed her cheeks, nuzzling her skin. Then he shifted and cupped her head in his hands to position her on her back. The movement triggered an explosion of agony so sharp she thought she might puke.

"Fuck." He bent over her, caressing her hair, and glanced over his shoulder. "Van."

Footsteps approached, and the mattress dipped on her other side beneath Van's weight.

"Where does it hurt?" Van slung a backpack off his shoulder and removed a huge zippered pouch with a medical logo on it.

"Everywhere. I think…" The constant pain trembled her voice, and she swallowed. "A shower would be nice if I had help."

He glanced at Tate, and something passed between them.

"We don't have time." Tate feathered his fingertips across her stomach and paused on the hem of her shirt. "We're leaving. But first, Van's going to examine you and make you as comfortable as possible to travel." He lifted her shirt, inching it toward her head without moving his eyes from hers. "I called Matias."

"What?" Her lungs slammed together. "Camila knows? She knows I'm alive?"

"I just called him, but yeah, I'm sure she knows now."

Anger shuddered through her. Not because Matias would take her away from her medicine. Her death was inconsequential. But she didn't want Camila to experience it. *Again.*

The thought jabbed into her wounds and tore them open. "You shouldn't have done that. Camila can't—"

"Camila isn't a fucking factor in this." The harshness in his tone contradicted the delicate way he inched her shirt up and off.

"That's bullshit." Her frail voice failed to express her distress. "You're here for her."

"Not anymore." The loaded press of his gaze sent her heart into a tailspin.

With a coughing smirk, Van left the bed and turned the water on at the sink.

"What does that mean?" she asked, aching to hear Tate say it, to taste the hope.

"I'm here for you and you alone."

Just like that, her wish for death was laid waste in the promise that hovered between them. Maybe she could find a cure. Maybe she could see Camila again, and her sister wouldn't have to mourn her death a second time.

Maybe Tate would love her the way he loved Camila.

She dreamed of a life where she could explore possibilities with him, where she could nurture their connection, grow it, and pour the entirety of her being into it. To do any of that, she needed to live.

He kissed the corner of her mouth, the injury on her cheek, and the trickle of tears spilling from her eyes. "The quickest Matias can get here is eight hours by helicopter. But he can't get into the neighborhood. We have to go to him."

Eight hours and she would be rid of this place.

Eight hours and I'll be dead.

"I have time for one more injection if—"

"No. You're not going near the compound." He focused on her jeans, releasing the fly and gingerly sliding them off. "Are you still not able to feel your legs?"

"No, I can't..." She searched his eyes, confused. "How did you know about that?"

Van returned with a wadded wet shirt and bottled water and removed two pills from the medical bag.

"For the pain." He helped her swallow the medication while exchanging a silent look with Tate.

What were they not telling her?

She stared into Tate's bloodshot eyes, wincing at the cut swelling his eyelid. "Why were you fighting?"

"I know what happened to you tonight. I was listening." He worked his jaw, his expression pained. "You've been wearing a bug."

He told her about the listening devices, how he planted them, how they worked, and why he hid them from her. His hands flexed as he detailed what he'd heard tonight and the fist fight that followed with Van.

"I can't tell you how sorry I am for failing to protect you." His voice broke beneath a tide of torment.

Desolation flooded his expression, and it hurt her to see it. She let her eyes drift shut and tried to process everything he'd said.

She didn't feel anger or resentment about being spied on. She felt...relieved. Safeguarded. Maybe even cherished. He didn't have to watch over her like that, but he did. Because he was here for her.

"Thank you," she whispered.

He gave her hip a gentle squeeze and ghosted his fingers along the edge of her panties. "I need to remove these."

She kept her eyes closed, knowing there was dried

blood and come between her legs. Since he'd heard her struggle and ultimate defeat in the basement, he wouldn't be surprised at what he found.

Once she was bare, he didn't make a sound as he used the warm wet shirt to clean her. Then he and Van worked together, washing and nursing the worst of her injuries. The gash on her cheek needed stitches, as well as two across her ribs. Brutal knuckles, the concrete floor, the steel toe of a boot... She didn't know which cruelty caused which wounds, but Van sewed them up. Considering he used to torture people for a living, she supposed he was an expert at tending injuries inflicted by a sadist.

As Van stitched, Tate wove his fingers through hers and kissed her hand. "Your paralysis is concerning, Lucia."

She cracked open an eye. "What time is it?"

"Just after midnight. If you usually get your medicine at dawn, we have enough time to go to the nearest hospital and —"

"All three hospitals in Caracas are infiltrated with Tiago's people. The doctors won't treat me. He would kill them if they did."

His eyes flashed dangerously. "Then we'll find a hospital outside of the city."

"Waste of time."

"Dammit, Lucia. I'm not giving up."

"This isn't about giving up. The country is in a major health crisis. The shortage of medical supplies and hospital beds is so awful women are giving birth in the waiting rooms. Patients are dying on the bloodstained floors of hospital hallways after waiting days to see a doctor. I've seen the newspaper headlines. They have three percent of the supplies they need to treat people. *Three* percent, Tate."

"Because of the limitations the President put on importations?" Van clipped the final stitch and packed up the medical bag.

"I think so," she said. "As a result, the hospitals have *nothing*. I'll be dead and cold long before I even get into an exam room."

The simple act of talking had stressed her body. Parts deep inside her stabbed and burned, but she didn't know what was damaged or how irreparable the damage was. The burning sensation in her gut spread outward, blanketing her skin in violent, sweaty chills. Her breathing labored, and her pulse weakened, as if her organs were shutting down. Soon, they would be of no use to her.

"I'm dying."

"Not if I have something to say about it." Tate released her hand, and his large frame retreated in the blotches of her vision.

As unconsciousness tried to claim her, his voice thrummed at the edges. He was on the phone, making angry demands and pacing through the room.

She floated in and out of awareness, shifting restlessly on the mattress in an attempt to escape the persistent pain. Tate's voice continued in the background as Van dressed her. She welcomed the warmth of clothes, until she became too hot, too clammy. She was burning up.

Then Tate's hands were there, smoothing back her hair and easing a cool damp cloth around her face.

"I just talked to Cole Hartman." He touched a kiss to her lips. "He's going to find a doctor outside of the city. Someone we can trust."

Her chest lifted, filling with lofty wishes and greedy reveries. She wanted to scream her excitement and hug him until they both grunted with laughter, but the most she could offer was, "'kay. Thank you."

"He'll call back and let us know where to go. But we need to move. Get out of this neighborhood. Are you ready?"

"Can't walk." Her words sounded garbled and slurred.

"Shh. I have you." He pulled a gun from the front of his jeans and twisted toward Van. "I'll follow you out."

Van stepped toward the passageway in the closet with a gun in his hand and a huge pack on his back.

Tate bent to lift her and stopped. "Did you hear that?"

The silence that followed strangled like a chokehold. Then Van said, "No—"

A deafening bang rattled the front door, and it blew open in an eruption of splintered wood.

Her heart stopped, and guns fired. A man screamed. More men swarmed in. Assault rifles and handguns and street clothes. Tiago's guards.

Tate stood over her, shooting, dodging, ducking, and shouting something at Van. Boots scuffed near the door. Bullets pelleted the wall. Then glass popped, and the lights went out.

Her vision fuzzed in the darkness, her brain sluggish, her entire body convulsing with panic and helplessness. She couldn't stand, couldn't defend him, and fear ate away her alertness.

She blindly stretched an arm across the mattress,

seeking her Berettas as the gunfire began to slow.

"Van!" Tate lurched off the bed and slammed into something just as a shot rang out from the doorway.

Then silence.

Icy, dead, ominous silence.

She broke out in a cold sweat, trembling in her effort to stay conscious. "Tate?"

The rustle of clothes, tread of boots, beam of a flashlight — there were people in the room. Was Van among them?

"Tate?" She blinked, but her eyes wouldn't work right. "Answer me."

Where was he? What happened?

He'd called to Van, jumped, and a shot was fired. *He was hit.*

Her heart collapsed, and the roar of blood thrashed in her ears.

No no no no no. He can't be hurt. He can't die. He can't. He can't. He can't.

Shadows moved in around her. Then footsteps. A lot of them.

She turned her neck and felt a cool hand on her cheek.

"Tate and Van." The low rumble of a man's voice. Tiago's voice. "I know a lot more than their names."

"Help." She cringed away from his touch, but his hand stayed with her. "I think Tate was shot."

"He was definitely shot." His fingertips crawled across her lips. "Directly in the chest."

She couldn't breathe. This wasn't real. Her body locked up, and her mind screamed in denial. "I need to see him. Let me see!"

A phone rang. Muffled and cheerful, the chirp

sounded close. Somewhere on the floor.

Cole Hartman. He was supposed to call back with an address for a doctor.

The hand on her lips slipped away. A moment later, the chirping grew louder, clearer. Then it died.

"Who's calling him?" Tiago's voice drifted from above.

"I don't know."

It didn't matter. That call was an invitation for believers and dreamers. There were no dreamers in hell. Only sufferers and tormentors, prey and predators, and she epitomized both sides.

She was also a fool. Because dammit, she still hoped.

She hoped Tate was alive as Tiago carried her away from him and out of the apartment.

She hoped to live as he sat her in the backseat of a car and drove her to the compound.

She hoped for strength as he hauled her into the basement chamber.

But as she trembled on the concrete floor, it was hard to hang onto hope. The pain in her body became intolerable when her muscles began to spasm and a seizure thrust her into the black void.

Voices and footfalls ricocheted around her, but her mind was a mass of wool. She couldn't focus. Couldn't fight. They would do whatever they wanted to her, and the slow pulse of time would be a new kind a torment.

At some point, her brain disentangled, and her senses came online. A pillow, hard and thick, bolstered the back of her head. She lay face up, squinting against the harsh lighting. And hurting. The pain concentrated in her stomach, constricting and twisting and threatening to take her under again.

Oh God, it hurts. Make it stop.

She shifted her gaze away from the lights and focused on what was directly above her. Broad chest, thick biceps, and a scarred and swollen face with silver eyes. As her mind sharpened, she realized her head was on Van's lap. With his back against the wall and his arms chained to a horizontal beam behind him, he watched the activity on the other side of the room.

Her heart rate exploded. If Van was here...

She gathered the strength to turn her neck and collided with the crystal blue fury engulfing Tate's eyes.

He's alive.

Her breaths seized, and her arms quaked to hold him.

Shirtless and heaving, his chest bore a ghastly wound that bled beneath the skin. But it wasn't the critical, penetrating type of injury she expected from a bullet. It looked like someone had swung a hammer as hard as possible against his ribs.

If he was in pain, he didn't show it. His red-hot expression suggested he had so much adrenaline and testosterone pumping through him he felt nothing but violent rage.

"He took a bullet in the chest for me," Van said quietly. "Saved my life. Only reason he's alive is because he was wearing an armored shirt. His ribs are probably broken."

She knew his soft tone was meant to calm her, but beneath the whispered words shivered something she knew too well. *Fear.* She felt it, too. Dread. Terror. The horrifying grip of doom.

Tate hung from chains that encircled his wrists and

connected to the rafters, his feet bare and raised on toes, as if to ease the strain on his arms. It was the same place, same position, same fate as the man who died there only hours earlier.

Standing beside him, Tiago held a phone in one hand and Tate's shirt in the other. He spoke in a low voice to Armando — the only other person in the room. When he tossed the shirt on the metal table in the corner, that was when she saw it.

The lethal razor blade curved from the end of his finger like a claw.

An artist's instrument.

His favorite weapon.

"No." A mangled keening sound wailed from her throat. "Tiago, please, I'm begging you. Don't do this. I'll do anything."

"You'll do anything for *him?*" He tipped his head toward Tate, holding her gaze.

"Yes. Anything."

"Hm." He teased the claw across Tate's pecs. "I'm more interested in finding out what he'll do for *you.*"

CHAPTER 23

The scent of blood stung Tate's nose. Not *his* blood. The death from earlier tonight hovered in the air and stained the concrete floor. He'd heard the man's tortured screams through the transmitter and could now see the source of that agony glinting on the end of Tiago Badell's finger.

The blade looked lethal enough to carve through muscle, and as it lightly scraped across his chest, he was certain it would.

His heart drummed a furious tattoo. Chains restrained his arms, and broken ribs made every breath excruciating. He had no defense, no way to protect Lucia and Van. No way out of this.

Fear should've been a hulking presence inside him, but it was crowded out by unholy rage. Lucia lay on the floor in dangerous need of urgent care. She'd just surfaced from what must've been a seizure, one that had convulsed her muscles so violently it banged her skull against the concrete. Van, with his arms shackled, had managed to wedge a thigh beneath her head. Meanwhile, Badell had stood there and watched her suffer like a morally depraved psychopath.

How would they get out of this? With Van and him

shackled and Lucia clinging to life, they needed a fucking miracle.

It would be eight hours before Matias realized there was trouble, and even more hours to organize a rescue party. Maybe Cole would suspect something since his call went unanswered. That wouldn't help them, though. He was in another country.

"There are no contacts stored on your phone." Badell set it on the metal table and met his eyes. "No call history."

At Cole's request, Tate had meticulously kept the burner phone wiped clean. Thank fuck for Cole's counsel. The man had laid out plans for every emergency, including instructions in the event Tate was captured.

"I can give you a contact." He hardened his expression, masking the pain in his ribs. "Call my brother." He rattled off a predetermined phone number that would alert Cole of foul play. "You'll get your ransom money."

"Your *brother?*" Badell casually strolled through the room, clasping his hands behind him and twitching that deadly finger blade. "Your shirt repelled a bullet, and your companion" — he glanced at Van — "doesn't carry a phone."

Tate had destroyed all the phones but one before they left the apartment. He'd also had the foresight to protect their friends and family in anticipation of repercussions for taking Lucia out of Caracas. If Badell were to discover Tate's identity, his friends' lives could be threatened. So when he'd called Matias, Matias vowed to send his local guys to collect Liv and Josh, Amber and Livana, and all of Tate's roommates. They should be safely on their way to Matias' Colombian estate at this very moment.

"You have high-tech weapons and medical supplies." Badell paused before him, head cocked. "But no IDs. No passports. Nothing to connect you to anything or anyone. We both know you won't be providing your *brother's* number."

A knot formed in Tate's throat. He'd given Badell too many reasons to be suspicious. The man might've been clinically insane, but he was smart. There would be no ransom demands, because he smelled the trap.

Across the room, Lucia's whimpers grew louder. She rolled off Van's lap and pulled herself across the floor, grunting and sobbing in her determination to get to Tate.

"Lucia, don't." He jerked uselessly against the restraints. "Stay where you are."

"No." Her legs dragged behind her, slowing her down, and she cried out in frustration.

It was gut-wrenching to witness, cracking things inside him that hurt far worse than broken ribs.

He gave Badell the deadliest glare he could manage for a man hanging in chains. "She needs medicine. A doctor."

"Whether she gets that is up to you."

"What do you want?"

"Tell me why you're here. In Caracas."

Given Tate's weapons and the bullet-resistant shirt, Badell knew this wasn't a pleasure trip. He also knew it was personal. He only needed to watch Lucia as she hauled herself toward Tate. Her anguished cries shuddered with heartbreak. And *love*.

Love.

She loves me.

229

The intensity of that realization sent waves of pain through Tate's fractured chest. At first, he didn't understand it. It made him feel desperate and terrified, but underneath the panic was something new, something wholly unexpected.

When she smiles, I feel a peace unlike anything I've felt in my life.

Van's words hit him with soul-deep comprehension.

Lucia's smile was his responsibility, his goal, his everything. Her life, her health, all of her was his to protect.

She didn't belong to Matias or Badell or any other man. If anyone even thought to lay claim to her, he wouldn't step aside. He wouldn't back down. He would fucking fight for her with every breath in his body. She was his.

I love her.

Not the kind of love he'd flirted with before. What he felt for Camila paled in the dense, feral glow burning in his chest. This was deep, consuming, world-changing love. His past, present, and future, his entire existence took on new meaning.

His reason for everything was right here, in this room, dragging herself toward him. Her pain was his pain. Her tears, her happiness, her fate—all of it was his. Protecting her wasn't an obligation. It was his purpose.

It was the most significant thing he could ever do.

In that moment, he knew he would endure anything to make sure she smiled again. He would kill, bleed, cry, break, and die for her. There was nothing, absolutely fucking nothing he wouldn't do for her.

Fortitude built in his mind and girded his spine. It

wasn't just a willingness to fight for her. It was an insistence.

"You know why I'm here." He leveled Badell with a look that encapsulated the depth of his conviction. "As for finding out what I'll do for her, the answer is yes."

"Yes?" Badell's eyebrows rutted together.

"Get her and Van out of here. Give her the treatment, let them go, and my answer is yes to anything you want from me."

Lucia burst into a sobbing wail and sped up her harrowing crawl.

"Fascinating." Badell stepped out of her path, studying her as she closed the distance.

"Tate." She collapsed beneath him and slid a trembling hand over his bare toes, along the arch of his foot, and curled cold fingers around his ankle beneath the jeans.

His eyes burned, and his heart rate skyrocketed. God how he wanted to cradle her against him and console her. He wanted to clutch her hair and press his face to hers and smell her and hold her and kiss her. His inability to do so filled him with such maddening anger he couldn't form words over the scalding heave of his breaths.

Across the room, Van wore a bleak expression, but there was something else in his eyes. His strength and redemption was rooted in his love for his wife. He understood.

"The human spirit intrigues me." Badell closed the blade on his finger and pocketed it. Then he leaned down and gripped Lucia's hips, lifting her until she was eye-level with Tate. "Show me what you want, Lucia."

Her hands immediately slid around Tate's torso,

and tears streaked her ashen cheeks as she tried to pull herself against him.

Badell adjusted his hold, hooking an arm across her stomach and giving her what she sought—contact, connection, togetherness.

Tate clutched the chains that suspended his arms and pressed toward her, chest to chest, breathing her in. Their lips met, and he fed her what they needed. Commitment and unity. Substance and meaning. Promise and love. His tongue rubbed against hers, dedicated, possessive, licking away the salt of her grief as everything inside him roared with desperation.

It was a kiss that would carry them through the night. A kiss that hoped for tomorrow. A kiss that would survive the end of time.

Too soon, Badell pulled her away and carried her back to Van.

"No! No, please!" She sobbed, thrashing her head and feebly wheeling her arms. "Let him go! Let him go! You can't do this."

She continued to cry as Badell positioned her on her side with her cheek on Van's thigh, facing Tate. The placement was deliberate and cruel. He wanted her to watch.

"You think you love her." He returned to Tate, his dark eyes gleaming with morbid curiosity. "I'm not convinced."

"Do we have a deal?" He gritted his teeth.

"She's a beautiful woman. And compassionate. If you're into that kind of thing."

"Give her the medicine, Badell." He yanked at the chains, coughing against the agony in his ribs. "She needs it now!"

"I understand your urgency." Badell cast her a passing glance. When he turned back, the indifference in his expression faded, replaced with impatience and a hint of anger. He sucked on his teeth, his voice dropping an octave. "Once I'm convinced of your feelings, when I fully understand the lengths you'll go for her, I'll give her the medicine. Then I'll let her leave. I'll set her free."

Lucia screamed her protests, her words too hoarse to be discernible.

"How can I trust you?" His heart stammered, dying a thousand deaths.

"Lucia?" Badell called over his shoulder. "Have I ever broken a promise to you?"

"No," she wept weakly, miserably.

"We should get started." He removed the blade from his pocket and attached it to his finger. "She doesn't have much time."

CHAPTER 24

Tate memorized the delicate lines of Lucia's face, the fall of glossy black hair around her tiny shoulders, and the love glistening in her deep brown eyes. He devoured her pain and beauty, anchored himself to it, to *her*, as hands grabbed him and spun him toward the wall.

The hands, as he'd learned when he was driven to the compound, belonged to Armando. Badell's torturer. The man who raped Lucia just hours earlier.

While Armando adjusted the chains, Tate played out all the slow, agonizing ways the rapist would die. Didn't matter the method. Blood would spill. More blood than that which coated the wall inches from his face.

Why was there a sheet of wood on this wall and not the others?

"The chains usually prevent movement." Badell tested the links that ran from Tate's wrist to the ceiling. "But you're a big guy. Strong."

His hand vanished from view, and his footsteps shifted behind Tate.

A featherlight scratch moved across his shoulder blade. Chills swept through him, stealing his breath.

It's the razor. He knew it. His clenching muscles

knew it, and he tried to relax, to convince himself to accept it. But dread turned his body into a shaking block of ice.

"Nooooo!" Lucia screamed just as shocking, fiery pain seared through his skin and muscle.

His head fell back as violence and fury roared from his throat. It was so excruciating his limbs convulsed and slammed him against the wall.

Fuck, fuck, fuck. Breathe. It was just one cut. Just one. I'm better than this.

"See, if you buck like that, you'll rip the chains from the ceiling," Badell said at his ear. "I can't have that."

He was still heaving with blinding pain when Armando wrestled his forearm against the wood above his head. Blinking away the spots in his vision, he watched in horror as Armando stabbed an icepick through his arm and pinned him against the wood board.

The pain was unimaginable, shooting through him in shocking quakes of agony. His head hung on his shoulders, and his knees buckled, causing his weight to pull on the arm nailed to the wall. Nausea rose, and his vocal chords shredded. He tried to stifle his screams, but they were constant. Or maybe it was Lucia. Her anguish had become one with his own.

When I fully understand the lengths at which you'll go for her, I'll give her the medicine.

He needed to breathe. Breathe. Breathe. In and out. Stay alert. Focus. He was strong.

As his lungs found their pace, he planted his feet beneath him, lifting on toes to minimize the movement of the icepick through his arm.

"Why do you care if I love her?" he growled in a

thick, guttural voice. "What do you gain from this?"

"Your loyalty to her intrigues me. I want to examine it. Challenge it." Moving into his line of sight, Badell studied him with a pensive expression. "To truly understand the veracity of love, a man must be tested. He must pay for it."

What is the price you're willing to pay?

Cole's question repeated in his pain-addled mind, and he spat the words. "I'll pay, you son of a bitch. Just name the price."

"The price of love is devastation."

"How the fuck would you know?"

A muscle bounced in Badell's cheek. "I've paid it a thousand times over."

The sick fuck wasn't capable of love. Not that it mattered. He was lord and king here, Hell's monarch in human flesh. There would be no mercy.

And so it began.

The blade sundered his flesh from neck to waist, striping, curving, digging, cutting. Cutting. Cutting. Hours of continual pain immersed him in a bottomless pit. He went into shock, but it didn't numb the insufferable misery.

He kept his feet firmly beneath him and cheek pressed against the wood, staring at the metal handle protruding from his forearm. Every breath caused slight movement, shifting tendon and bone around that spike.

Everlasting fire incinerated his back, his ribs, his arm. Dizziness dulled his thoughts. But at the outskirts of his senses, he tracked the clang of Van's chains and marked the moment Lucia's weak cries dissolved into wheezing breaths. God willing, she must've passed out. He couldn't imagine what his back looked like and didn't want her staring at it.

How much blood could a person lose? Was he reaching his limit? It drained from his arm in steady red rivulets, leaving tracks down his bicep and ribs and soaking his jeans. The same wet warmth flowed from his back beneath the relentless slice of the blade. There was so much blood his feet slipped in the sticky pools cooling on the floor.

"How long have you known her?" Badell traced a soft finger through the agony along his spine.

He swallowed, tried to clear his head. Five days? That was when they met. But he'd known her for six years through photos, Camila's stories, and the depths of his investigations.

"Long time." He choked on a throat full of phlegm and bile and spat it out.

"And Van? How do you know him?"

Another stroke of that finger down his back, a gentle taunt that fired muscle-flinching pain. But Badell wasn't cutting. Conversation meant a reprieve from the blade.

Tate tried to make his mouth work, to give an answer that would delay the torment. Words eventually slipped out, but they were strangled and unintelligible.

"I kidnapped him," Van said from across the room.

"Explain." Badell shifted, creaking the stool beneath him.

Van outlined the sex trafficking operation, focusing on the training and the network of slave buyers. His words were carefully chosen, avoiding details that might've suggested they had friends or family. He also didn't explain why or how it ended. As far as Badell knew, it had been just Van and Tate and a dozen other faceless slaves.

He wasn't sure why Van shared any of it. Maybe Van was angling to connect to their captor in a companions-in-kidnapping way.

Badell listened, but he wasn't distracted from his mutilated canvas. The vicious, incessant cutting continued, shoving Tate into a hazy fog of gasping, retching distress. He vomited everything he'd eaten in days, heaving until blood vessels burst in his eyes. His suffering was so acute he felt every twitch of the blade, every notch, slash, slice, and cleave.

He was cold. So fucking cold he feared he was nearing the dark dismal nothingness Lucia had talked about. His lungs produced weak, shivery sounds, and the breaths trembling from his throat cracked his dry lips.

But he still had his mind, and he let it travel to the quiet woman across the room, absorbing himself in hallucinations—the softness of her hair as he ran it between his fingers, the ferocity of her expression as she argued, and the sweet perfection of her submission as he commanded her to kneel. A man could get lost in a dream like that, and he did, for a time.

Badell and Van continued their conversation while the dissection stretched over the expanse of his back. There wasn't an inch that hadn't been carved. He'd been in excruciating pain for so long he'd forgotten what relief felt like. The razor penetrated again and again, and he no longer had the energy to tense or resist. The fight had bled out of him. His life would soon follow.

It must've been nearing dawn when the last of his alertness faded. His groaning had become a heavy, hollow drum in his ears, booming in the black cavern of his mind. He was stuck there in that desolate vacuum, unable to escape the throbbing pressure. It was the only thing that existed. One continuous, torturous throb.

Throb.

Throb.

Throb.

Then he was cold again. A suffocating, liquid kind of cold that washed over his face and seeped into his nose. He choked and hacked, fighting for air.

I'm drowning.

It wasn't real. He wasn't under water. He just needed to return to that room. To Lucia.

Open your eyes.

Wake up.

More icy water. He coughed, taking the cool liquid into his mouth. His throat filled with shrapnel.

"Open your eyes." A deep voice breathed at his ear. *Badell.*

He blinked, moaning against the bright light as he tried to find his bearings.

Pain flared and flamed everywhere, but the pressure on his arms was absent. Nothing cinched or tore at his wrists, and his legs weren't pulling him down. He was weightless.

I'm on the floor.

Concrete pressed against his cheek and shoulder. He lay on his side, his good arm stretched toward the closed door. The other arm extended from beneath his torso and tucked against his stomach. He refused to glance at it, couldn't bear to see the ruin from the icepick.

And his back... Fucking God, his back felt skinless and exposed, as if the flesh had been shaved off and the muscle had been torn from bone. Grisly images of a bared spine and vertebrae flooded his mind.

Footsteps circled around his head as he tilted his neck back, aching, needing, searching...

There she is.

Eyes glazed, face blotchy, and frail body shaking violently, Lucia reached for him from a few feet away. Her fingers stretched toward his, too far, and her head lolled on Van's lap.

She was still alive. He was still alive. They still had a chance.

What time is it?

He tried to ask, but his vocal chords had been reduced to rock and gravel. "T-t-time?"

"An hour till dawn." Badell crouched in his line of sight, blocking his view of her.

Then he lifted a bucket and trickled cold water over Tate's face. When the rest was dumped on his back, the frigid drops felt like razor blades slicing across his skin. He bit down on his tongue, trapping a godawful bellow.

"You are my greatest masterpiece." Squatting with his sleeves rolled to the elbows, Badell rested scarred forearms on his thighs. "I haven't decided your fate. Quite frankly, I loathe the idea of destroying such a beautiful creation. If you live, you might one day come to value the artwork." He ran a hand along the welts covering his own arm. "Took me twenty years to appreciate mine."

Since he didn't wear a mask, Tate could identify him. The nutjob had no intention of letting him go.

"You promised," he ground out. "Meds." *Her medicine. Give her what she needs.*

"My promise was," Badell said, setting the bucket aside. "Once I know how far you'll go for her, I'll give her the medicine." He stood, slid his hands in the pockets of his blood-stained trousers, and paced the room. "I was going to have Van fuck her while you watched, but after hearing the history between you and him, I have a much better idea."

Profound relief mixed with overwhelming dread, curdling a venomous concoction in his stomach. The darkness in Badell's expression was sinister. Haunting. Whatever he had in store would threaten to break Tate's mind. He was certain of it.

He shifted his gaze across the floor and found Lucia staring back. Silent tears spilled from her eyes, and her mouth trembled with heartbreaking fragility. Her arm still lay outstretched toward his, fingers twitching to close the distance.

His chest heaved as he strained toward her, extending useless joints and failing to erase the inches between them. Goddammit, he just needed to touch her. Fury rose above the anguish, hardening his body into stone.

"Make your demands, Badell." He flexed his jaw, battling the never-ending pain that dotted his vision.

"One more trial." Shiny, blood-splattered shoes paused inches from his face. Badell lowered to a crouch and rested a hard, cool hand against Tate's jaw. "Van will take his pleasure in your body. Then you will take pleasure in his. Come inside him, allow him to release in you, then I'll know how far you will go."

"No-no-no-no-no…" Lucia chanted in a scratchy, tear-choked voice.

The hammering bang of his heart drowned out her cries. He was sprawled on the floor with his cheek against the concrete, frozen in place, silent and breathless as his vision lost focus.

Deep down he knew it would come to this. Badell wanted a trial, one Tate was sure to fail.

Hot moisture dripped from his unblinking eyes and traced a sodden stripe across his face. Such a strange sensation, that warm soundless trickle. He couldn't remember the last time he cried.

He would never be able to perform, let alone ejaculate. Not with a mutilated body. And not with Van.

But it was better than the alternative. If Van were forced to rape Lucia, Tate wasn't sure he'd ever get back up again.

Was that why Van had volunteered so much information about Tate's time in the attic? Perhaps he'd predicted Badell's plan for Lucia and steered him in a different direction. It took a sadist to know a sadist. Van probably saw the blood-smeared writing on the wall from a mile away.

Shifting his gaze, he sought the man who'd become his friend.

Van sat against the wall with his arms shackled, head tilted back, and eyes closed. Tate didn't have to be a mind reader to interpret the conflict twisting his face.

If Van participated in this, it would be a betrayal to Amber. If he didn't, they were all dead. He and Tate were probably dead regardless. But Lucia had a chance.

With her cheek on Van's thigh, she silently shook with full-body tremors. Tate gave her intense, meaningful eye-contact that said all the things he couldn't. *I'll kill for you. Die for you. You'll be okay. You're the strongest woman I've ever met.*

Van lowered his head and shared a look with Tate, a miserable moment of commiseration. Then Van

243

acceded with a single nod.

Tate closed his eyes, steeling himself. He felt completely and utterly defeated, his body a broken, worthless mess. He could handle the physical damage. He could survive it. It was the emotional blows that would bring him to his end.

He needed a mind-over-matter pep talk. If he were brave enough, the strength of willpower would help him overcome. He'd survived ten weeks beneath Van's thrusts. He could endure a few minutes, or hours, however long it took.

Reciprocating, however, was something entirely different.

"I found your limit." Badell stood and leaned against the wall. "It seems you won't, in fact, do everything—"

"Yes. The answer is yes," he whispered. "Send her out of the room."

Badell straightened, his brow lifting in shock before he emptied his expression. "She'll witness your undoing. That's nonnegotiable."

He stepped to the door, opened it, and spoke quietly in Spanish to whoever waited on the other side.

With a hard swallow, Tate returned his attention to Lucia, focusing on their hands and the dismal inches that separated them. "I'm sorry. I don't want you to see this."

Her mouth moved, and her chest rose and fell with the effort to speak, but nothing came out. She directed her eyes at her fingers, where they stretched toward his, and returned to his gaze.

"Shh. I know." His breathing accelerated, and he fought to calm himself down. "I'm here. No matter what happens, I'm with *you*. Only you."

The door closed, and Badell prowled toward him with three armed guards in tow. The men went to Van, two aiming rifles while the third unlocked his shackles.

Once free, he pulled his arms in front him, rubbing his wrists.

Please, Van. Don't do anything stupid.

Van thought about it. Tate saw the calculation in his silver eyes as he glared at the weapons pointed at his head. Then he turned to Lucia and lifted her fully onto his lap.

The guards kept their guns trained as he stood, taking her with him. Badell didn't stop him as he carried her closer and placed her on the floor, on her back, aligning her body against Tate's.

Thank you. Tate edged toward her with deliriously painful movements until the only thing separating them was his injured arm.

The press of her skin against the wound ignited unfathomable anguish, but he didn't care. He held the arm against his stomach and wrapped the other across her torso.

Fuck, how he'd needed to hold her like this. He needed *her*. More of her. More touching. More talking. More smiles. More time.

Their five days together had been the best days of his life. They'd lived in dearth and turmoil in a windowless room, yet they'd craved nothing but each other. It was confounding the way he connected to her so effortlessly, the way she fit so perfectly in his arms, against his body, and inside his heart.

Five days hadn't been enough. He wanted to laugh with her, fight with her, make up with her. He wanted a life with her. A lifetime. A forever.

Sweat beaded on her sallow face and drenched her t-shirt and jeans. Van had dressed her in those clothes while Tate had been on the phone with Cole. It felt like an eternity ago.

For the past five days, he thought he had this rescue mission under control. He'd sent off the blood samples and just needed a couple more days to receive the results. But it was too late for that.

He should've called Matias the moment he made contact with Lucia. Her illness, though… It was an endless, looming threat. Not even Matias had the means to cure her in time. Without the medicine, her fate was dire.

After she was raped, however, all bets were off. Tate had contacted Matias sometime before midnight. If dawn was an hour away, he'd been in this room for seven hours.

And so had she.

He called forth the energy to hug her tighter, savoring the flow of her breaths, the sweet scent of her hair, and the pulse in her throat as he kissed her neck. He ached to see her healthy and smiling and free. It would be the greatest gift, the ultimate definition of happiness.

"I love you," he whispered.

Her eyes squeezed shut, and her face crumpled with a weak nod.

Badell moved to the far side of the room and perched on the stool. His shoes left deep footprints in the thick puddles of blood.

My blood.

It ran from his body to the wall. There was so much of it on the floor, the wood board, and his jeans, he didn't understand how he was still breathing. He wasn't just physically spent. His emotions had run the gamut for hours, churning from intense trauma and helplessness to scathing wrath and hatred. The latter simmered anew as he met his tormentor's soulless eyes.

"You'll give her the medicine and let her and Van leave Caracas alive and unharmed." He lifted his chin with might and rage, eyes hard and breaths seething with vehemence.

"You have my word." Badell curled a hand beneath his chin, watching him, as if studying a curious object.

He looked away, vanishing the demon from his sight and his mind. As far as Tate was concerned, Badell and his guards were no longer in the room.

That left Van, who circled his feet and lowered to the floor behind him. "Stay where you are."

It wasn't like he could go anywhere. The constant state of his throbbing, bleeding torment would prevent him from getting his legs beneath him.

"I don't want to do this," Van said in a dead tone.

"I know."

"It's karma. I've carried this debt for so long. For the crimes I committed against you." Van leaned in, whispering at his ear. "When this is over, you and I are even. No more bad blood between us."

Tate nodded, but his thoughts were elsewhere, wholly occupied by what was about to happen.

"Give me permission." Van rested a hand on the button of Tate's jeans.

There had been a time when Van got off on taking without consent. And while every fiber in Tate's body screamed in horror, there was only one answer. "You have it."

"I'll only touch you where I need to." A crack in Van's monotone voice.

The hand on Tate's zipper moved efficiently, opening the jeans and pulling them down with the briefs to gather at mid-thigh. Then he lifted Tate's leg as far as the denim would allow and rested his thigh across Lucia's.

"Too heavy." Tate groaned through horrendous tremors.

"Stay." Lucia's whisper was barely audible as she curled a weak hand around his leg.

He wouldn't deny her the closeness, but once this began, there would be no eye contact. If he survived the night, he didn't know how she would be able to look at him the same. He couldn't bear to see that shift in her gaze now.

Van leaned away, leaving Tate's body wrapped around the side of hers. His cock and balls lay exposed and lifeless against her denim-clad thigh, his legs slightly spread, and his backside bare and vulnerable.

With his bleeding arm trapped between them, the pain was a sharp, constant presence. But it was nothing compared to the unholy dread amassing inside him.

Van's zipper sounded at his back, followed by the slapping of a fist against flesh. Van was stroking himself to get hard, and there was a measure of comfort in that, knowing his friend wasn't aroused.

"Tate." Her lips trembled through words that found no voice.

He tried to read her mouth.

Me... Look at me...

He didn't need to look at her to see her, sense her, feel her. She was inside him, part of him, embedded in his being. Curled around her delicate frame, he kissed her cheek, buried his face in her neck, and waited.

Several minutes passed before he heard Van spitting. Then a wet finger forced its way into his rectum.

Unbidden, he tensed up and stopped breathing.

"Was I the last person here?" Van asked quietly.

Six years ago. More than enough time to physically heal.

"Yes," he grated through clamped teeth.

"Don't clench." Van removed his finger and replaced it with something much wider. "You remember what to do."

Breathe. Relax. Push back.

The instant Van pushed in, Tate couldn't help it. He fought. The instinct to buck, kick, spit, and punch was uncontrollable. But he had no stamina, no energy, and Van easily subdued him.

"Hold still." With a grip on his hair, Van pushed his head toward Lucia, pressing his face into her neck.

Then the hand was gone, and all that remained was the invasion.

Slow and cautious, Van buried himself to the hilt. The burning fullness was much like Tate remembered, but also different. Maybe because his back, his ribs, his arms, everything was on fire. Or maybe it was the comfort of Lucia's hand on his leg and the rasp of her breaths at his ear.

Van held his body away as he drove in and out, no part of him touching Tate's back. Fingers clutched his hip for leverage, but this wasn't a dominant fucking. It wasn't taunting or cruel with the purpose of degradation.

It was efficient, merciful, and far gentler than anything he'd ever experienced with Van Quiso.

249

But it still hurt. A shameful, defenseless, lasting hurt that annihilated a man's dignity in one desecrating thrust.

He clung to Lucia, rubbing his lips against the tears that found their way to her neck. Her tears. And his.

Then it was over.

Van quickly pulled out and rolled to his back. Silent. So quiet it didn't sound like he was breathing.

"Show me." Badell leaned forward on the stool, craning his neck.

He wanted to see evidence of Van's release.

With a shaky hand, Tate reached behind him and spread his cheeks to expose the wetness Van left behind.

"Very good," Badell said. "Now switch."

Switch places.

He lay like the dead, half on top of Lucia's body, no doubt crushing her damaged organs. He didn't have it in him to move, let alone do what Badell demanded.

His physical self teemed with brutal spasms and fever. But his mind was numb. Detached. Unresponsive.

Unending pain, exhaustion, and humiliation had taken its toll. He'd finally reached the limit of his ability. He couldn't even will himself to look into her eyes.

"I failed you," he whispered.

Her head twitched side to side, knocking more tears free. The hand on his leg squeezed, and her other one fumbled between them.

When she bumped into his punctured arm, he swallowed an agonized roar. She whimpered and sucked in a breath, reaching her hand lower, sliding along his thigh until she found what she sought.

Trembling fingers encircled his flaccid cock. Then she began to stroke.

He couldn't. Even if he were able to send blood to that part of himself, how would he thrust? How would he stay hard inside of Van's body?

But she was determined. Why was that? She wouldn't push him into this depravity just to save her own life.

Suspicion aroused his senses.

Shifting his hand from her shoulder to her jaw, he turned her head and leaned up. Vertigo threatened to knock him sideways, and the cords in his neck quivered to hold up his skull. But he pushed through the pain and met her gaze.

Something flashed in her eyes, a fierce spark of perseverance.

If he were somehow able to satisfy Badell's demand, she would leave this place. She would have to leave him behind. But that wasn't what her expression conveyed.

He let his head drop, returning his mouth to her ear. "Don't you dare put your life on the line for me. Understand?"

A feeble nod.

"I can do this." He reached between them, nudged her arm away, and took his cock in hand.

The task was grueling. Each stroke aggravated the mangled muscles in his back. Every exerted breath squeezed the cracks in his ribs. There was no pleasure in it. And no blood. His dick refused to harden.

Then her hand was there again, wrapping around his, sliding in tandem, and lending him strength. He focused on her touch, on her slender weight beneath him, and on the sigh that parted her lips. He narrowed all his concentration on the pleasure and filled his mind with one image: Her pussy.

Her soft pink folds swelled so beautifully when she was aroused. She was too small for him, and he had to work himself in, but she was a greedy little thing, and she would spread her creamy thighs and welcome him, gasping and trembling as he seated himself to the root.

Christ, she turned him on. Her exotic beauty, resilience, and submissive nature was a trifecta of perfection. She was his ideal mate in every way.

She was his.

He slid his fingers over the top of hers and rocked into her fist. His breathing sped up. His pulse accelerated, and fuck him, but he stirred to life. It was medically impossible and beyond disturbing, but he had an erection and intended to keep it.

Grinding harder against her grip, he angled his neck until his lips found hers. The kiss was clumsy and languorous, but holy hell, her taste. The salty sweetness of her mouth aroused him further, heating his blood and driving his hips.

"I want you," he breathed against her lips.

"Van," she gasped weakly and looked at the man leaning over his back.

Van. That was who he needed to want right now. How? How the ever-loving fuck would he do this?

She tightened her hand around his shriveling erection and hardened her eyes. Goddamn, he loved her spirit, but it was going to take a lot more than a glare to push him past the physical and mental blocks.

"I have to rearrange us." Van moved to kneel on the other side of Lucia, with his jeans partially zipped up. "Lucia, he'll need his good arm to brace himself. Keep him hard and…positioned."

Her chin trembled as she attempted a nod.

Van looked at Tate with an expression that didn't belong on his face. Even in his worst moments, he was power and passion and dominance. But now... Now, he wore a mask that didn't fit. A facade that buttoned up his emotions and sucked the life from his eyes.

"When we start, don't look at me," Van said coldly. "Keep your eyes closed. Focus on her hand. I'll do the rest."

Shame coiled inside him, and it quickly spiraled into rage, whipping his heart against broken ribs and chopping his breaths. He gnashed his teeth, hating this for Van and hating himself for being so goddamn weak.

"Listen to me, dickhead." Van's voice was sharp and menacing—a tone Tate hadn't heard since the attic. "You're going to stop being a pussy and power through this. Close your fucking eyes and don't open them until you come."

He clenched his jaw and squeezed his eyes shut. *Her hand, her hand, her hand...* He felt the stroke of her fingers, appreciated it, and wrapped all his thoughts around it as the sounds of shuffling moved around him.

The comforting press of her body slid away. Then her touch was gone, too. He kept his eyes closed and tried not to imagine how this would work. Van used to arrange his captives in all sorts of vulgar positions. It was difficult not to think of that as limbs and bodies bumped against him.

He balanced on his side with his head on the floor, his throbbing arm pressed against his stomach, and his limp cock in his hand. Someone shifted close against his front, and he knew it wasn't Lucia. The breathing was too controlled, the physique too wide and hard.

As he tried to stimulate his dick, his knuckles brushed against skin and rigid muscle. Given the position and shape, he didn't have to open his eyes to see Van's bare ass. He suspected Van was face down beside him, with Lucia on the other side of Van.

Her hand wrapped around his shaft, her arm stretching over Van's backside. He didn't look as she rubbed and fondled him. Didn't open his eyes as she coaxed the blood back into his cock. He kept his thoughts on her and her alone, fantasizing about every dip and curve on her body, the taste of her lips, and the noises she made when he got himself off inside her tight cunt.

It took a lifetime to bring him to hardness, and by the time he was stiff enough, he'd fucked her in his mind in every position, in dozens of places and scenarios.

She held onto his erection as he shifted his weight and crawled over Van's prone body. The muscle tone, the masculine scent, even the feel of the t-shirt was wrong. Add to that the blazing pain across his back and down his arm, and he started to soften.

But he'd made it this far. He just needed to…lift…adjust… His good arm shook like a bitch as he braced it between Van and Lucia and supported the weight of his torso.

A sheen of sweat formed on his face, and his lungs huffed and wheezed with agonizing effort. He held his useless arm against his chest and dragged his knees into the *V* of Van's spread legs beneath him.

Then the real torture began.

Lucia, who was right beside him now, put all her strength and energy into rousing him. When he hardened, she lined him up. When he softened, she went at it again, stroking, squeezing, and encouraging with determined fingers.

Van must've already lubed himself with spit because his opening was wet. But Tate couldn't get it done. Every time he pressed in, his semi deflated.

Minutes passed. Too many to track. The countless starts and stops and position adjustments put enormous stress on his already weak body. He'd lost so much damn blood. Eventually, his muscles tired. His arm gave out, and he collapsed on top of Van's back.

Then he opened his eyes.

Van lay face down on the floor beneath Tate, braced on elbows with his head bent and his face pressed in the cup of his hands. Discomfort and strain flexed across his back beneath the shirt. His entire body was a concrete slab of tension.

This man wasn't a bottom. Not even close. He'd been sexually abused as a child and probably hadn't taken a man this way since he escaped that trauma.

"I'm so fucking sorry." Tate rested his cheek against Van's spine, his eyes burning with regret.

"Don't." Van pulled his arms beneath him and slowly lifted to hands and knees.

The position slid Tate to kneel behind Van, the weight of his upper body resting on top of Van's back.

"Instead of apologizing," Van said in a cruel voice, "think about all the times I pounded you into the floor. All the times I held you down while you begged me to stop until your throat was raw and your ass was bleeding. Think about that, Tate, while you fuck me."

The first time Van forced him was forever branded in his brain.

His insides ripping and tearing around Van's ruthless thrusts.

255

PAM GODWIN

Arms and legs restrained.
Mouth gagged.
His body no longer his own.

He'd wanted to kill Van then, but beneath that sinister wish lurked even darker thoughts. So many times, in the isolation of that attic, he'd imagined doing to Van all the things Van had done to him. He'd imagined fucking his captor until his cock dripped with blood.

He didn't want that now, but he harnessed those feelings — the vengeance, the violence, and the brutal urge to reclaim his dominance, to reclaim himself.

He wasn't a pussy. He wasn't emasculated. He controlled how this ended.

With a surge of empowerment, he balanced on his knees and grabbed Lucia's hand, showing her the speed and pressure he needed to get hard. It took a while. Fuck, it took goddamn forever, but he stayed focused, clear-headed, and finally hard.

He sank into Van's body in a single stroke, pushing with a grunt that made Van gasp and shudder. He found Lucia's eyes, gripped her hand, and held onto both as he gave into the forbidden pleasure and chased his release.

It was the longest minutes of his life. The climb was a battle of concentration. The peak was short-lived and cathartic, and the downward spiral dropped him into guilt-ridden hell.

He fucked, and he came, and he despised himself for it.

Van lowered him to the floor on his side as Badell stepped toward them and examined the evidence.

Every cell and nerve in Tate's body shivered with scorching pain. A shroud of darkness tried to pull him under, and he fought it, rapidly blinking as he sought

Lucia.

When their eyes connected and locked, the spinning, wobbly world righted itself. He fucking loved her, and as long as she lived, everything would be okay.

"You did well." Badell's voice reached his ear, distant and muffled.

"You made a promise," he tried to say. His lips felt numb.

"I will honor it." Badell lifted Lucia's lethargic body from the floor and carried her out of the room.

CHAPTER 25

Lucia lay on the mattress in Tiago's room, feigning sleep as her mind whirled and panicked.

A few feet away, Tiago grunted through an upper-body workout. Dumbbells lifted and hit the floor. His footsteps paced. Then he started again.

She'd passed out before she received the injection, then again after. Though she'd been awake for the last hour, she'd held herself still and quiet, waiting for the medicine to saturate her system. Waiting for her strength to return and her brain to fire on all cylinders. With her eyes closed and the desperation to get to Tate gnawing at her nerves, the wait had been brutal.

But she was fully alert now. Perhaps eighty-percent back to health. Very little pain in her abdomen. No paralysis.

She was alive.

Physically.

Emotionally, she'd died a hundred times over. Died every time the blade had made a new cut in Tate's flesh. She'd died in that torture chamber and continued to do so.

The monstrosity inflicted upon his back, the icepick

in his arm, his screams, the blood, the sodomy, the heartbreak… It replayed and fermented and thrashed inside her, crushing her chest and blackening her thoughts.

Whether Tiago let her go didn't matter. He would never free her heart.

Her person.

The man she loved.

The man who proved his love in the most excruciating ways imaginable.

Tears simmered beneath her eyelids. She willed them away, relaxed her face muscles, and continued the ruse of sleep.

Tiago had imprisoned her for eleven years. He would do the same to Tate just to rest his gaze on his macabre artwork every day. That knowledge had plagued her in the basement, and she'd spent those gut-wrenching hours devising a different ending.

She would walk out of the compound today, and Tate and Van would be with her. She knew exactly how she would do it.

Except she hadn't expected to wake on Tiago's bed. She needed to be near the chairs, so she could use one as a weapon.

There were other surprises, too. Tiago never lifted weights in her presence. Never allowed her in his room for this long. And never, never, never permitted her to wear clothes in here. The fact that she was dressed meant he'd been in a hellfire hurry to give her the injection.

But she didn't have her guns.

The thud of a dumbbell against the floor resounded through the room. If one of those was twenty or thirty pounds, it would be light enough for her to lift.

And heavy enough to crush a skull.

She peeked across the room from beneath barely raised lashes.

Tiago hissed through a set of curls, his bicep flexing with each heave of the dumbbell. Covered in sweat and dressed in a tank top and athletic shorts, he was angled toward her with his eyes down and his brow creased.

He was disgustingly handsome, sculpted all over, and evil down to the morrow of his bones.

She hated him with a seething passion that clouded her vision and poisoned her blood. Murder was the only way to relieve the pressure swelling behind her eyes. When she killed him, she wouldn't feel an ounce of remorse.

Multiple dumbbells of various sizes scattered around his feet, and several of those looked like the weight she needed.

She twitched the muscles in her legs and arms, testing responsiveness. Everything moved as it should.

The plan will work.

Her insides tangled in a heap of nerves, making it harder and harder to initiate the first step. Once she alerted him she was awake, it would be go time. No turning back.

She pulled in a deep breath, sharpened her mind, and deliberately released a sickly moan.

The dumbbell paused mid-curl. He lowered it to the floor and prowled toward her. The mattress sloped beneath his knee, and his hand cupped her face.

"How do you feel?" His fingers, sweaty and vile, crept along her jaw.

"Where's Tate?" She widened her eyes in a

semblance of panic and wheezed a cough from her throat.

"You need to rest." He gripped her chin, a gentle pressure.

"No." She bowed her back and flailed as if trying to sit up but couldn't.

Except she could. The flexing of muscle in her core and limbs gave her hope. She was strong enough. Definitely determined enough. She could do this.

"I want to leave." She shot him a fierce look, one he'd come to expect from her. "You promised."

"I'll let you go, *after* we have a conversation."

Restlessness trembled through her. She didn't want to spend another second with this man. Didn't want any part of his slippery tricks or mind games.

"You're going to leave Caracas without Tate." He tightened his fingers on her face, as if expecting her to jerk away.

She didn't have to fake the quiver in her lips. If her plan failed, Tate and Van would never see outside of these walls again.

"You care for him." His touch softened, ghosting across her cheek. "You might even love him. Those feelings will eat at you and consume you and you'll return to Caracas with a half-cocked rescue plan. You'll probably attempt to kill me, and you'll die trying."

Her jaw clenched. *He has no idea.*

"I won't. I'll stay away." She made her voice shake. "Please. Just let me go."

"I investigated your friends." He stood from the mattress where it lay on the floor and paced away. "I learned that Tate Vades and Van Quiso are missing persons, living under the radar in Austin, Texas."

Her stomach folded in. Tiago had been with her the entire night. An investigation like that would've taken time.

"How long have you known?" Her voice fractured.

"Six days." He shot her a disapproving glare. "I investigate every man you fuck at that club."

Oh God, oh God, oh fuck. Did he know she'd sneaked out the back door that night? Or that she spent five days with Tate? Or that Tate was close to her sister and her sister was alive?

Why did he wait six days to capture Tate?

Because he loves his twisted mind games.

"I know Van Quiso's married," he said. "But I didn't know about his criminal history until he told me."

Van's married?

Her fingers clenched at her sides. The forced sex between Van and Tate had been harrowing enough. The fact that Van was married made it even worse. She wanted to scream and kick at the unfairness of it, but she kept herself lethargic. She needed Tiago to believe she was too weak and defeated to be threatening.

He went on to describe Tate's roommates, their house, and the two-hundred-acre property Van shared with his wife. Not once did he mention Camila or Matias. He either hadn't made the connection between Van and Camila or he was deliberately fucking with Lucia's head.

The scariest part was his discovery of Van's wife and Tate's friends. Tiago knew where they lived and was vindictive enough to go after them.

Even more reason to kill him.

"I'm relocating." He stood in the center of the room, arms crossed with a knuckle resting beneath his pensive frown. "I found something…a new interest I'm pursuing."

That was fucking cryptic. And inconsequential. He wouldn't be leaving this room alive.

"When I let you go," he said, "you can try to come back for Tate, but he won't be here. I'm taking him with me."

The hell he was.

He stared at her like he expected a reaction, and she was more than ready to give him one.

In a series of intentional movements, she surged upward, swayed dizzily, and tumbled back down like a rag doll.

"Lucia." He watched her in that way he always did, head tilted and eyes tracking her with unfeeling curiosity. "You're not ready to get up."

Swinging her legs to the floor, she exaggerated every motion as she climbed to her feet. With staggering steps, she made her limbs look cumbersome and awkward.

While she didn't glance at the dumbbells, her senses narrowed on the one she wanted. Each weaving, uncoordinated stumble brought her closer, closer…

Close enough.

She let her ankle twist without injuring it, pretended to lose her balance, and angled her fall so that she landed with her fingers next to the dumbbell.

"Always so stubborn." He strolled toward her with his hands behind him.

Lowering into a crouch beside her hip, he trailed the softest touch down her spine. The glide of his fingers became a rubbing hand that traveled the length of her back. The same hand that had tortured and scarred Tate without mercy.

She lay still beneath the affection, pushing air in and out of her lungs noisily and intentionally. If Tiago would just lower his head a little more, she wouldn't have to swing so far.

"I've treated you badly." He smoothed his fingers through her hair, gently and rhythmically. "Sometimes, I wish I could undo the things I've done. I wish…" His hand paused, and he let it fall to the floor beside her shoulder. "Well, I can't change my plans for Tate, but *you* have the power to give him what he wants most. You can start over, stay alive, and move on. He wants you happy, and you can be that for him. His survival is up to you."

She would do better than that.

With a sweep of her hand across the dumbbell, she curled her fingers around the bar and jerked it from the floor. It was heavier than she expected, and she gritted her teeth, accidentally releasing a warning grunt before swinging it toward his head.

It connected with his temple, and his eyes widened with a gasp. The heavy force of the momentum sent him backwards, and his arms flew up to grab her. But she was ready for it, dodging his hands, rearing back, and striking again.

The second hit landed higher up on his skull, with a crunch of bone, a wet smack, and a dead fall to the floor. He slumped on his back, eyes closed, with his legs bent beneath him. Blood saturated his black hair and spread a slick red pool beneath his head.

I did it.

The weight fell from her shaking hand, and her breath hung in her throat. She waited for him to rise up and attack. Waited for the guards to rush in. Waited for this to not be real.

I actually did it.
I killed him.
I fucking killed Tiago Badell.

Bile rose up, and she dry heaved. No sound. No vomit. Just cold, paralyzing shock.

And sorrow.

It stitched through her chest in pinprick stabs, causing her to double-over.

She didn't want to feel a damn thing for him, didn't want to dwell on the tenderness he'd shown her or the soft words he'd whispered. She needed to slam the weight against his head over and over until his face was as mutilated and unrecognizable as Tate's back.

But she couldn't.

She wasn't a monster.

You're a pretty little flicker of compassion, begging to be extinguished.

She scrambled away from his lifeless body and ran toward the safe in the closet. The detour would be a waste of time, but she couldn't leave without checking.

Her hands fumbled with the lock's dial, spinning through number combinations and testing the lever. She would never guess it, and every second she delayed was a risk to Tate's life.

She stepped back. Leaving behind the medicine had been part of her plan. She couldn't do anything to change that.

With a resolved breath, she pivoted and faced the body.

The sticky puddle beneath his head had doubled in size. The sight of his slack face, matted hair, and gory wound on his skull made her feel sick. Villainous. Her stomach knotted, and her scalp tingled with unease.

She'd killed him in cold blood.

So much for not feeling remorse. God, I'm so fucked up.

Turning on her heel, she strode toward the door.

She still wore her boots, jeans, and shirt. Dried blood stained her chest and arms. Tate's blood. If Tiago's death had splattered on her, it wasn't noticeable.

At the door, she rested a hand on the knob and checked the line of sight between her position and the body. The guards wouldn't see Tiago unless they pushed the door all the way open.

It would be easy to enter the hall without being questioned by them. She did it every morning after every injection, and Tiago rarely followed her out. Today would be the same.

She swallowed, emptied her expression, and turned the knob.

Her Berettas weren't on the bench in the hall. Being unarmed would suck for the next few minutes, but it worked in her favor.

The guards gave her a cursory glance. She returned one of her own as she slipped out, shut the door behind her, and made her way down the hall.

All they had to do is peek inside his room. If they were suspicious or simply had a question for him, the door was unlocked. With just a turn of that knob, they would know what she did. And they would kill her.

Fucking hell, she trembled. Her hands shook, and she clenched them. Her heart beat so fast she felt dizzy and overloaded with tension.

She didn't know what Tiago's plans had been for her once he released her. But on a normal day, two guards would be waiting in the lobby, watching for her so they could escort her back to the apartment. Escaping them wouldn't be an option. She would have to neutralize them quietly and discreetly.

She weaved through the labyrinth of corridors, passing countless men—thieves, kidnappers, murderers, rapists. The worst of humanity. And they had no idea she'd killed their commander.

As the lobby came into view, she veered to the left and slipped into the kitchen.

Food and cookware scattered steel counter tops without a single person in sight.

Yes! I lucked out.

She rushed toward a rack of utensils and snatched the biggest knife. Then something moved in the pantry behind her, the squeak of sneakers on tiled floors.

Quickly and carefully, she concealed the blade in her boot and spun toward the sound.

"*Qué buscas?*" Roberto, the oldest of Tiago's chefs, paused in the doorway of the pantry.

If he'd seen her steal the knife, she would have to kill him. More blood. More death. She braced herself for it.

"I'm hungry," she said in Spanish.

He strode toward her, carrying a bag of rice while eying her from head to toe. His graying mustache twitched with the roll of his lips.

"You eat when everyone else eats." His Spanish dribbled with disdain as he thrust his chin at the door. "Get out."

Gladly.

She fled the kitchen, fighting the urge to glance down and make sure the knife was hidden until she stepped into the vacant hall.

The stairs to the basement waited just around the

corner. She kept her gait even, casual, as she walked, turning the bend and —

A hand clamped onto her shoulder, propelling her heart to her throat.

"Are you ready to leave?"

She didn't recognize the masculine voice but knew it was one of her Spanish-speaking guards before she turned to face him.

"I left my Berettas in the basement," she said in Spanish and stepped out of his grip with a racing pulse.

Her guns were probably still at her apartment. If this tattooed, baby-faced thug had been involved in the gunfight last night, he would know that. Unfortunately, she'd been in too much pain and shock to recall the details of Tiago carrying her away.

She held her breath as he studied her with bloodshot eyes. She could really use a 9mm with a silencer. Most of the guards carried them, but not this one. The sawed-off shotgun on his hip wouldn't help her if it alerted every gang member in the compound.

"Fine," he said in Spanish and pulled a cigarette from his shirt pocket. "Be quick."

Forcing her boots to move as if reluctant and bored, she shuffled toward the stairwell.

CHAPTER 26

There were benefits of being a high-ranked gang member for Tiago Badell. One, Lucia had access to every hallway, room, and dark corner in the compound and no one questioned her. Two, she had deep insight into how Tiago ran his security.

Since there were two prisoners, there would be two guards in the basement. No more. No less. They would be armed and separated. One at the door to the basement corridor and one at the entrance to the chamber.

She was so damn nervous her shoulders tried to hunch around her ears. The tension in her neck tightened to the point of pain.

I can't fail. I can't fail. I can't fail.

With a steeling breath, she opened the door to the stairwell and found the dank, narrow space quiet and empty.

So far so good.

Closing the door behind her, she grabbed the knife from her boot and flattened the blade against the side of her leg. There was no way to conceal it, so whatever happened next needed to be swift and soundless.

The almighty pound of her heart threatened to

liquefy her knees as she rounded the first bend in the staircase. Her senses buzzed on high alert, making every step more arduous than the last.

One more corner to go.

Her soft treads whispered along the stone walls, but there were other sounds, too. The rustle of movement. The faint rasps of breathing. There was definitely a guard waiting at the bottom door.

The knife handle slicked in her clammy fist. She squeezed her fingers, shifted it out of sight behind her thigh, and edged around the last bend.

Perched on the bottom few stairs, the guard pulled his attention from the phone in his hand and glanced over his shoulder.

Armando.

Panic, disgust, vengeance—all of it blazed through her, feral and venomous.

His eyes widened. *"Donde esta* Tiago?"

Where's Tiago?

He's dead, and you're about to join him.

He knew, even as he'd asked the question, something wasn't right. He'd been in the torture room and witnessed her despair. He knew she was here for no other reason than to rescue Tate.

It happened so quickly—that realization on his expression and her sudden lurch forward. He tried to rise to his feet, but his movements were too slow, his belly too big, and she was faster.

Her higher elevation on the stairs gave her an advantage as she jumped and collided with his back. The strength and direction of her attack knocked him off balance. He stumbled, bumped against the wall, and went down. She followed him to the floor, clapping a hand over his mouth, wrenching his head back against her shoulder, and thrusting the blade upward, right into the soft part beneath his jaw. She pushed hard and fast, aiming for his brain until the hilt met his throat.

Hot blood soaked her fingers as he sagged. Soundless. Breathless. Dead.

She held onto the knife, frozen and listening for footsteps over the thrash of her pulse.

Blessed silence.

His phone lay on the floor at his feet. A 9mm with the extended barrel of a silencer sat on his hip. She needed both and waited several torturous seconds, concentrating on her surroundings. When she was certain no one had heard, she pocketed the phone and chambered a round on the gun.

That was the easy part.

Any second now, the guard upstairs would finish his cigarette and come looking for her.

With trembling hands, she positioned herself on knees at the bend in the staircase and raised the gun, ready to shoot anyone who rounded the corner.

The wait lasted an eternity as her mind swam through worst case scenarios. If Tiago's guards checked on him, she would fail. If multiple men entered the basement and outnumbered her, she would fail. If the gun in her hand misfired, she would fail.

Tate's fate rested entirely on her ability to not fucking fail.

When the door at the top of the stairs finally scraped open, every pore in her body beaded with sweat. Her lungs froze, and her limbs locked up.

Breathe, dammit.

The sound of footfalls grew louder, clomping,

descending, speeding up. One threatening gait. Only one.

He would see Armando's body the moment he turned the last bend, but she wouldn't give him enough time to react.

Resting her finger on the trigger, she breathed in, timed his steps, and waited, waited...

His chest came into view, and he jerked to a stop, spinning toward her.

She squeezed the trigger on her exhale, point blank range, right in the chest.

The bullet casing pinged against the stone wall behind her, and the report of suppressed gunfire ricocheted through the stairwell. The echo sounded like a metal ball bouncing on concrete.

It's too loud!

The guard was dead before he hit the floor, but the racket would've been heard in the basement. She didn't have time to pause.

Stepping over the bodies, she cracked the lower-level door and spotted a man charging toward her, maybe ten feet away. He reached for the gun in his waistband, but hers was already aimed.

She fired at his torso, and the suppressed bang reverberated through her.

He dropped before he pulled his weapon, but his hand was still moving, reaching for it.

Adrenaline kicked in as she sprinted toward him and shot again, directly through his heart.

His arm fell to the floor with the slump of his body, his eyes fixed, glassy and frozen, at the ceiling.

This was far from over. Even with a silencer, those three shots had made noise. If the reverberation had reached the main floor, she didn't have much time.

She raced toward the chamber where Tate and Van waited and slammed to a stop mid-stride.

Keys!

Spinning back to the dead guard, she grabbed his 9mm and unhooked the keyring from his belt.

Then she ran, stretching unused muscles in her desperation to get to Tate. At the door to the chamber, she released the bolt and rushed into the room.

The overpowering scent of blood hit her in the face, causing her to stumble. Van sat against the wall, arms shackled to the beam. Tate lay on his stomach beside him, free of restraints because...

Oh God, his back was a gruesome tapestry of tattered flesh and gory illustrations too shocking to focus on. With his cheek against the concrete and his wounded arm lying like a dead thing beside him, he didn't move, didn't react.

Waves of heartbreak crashed through her, wrenching a whimper from her throat.

His eyes were open but glazed over, expressionless, utterly catatonic.

With panting breaths, she forced her feet to keep moving, skidded to her knees beside Van, and set the guns on the floor.

"We have to hurry." She fumbled with the key in the locks, losing precious seconds before the chains fell loose.

"Badell?" Van pulled his arms free and grabbed one of the guns.

"Dead. In his room. No one knows. *Yet.*" From her pocket, she handed him Armando's phone. "I'll get us out of the compound, but we need help leaving the city. This won't be a stealthy getaway."

"Matias should be close, but I don't know how to contact him." Van inched toward Tate and stroked a hand over his unmoving head. "Tate? I need Matias' number."

Tate's lashes twitched, followed by a sluggish blink. The muscles in his jaw bounced, like he was trying to respond and couldn't.

Her heart shattered, and it took every ounce of willpower she had left to keep her emotions in check.

"He's been unresponsive since you left." Van stood, stepping out of her way.

"Tate." She stretched out on the floor beside him and put her face in his. "We're getting out of here, but we need Matias' number."

His eyes tried to track her voice, focusing and clouding over. Then his lips moved, whispering the digits slowly and painfully in a shredded voice.

As Van made the call, she moved down Tate's legs. His jeans gathered just beneath his butt, as if the task of righting them had been interrupted. She carefully dragged his pants into place, focusing on her hands rather than the horror painting his back.

"It's Van Quiso," Van said into the phone. "We're in trouble."

Tate groaned weakly as she slid a hand beneath his hips, tucked him inside the boxer briefs, and zipped the fly as much as she could manage.

Van quietly and efficiently outlined the situation to Matias. A few seconds later, he turned the ringer off the phone, pocketed it, and rested those sharp silver eyes on her.

"He's twenty minutes outside of the neighborhood." He crouched at Tate's side. "We need to head north, and he'll meet us at—"

"M-mmeh..." Tate inched his hand toward her, dragging his injured arm along the floor and hissing, "Medsss...you..."

"I got the medicine." She caught his hand in hers and found his swollen blue eyes, blinking back tears. "I'm good, Tate."

"Extra?" he slurred. "More mehhs...sinnn?"

Extra medicine?

Despite her efforts, her strung-out misery flowed down her cheeks in hot streaks. She couldn't imagine the amount of pain he was in, yet his concern was entirely focused on *her*.

She knelt over him and put her mouth against his. "The syringes are locked up, but it's okay. Matias will find me a good doctor." She kissed his cracked lips, lingering, savoring the connection. "I have twenty-four hours. Plenty of time." *Not near enough time.* But she wouldn't dwell on that. "Van's going to carry you. We need to go."

Tate closed his eyes, his expression contorted in pain. When he refocused on her again, he looked fiercely determined and brutally handsome.

Flattening the hand of his good arm against the floor, he tried to push up. Van was there, lifting and adjusting to position Tate's body in a fireman's carry. Though Tate didn't make a sound, his agony was palpable in the tenseness of his muscles and the creases on his bruised face.

She lost her breath through the grueling process of dragging him to his feet. His back was one massive, open, chewed-up wound. His ribs were broken, and the hole near his elbow slicked his forearm and hand in fresh blood. Moving him without causing extreme pain was impossible.

Sliding behind Van, she cupped Tate's jaw and kissed his mouth, tasting his torment and love and wetting his lips with promises.

"Netflix, a rescued dog, and a road trip to wine country." Squatting beneath the droop of his upper body, she kissed him again. "It's all waiting for us."

The corner of his mouth twitched—a heartbreaking attempt at a smile.

"Lay out the escape plan." Van hitched Tate higher on his shoulder, with the guard's gun held tightly in his hand.

Thank fuck he was strong, because Tate wasn't a small guy. Carrying him through the compound would be a feat in and of itself.

"There are two ways in and out." She strode toward the door, trembling violently with nerves. "We'll take the stairs up, turn right down the hall, and go out the back exit. Less guards."

She opened the door and peeked down the basement corridor. Other than the dead man, it was empty.

"Since I have the silencer, I'll do the shooting." She checked the magazine in Armando's 9mm. "Five rounds left."

"When we make it out, what then? Is there gate in the rear?"

When not *if*. She could've hugged Van for his confidence.

"No gate. Just guards. It's a service entrance. We'll have to shoot and run." She rested a hand on Tate's backside, where he hung over Van's shoulder. "Can you manage?"

"I've got him." Van gripped the door, opening it wider. "We need to head north. It's quicker and easier for us to leave the neighborhood than for Matias to fight his way in."

He gave her the address of the meet spot, which was about a fifteen-minute sprint. Half that if they stole a car.

Her stomach turned to ice as she led him down the hall and into the stairwell. She paused at the bodies long enough to snatch the sawed-off shotgun and holster from the dead guard. She strapped it on her hip and crept up the stairs with Van at her back.

At the top, she met his eyes and whispered, "Don't let him get hit."

"I'm more concerned about you," he whispered back. "He'll kill me if something happens to you."

Tate released a low, deep sound in his throat, and her lips quivered in a smile.

She stroked the back of his leg, her chest aching with an outpour of things she wanted to say to him. But this wasn't the time.

We'll make it out. Then she would have a lifetime to tell him how much she loved him.

She cracked the door to the main floor and scanned the empty hall through the opening. "Clear."

They ran. Down the long hall, guns raised, footsteps soft, the sprint zapped the air from her lungs and turned her stomach to lead. Adrenaline soared through her blood, and her hair flicked against her face as she swung her neck side to side to watch their backs and fronts.

A shadow moved across the wall of the

intersecting corridor up ahead, and an all-over tremor shook her aim. She locked her elbows and honed in on the approaching threat.

The guard stepped from around the corner and paused in her sights. He gasped, and she fired. The bullet hit his chest, and he dropped just as another man emerged behind him.

This one managed to release a warning bellow and draw his weapon before she shot him in the face.

Fucking shit and damn! The back door was close now, only ten paces away, but the commotion was too loud. Soon, they would be swarmed by armed men.

A glance behind her confirmed Van was on her heels. She grabbed a gun off a dead guard, shoved it into her waistband, and cut the corner.

The din of distant footfalls pounded behind her, intensifying the terror that gripped her neck and shoulders. They were feet away from the exterior door when two more guards entered the hall at the opposite end.

"Go, go, go," she shouted at Van. "Get outside."

Breathless and sweaty, she ran past the exit and fired three shots at the men. One guard went down as Van threw open the door and slipped outside with Tate.

The second guard fired back, missing her by inches. Tate's hoarse roar sounded over the bang of gunfire, and she fired again.

A hollow click stopped her heart. *Out of ammo.*

The man at the end of the hall had paused to check on his friend. But he was moving now, running toward her with his pistol aimed.

A bullet pelleted the plaster beside her head as she dropped the silencer, drew the short-barrel shotgun, and blasted a huge hole through his chest.

Her ears rang with the explosive noise. She tossed the gun and pulled the pistol from her jeans, needing the 9mm to cover the distance between her and the throng of men tearing around the corner.

She backed through the doorway and into the sunlight, angling around the door jamb and spraying bullets into the chaos inside.

More gunfire ricocheted behind her, spiking her heart rate. She turned and found Van shooting down two approaching men in the alley. He crouched beside the open rear door of a small car. Tate lay face down across the backseat.

"Let's go." He scanned the barren street and ran toward the driver's side.

Can he hot wire that car?

She didn't have time to ask. More men flooded the corridor. Too many to shoot down. She slammed the steel door shut and hauled ass toward the car. Van bent under the steering wheel and yanked on wires as she pulled Tate's feet into the backseat with her.

"Hurry!" She closed the door and ducked just as the window exploded in shards of glass. Bullets pinged the side of the car, and the report of gunfire shuddered the air.

"Van!" she shouted, petrified. "Can you do it?"

The car roared to life and jerked forward, slamming her against the seat back and tossing her on top of Tate's prone body.

Van sped out of the alley, sideswiped another car, and bounced over a curb. Bullets rained down upon them, blowing out the rear window and riddling the metal exterior.

Keeping as low and concealed as possible, she curled up near Tate's head and rested his cheek on her lap. His lower half hung off the seat, his knees bent on the floorboard at an awkward angle.

"Which way is north?" Van swerved around a pedestrian and hit the gas.

"Left." She craned her neck to look between the front seats. "Not this street. Turn left at the next one."

He followed her directions, and as her panting breaths slowed, so did the bullets and yelling behind her, until...nothing.

We lost them.

We escaped.

The glory and relief in getting away settled through her in great shivering waves. She combed a hand through Tate's hair and bent to rest her lips against his feverish brow as she caught her breath.

But they weren't out of the woods yet.

"They have motorbikes," she shouted at Van over the gusts of the wind through the windows. "They'll catch up."

He took the corners at high speeds, lurching in and out of traffic, and whipping her around the backseat with the starts and stops of g-force.

The pungency of fuel and burning rubber saturated the cab, and the taste of blood soaked her tongue from her stabbing teeth.

"It's going to be okay. We're going to make it." She whispered the chant at Tate's ear.

She didn't have medicine and probably wouldn't live through tomorrow, but she had today. She had Tate, and he would survive this. He had to.

His eyes were closed, his lungs laboring for every

intake of air. Clots of blood coated his back in a gruesome reminder of the prior night, and beneath the gore lurked a picture carved into flesh and muscle. Through the shimmer of tears blurring her vision, she could make out images. A massive gate opening outward and... Was that a silhouette floating through it?

"We're close, right?" Van pointed at the motorway that emerged up ahead.

"Tiago's domain ends there. Just a few blocks away."

She twisted to see out the broken rear window. No one chased them. No motorbikes. No speeding cars. No guns.

Dread buckled her stomach.

The escape was too easy. Even if Tiago's men had discovered his death, they wouldn't just let her go. Something was wrong.

"Call Matias," she said urgently. "Tell him where we are."

"A little busy." Van's laugh strained with tension as he swerved the car side to side, dodging motorists.

She cradled Tate's head and scooted forward to reach between the seats and search for the phone in Van's pocket.

"Fuck!" He slammed on the brakes, throwing her back against the seat. "Fuck, fuck, fuck!"

Up ahead, police cars skidded onto the street, blocking their path.

"Turn back!" Her pulse exploded as she twisted around, searching for a side street. "Take that one!"

She caught Van's eyes in the rearview mirror and pointed at the alley behind them.

"We can't trust these cops?" He shoved the car in

reverse and sped backward. "What happens if they catch us?"

Tires squealed behind them, followed by the rumbling sounds of motorbikes. Her scalp crawled, and a chill spread through her cheeks as she looked back and found a roadblock of armed officers.

"Get to that alley." She gripped tight to Tate's head and shoulders, shaking and nauseous. "They wouldn't be here unless Tiago called in a favor."

"What?" Van spun the car around and veered into the alley — the only way out. "I thought Tiago was dead."

"He is." Her breath came in wheezing pants. "I smashed his head in with a dumbbell. I thought... Oh God, I didn't check. I couldn't..."

His pulse. I didn't check his pulse. Was he still alive?

If the police caught them, they would die in prison. Or they would be taken back to the compound, where they would be tortured before they died.

"If they surround us, we're dead." She tightened her arms around Tate's limp body.

"Goddammit." Van slammed the shifter through the gears and recklessly weaved around dumpsters and metal stairs in the alley.

The motor revved, and the end of the alley glowed like a beacon. Police on motorbikes zoomed in behind them, but there were no barricades up ahead.

They can make it. They can make it. Go, go, go...

The air vibrated with a rumbling reverberation right before the end of the alley filled with half a dozen police on bikes.

"Hold on." Van accelerated.

Twenty feet, ten feet... Holy fuck, he was going to plow through them.

Heart pounding, she bent over Tate's head, wrapped her arms in a death grip around him, and braced for impact.

A ringing sound split her eardrums, buzzing with the clamor of gunshots and Van's shouting. Then sirens.

Sirens on a police car, in the alley, careening toward them head-on. The alley was too narrow, and they were traveling too fast and close to avoid collision.

Van jerked the car, hit the side of a building, then slammed into something else. The world spun, and time became heavily compressed and fractured.

The jarring impact catapulted her to Peru, shackled in the back of a transport, falling, rolling, flailing in the memory of twisted metal, broken bodies, crushed bones, and the scent of blood.

CHAPTER 27

Tate surfaced to a muffled symphony of pandemonium. Banging, shouting sounds pulsed in and out, as if trying to penetrate the cotton stuffed in his ears. He lay twisted in a mangled car, covered in glass and throbbing in excruciating pain.

Lucia was there, her tears drenching his face and her hand stroking his hair. Her agony was unbearable, her fear palpable. He couldn't swallow, couldn't breathe as he tried to make sense of the clamor around him.

He remembered gunfire and running and the speeding car. The front hood was bent against the broken windshield. The dash was too close to the front seats, and the pungency of coolant, gasoline, and burnt chemicals fumed the air. They must've crashed.

Black spots dotted his vision as he dragged his good arm beneath him and lifted. He blinked. And blinked again.

Multiple rifles pointed through the shattered window beside Lucia, aimed at her head. The armed men shouted something, and she screamed back at them, sobbing and shaking uncontrollably.

His pulse raced, and his senses sharpened. The

men wore helmets and uniforms with arm patches and name tags. They surrounded the car, training rifles through every window and shouting in Spanish.

Where was Van? The airbags were deployed, and the front seat was empty.

Overpowering pain tore through his body and stole the strength from his neck. His head dropped onto her lap, and his muscles trembled with never-ending agony.

This wasn't him. He wasn't weak or puny. He was physically fit, stubborn, aggressive. He was a survivor. He needed to get the fuck up. He should be able to protect her.

The door beside her opened with a godawful squeal of grinding metal. Hands dove in, yanking her out of the car. She fought and kicked and screamed his name, but he couldn't reach her. His arms wouldn't respond to his urgent orders.

"Lucia." Seething with pain, he tried to scramble after her.

His limbs wouldn't cooperate, moving sluggishly, inch by inch across the seat. He reached his working arm through the open door and clawed at the pavement, yanking himself forward in a fevered frenzy of ripping flesh and dizzying anguish. He felt things tearing and breaking inside him, but he was separated from his body, completely fixated on getting to her and nothing else.

With his torso hanging out of the car and his legs caught within, he watched uniformed men with guns haul her away. Police cars and motorcycles filled the alley, and at the far end, several cops wrestled Van into the backseat of an armored transport.

If they were incarcerated, she wouldn't see a

doctor. Wouldn't have access to medicine. Maybe Matias or Cole would find them and grease the right palms to get them released, but it would be too late for her.

She would be dead by tomorrow.

A roar ruptured from his throat as he twisted around, searching the car for a weapon and coming up empty. A seat belt tangled around his leg, and he wasted miserable seconds and precious strength to free himself. Then he crawled on one arm, rolling onto the pavement and nearly blacking out. He muscled through it, compartmentalizing the pain and fumbling forward, scraping his chest along the ground.

She thrashed and swung her legs in the clutches of the men who carried her. When she found his eyes, her expression hardened, and she redoubled her efforts. But she was outnumbered, and he was too slow, too fucking weak.

He couldn't reach her, couldn't touch her, couldn't save her.

But he tried, and tried, and kept trying.

Goddammit, he would never give up on her.

CHAPTER 28

Crammed inside a cell in the municipal police station in eastern Caracas, Lucia struggled to breathe amid the sweltering heat and the reek of body odor, shit, and urine.

She didn't know where the police had taken Tate. Didn't know if Tiago Badell was orchestrating their fates. Didn't know if Matias would be able to find them or if he even had the power to get them out of this place. Her nerves were shot, and with every hour that passed, she felt the tendrils of despair taking root.

When she and Van were thrown in here, they were shell-shocked and manhandled. The guards took his shirt and shoes and her bra and boots. But they let her keep the rest of her clothes. Then they were shoved to the back of the prison cell by dozens of restless, hungry prisoners.

Van had dragged her through the crowded bodies, fighting his way back to the front to yell at the guards through the bars. Though he spoke good Spanish, his pleas for a doctor fell on deaf ears. He'd tried to explain her illness and her need for medical attention, tried to argue for her human rights, but there were no rights here. Within the walls of the *calabozo*, no one was human.

Shirtless men and barely-dressed women stood shoulder to shoulder against one another, with no room to sit. They took turns resting on hammocks made from sheets tied to the bars. A few managed to squat along the back wall.

Every hacking cough was a reminder of the diseases that lurked among them. Tuberculosis. HIV. Influenza. Not to mention the red scabies-like rashes that blistered the arms and legs around her.

A small window outside of the cell sat high on the wall. The sun had set forever ago. The guards had changed twice. Dawn would come soon.

She stood with her back to a corner. Van had wedged her there, using his body to separate her from the others. With his arms braced on the walls above her head, he worked his jaw rhythmically.

Neither of them had eaten, drank, or gone to the bathroom in over twenty-four hours. Her bladder cramped painfully, but relieving it would require peeing in a plastic bag while everyone watched. She would have to submit to that eventually, but she wasn't mentally ready.

"Still no symptoms?" Van asked for the hundredth time.

"No."

There were some nights, though rare, when she didn't experience nausea, abdominal cramps, or any pain at all.

Tonight, she felt a different kind of pain. A deep, emotional torment that festered and cramped in every part of her.

Tate was probably in a prison cell like this one, alone, unable to stand or defend himself. Were prisoners stepping on him? Was he bleeding out on the filthy floor? Would he take his last breath while prisoners stood on him unaware and unconcerned? She couldn't stop imagining it, and it was slowly killing her from the inside out.

Beside her, a man leaned his back against the wall, sobbing as he pulled on his hair and scolded himself for robbing a merchant to feed his starving family.

"I can't believe places like this exist," Van muttered, staring at the man. "That's saying something, considering I grew up in the shittiest shit hole on Earth."

Her chest pinched. "I'm sorry you got pulled into this. This wasn't your fight."

"I volunteered." He bent his knees, bringing his scarred, bruised face into her line of sight. "I've committed so many crimes, and this is the first time I've been behind bars. This is justice, don't you think?"

She shook her head. "You're a good man."

He laughed and returned to his full height, looking away.

"No." She gripped his bicep and pulled him back down. "What you did for Tate last night, especially knowing you have a wife—"

"How the fuck do you know about her?"

She yanked her arm back and swallowed. "Tiago knows. I'm sorry. I don't know if he'll go after her or—"

"She's safe." His entire body turned to stone, and he dragged a hand over his face, breathing through his nose as if trying to rein in his temper. "Matias has her. He's protecting everyone connected to Tate."

Oh, thank God.

She closed her eyes and inhaled. Then she looked up into his silver-bladed gaze. "I probably won't make it through the morning—"

"Lucia," he growled.

"I just want to thank you for what you've done for him. You didn't have to come to Caracas. You didn't have to participate in Tiago's demands last night. If you hadn't done those things, I wouldn't have made it this far."

"*This* far? To a prison?"

"I had five days with him." Her voice quivered. "I got to experience love. Do you know that feeling?"

"Yeah." His eyes closed briefly, and when they opened, they glimmered.

Jesus, this mean-looking ex-kidnapper was head over heels in love. Who would've thought? She certainly wouldn't have recognized it before, but now... Now that she knew what it felt like, she sensed this man's love for his wife all the way down to her toes.

Neither of them was in a position of hope, and maybe that was why she felt the need to say, "Promise me you'll see her again."

"Easy." His expression hardened with conviction. "I'm counting every breath until I see her again. I promise." He cupped the back of her head and held her face against his chest. "Your turn."

"I'll see him again." *In my memories. His face will be the last thing I see before I die.* "I promise."

CHAPTER 29

Four nights. Three days. One room.

Tate marked the loss of time by the ebb and flow of sunlight through the cracks in the wood walls. He lay face down on a thin blanket, his muscles trembling and his back a throbbing, burning, spasmodic ripple of pain.

His prison was a windowless shack with a dirt floor, a bucket to shit in, and a door that locked on the outside.

After Lucia had been taken from him in Caracas, the police put him in the trunk of a car. He'd traveled about a day in that dark cramped space. When he arrived here, he was blindfolded and carried into the shack by two men he couldn't see.

During those few seconds outside, he'd felt the warmth of the sun on his skin and the dry heat in the air. It smelled like a desert — dusty, hot, barren.

Maybe he was near the coastline, but he didn't hear the tide or the sea birds or any insects. He didn't hear anything at all through the walls of the shack.

Except when the doctor came.

Twice a day, a car rolled up outside. The bar slid from the door on the shack, and an old man shuffled in to tend to his wounds.

Always escorted by two armed guards, the black-skinned doctor spread a numbing cream into the cuts on his back, cleaned the stitches on his arm, and bathed him from head to toe. Then he was fed broth and tea.

One guard emptied the shit bucket while the other patrolled the door. Tate could barely crawl, let alone stand. But they weren't taking chances.

No one spoke. In those first couple of days, Tate couldn't, either. He wasn't sure any of them knew English. The guards resembled the thugs in Badell's compound, and the doctor matched the descriptions Lucia had given him of Badell's medical team, down to the scarification welts on his arms.

My back will look like that someday.

If I live.

Though he'd heard Lucia say she'd killed Badell, he knew the gang leader was the reason he was here. Either someone had taken over the operation or Badell was still alive.

When Tate could finally manage raspy words, he badgered his visitors with questions about his location, Badell's whereabouts, and Van and Lucia.

Where's Lucia? was the question he demanded most, and during the visit this morning, one of the guards had given him a single English answer.

Went to prison.

He'd blown a gasket when he heard the response, seething and thrashing and reopening wounds in his fit of rage. The guards had to restrain and gag him while the doctor patched him back up.

If he counted the day it took him to travel here, it'd been four days since he'd been separated from her. If she was imprisoned, she would be dead now.

His brain struggled to process that. His heart flat out refused.

He ran through a range of conflicting emotions in his isolation, from fury and guilt to determination and hope, and chief of all was helplessness. He'd failed her. Failed to protect her. Failed to rescue her. Failed to make her smile.

His shame and self-pity made him resent the healing of his injuries. He resented every fucking breath he took. Why bother?

But what if she lived?

He wore himself out trying to stand. Felt the wounds on his back tearing when he tried to stretch. He was imprisoned in a horizontal position, lost in the destructive fabric of his thoughts.

In hopeless conditions, the mind deteriorated. He knew that was happening, knew he needed to shut down parts of it to survive.

So he did.

CHAPTER 30

I'm still alive.

Lucia didn't know how or why her illness up and fucking vanished, but she hadn't experienced a single symptom since the night Tate was tortured. Tiago must've given her a cure in the last injection. It was the only logical answer.

She and Van spent a week in that overcrowded jail, living in a cesspool of feces, disease, and despair. Now they were on a prison bus, being transported to a permanent penitentiary. There were no phone call allowances, no lawyers, no judicial process. No human rights. This was the underworld, and corruption pulled the strings.

She wasn't sure if their case had even made it to the courts. She still didn't know what they were being held for. Tiago was behind this. He was powerful enough. Vindictive enough. She expected nothing less after bashing him over the head with a dumbbell. Killing her would've been too merciful for his brand of revenge.

Did she regret attacking him?

Maybe he'd truly meant to give her freedom.

Freedom from him.

Freedom from her illness.

But without Tate, she would've never been free.

The only thing she regretted was not bashing him again and again until his brains spilled onto the floor.

She sat beside Van on the bus, hands and legs shackled with a chain between the restraints to limit movement. Dozens of prisoners crowded in around them, all traveling to the same horrific fate.

Sadness hung like a fog in the humid air. The entire bus smelled like defeat. But she refused to subscribe to it. Her feelings had been all over the place for the past seven days, but she hadn't let herself break. She hadn't given up. Eleven years ago, she'd entered Tiago's world much like this and worked her way to the top. She would do it again.

But could she do it with a broken heart?

Thinking about Tate, missing him, craving him, loving him—her need for him didn't come and go like her illness. It was a building, growing, continuous escalation, and she couldn't break away from it. She didn't want to. She'd never experienced such deep-seeded torment in her life. But it was *her* torment, and she would endure it for as long as she was separated from him.

About an hour into the drive, the bus rolled through an urban town. High-rise buildings lined the street in a mishmash of historical and modern architecture.

There were over a hundred prisons in Venezuela, and she didn't know which one they were assigned to or where this town was on the map. But as the bus stopped in front of a towering office building, it didn't feel right.

She exchanged a confused look with Van.

"Where are we?" he asked.

"Hell if I know."

The driver rose from the seat and opened the door. The two armed guards in the front also stood.

Footsteps announced someone boarding the bus. She craned her neck and spotted a mid-thirties Caucasian man. His short brown hair was a military-type cut. He wore aviator glasses, a black leather jacket, and dark jeans. Strong jawline and muscled physique, he looked like a hot DEA Special Agent from the States. *Wishful thinking.*

Why was he talking to the driver?

She glanced at Van, who watched the man with a grin tugging at his lips.

Her heart rate skyrocketed. "Do you know him?"

Without looking at her, he gripped her wrist above the chains and squeezed. Hard.

Oh my fucking God. He knows him!

Was it Cole Hartman? The man who helped Tate locate her? Who else could it be?

The bus hadn't been forced to the side of the road. This was a preplanned stop. An arrangement negotiated in advance.

A rescue.

One of the guards turned and strolled down the aisle. Her lungs crashed together as he stopped beside Van and unlocked the restraints from the seat. He did the same for hers and stepped back, motioning for them to go.

Her legs trembled, and her pulse hiked as she followed Van off the bus. The man in sunglasses led them into the building without a word, his gait efficient and quick. Too quick for her shackled, shuffling feet to keep up. Van managed only slightly better with his stronger legs.

Once they were inside the vacant lobby, the stranger crouched before them and unlocked the chains with a key.

"Where's Amber?" Van kicked his feet free.

"With Matias." The man unlocked her shackles and rose to free her wrists. "I'm Cole Hartman."

Her heart tumbled and flipped.

"Do you know where Tate is?" She dropped the last of her restraints and sucked in a breath.

"Tiago Badell has him." He freed Van's hands, strode to the bay of elevators, and pushed the *up* button. "I don't know where."

Her heart shattered into a million pieces. "Is he alive?"

"I don't know," Cole said. "When I leave here, I'll find him."

"Who's funding that?" Van prowled toward him, head cocked.

"You are." Cole smirked. "Your wife approved it. Matias is chipping in on the extraction fee."

"Extraction." Her voice cracked with tears, and she cleared it. "You know he's alive?"

"I don't want to get your hopes up."

"Hope?" She gripped the front of her shirt, drawing his attention to the dark red stains. "I've been wearing his blood for over a week. I left him crawling in an alley with broken ribs, his back carved to hell, and a hole from an icepick through his arm. Hope is all I have left."

"Okay." Cole's brows drew in, and he stood taller. "What I know of Tate Vades is when he's determined to do something, he does it. If he wants to live, he will."

The elevator dinged, and the doors opened. In a swirl of tears and long brown hair, a beautiful woman shot out of the lift and collided with Van's chest.

He grunted a noise that sounded a lot like a sob as he yanked her up his body and buried his face in her neck.

"Amber, you were supposed to stay upstairs." Cole stiffened as he scanned the street through the glass doors. "It's not safe."

She wrapped her legs around Van's waist, crying as she peppered his face in kisses.

"Where's Livana?" Van caught her chin and stared into her eyes.

"She's in Colombia. Liv, Josh, they're all there, except Kate. Matias has a team of men looking for her."

Kate. Tate had told Lucia about his roommate, but he never mentioned Livana.

Amber went back to kissing his face, covering the length of his scar and the bruises around his eye. When their lips met, he kissed her hard and deep, eating at her mouth with a passion that heated Lucia's cheeks.

"Who's Livana?" she asked Cole.

"Van's daughter. Get in the elevator." He shooed her in.

Van has a daughter?

She didn't move. "I'm not going anywhere without Tate."

"We'll discuss it upstairs." He gripped Van's arm, guiding him onto the lift with Amber in his arms.

"Lucia." Cole lowered his voice to a threatening tone. "If you die in this lobby, you won't be able to help him."

She gritted her teeth and stepped onto the lift. He pressed the button for the top floor, and the elevator started its slow crawl upward.

"Who gave you a black eye?" Amber cupped Van's face as tears streamed down her own.

He kissed her again, pressing her back against the wall and tangling his hands in her hair.

Watching them together ripped open the hole in Lucia's chest. She'd been kissed like that once. For five days. Not only had Tate given her a blissful taste of happiness, he'd also fought for her, bled for her, and reopened his own emotional wounds. For her.

She owed him her life, her freedom, and she intended to pay that debt. She wouldn't neglect it or abandon it. She would never walk away from him.

"What's on the top floor?" When she glanced at Cole, her horrific, puffy-eyed face reflected back in his sunglasses.

"Helicopter," he said. "Matias is taking you to Colombia."

Camila might be here with Matias, but it wouldn't change anything. Lucia's mind was made up. "I'm not getting on that helicopter."

He slid the sunglasses to his hairline and pinned her with the intensity of his brown eyes. "I didn't just spend seven days getting you out of a Venezuelan jail to let you stay here."

"I'm going with you."

"No. Absolutely not." He set his jaw. "I work alone."

"Work alone then. I know Tiago better than anyone. I'll find him on my own."

The elevator bounced to a stop, and the doors

opened to a waiting room filled with half a dozen people. Some she didn't recognize—Matias' cartel members by the look of them and the weapons they carried. But there were two familiar faces.

Sitting on a couch beside Matias, Camila lifted her head toward Lucia. Their gazes caught, locked, and connected in a way only two sisters could.

Camila stood, and Lucia stepped off the lift, her legs numb and throat tight.

I'm not going to cry. I will not cry.

Tears welled in Camila's huge dark eyes. God, she was beautiful. Gone was her sweet baby face and spindly limbs. She'd bloomed into a curvy, toned beauty with long black hair and a healthy glow that radiated around her like a halo.

She paused within arm's reach of Camila and tentatively touched her soft hair and tear-soaked cheeks.

"You're as tall as me." Lucia laughed through a sob. "I told myself not to cry."

It'd been twelve years since Van had taken Camila from their citrus grove. Twelve years since Lucia last saw her. But it felt like only yesterday when they were running through the maze of orange trees, laughing and screaming as Matias chased them.

"You're thinner than me, bitch." Camila grinned through her tears.

"And you're still bitchier."

They reached at the same time, crashing together in a hug that constricted her ribs and wrenched a sob from deep inside her.

"I thought you were dead." Camila cried, soaking Lucia's neck.

"I thought you were dead, too. This doesn't feel

real, does it?"

Camila shook her head and tightened her embrace. "I'm taking you to Colombia with me. You need food and a doctor and… Goddammit, Lucia." She leaned back and wiped her cheeks. "I'm so sorry. I should've looked harder. Done more. And Tate…" Her face crumpled.

"Don't do that." She brushed Camila's tears away. "Tate told me all about your vigilante work. I'm so fucking proud of you."

Matias stepped in, nudging Camila aside to wrap his arms around Lucia. "So damn good to see you, *bella*."

"You, too." She hugged him back. "Thank you for taking care of my sister."

"She's my life." His head turned toward Camila.

She followed his gaze and watched Camila pull Van into a tight embrace. His hands hung awkwardly in the air for a moment before they slid behind her and patted her back.

"I still want to kill him," Matias growled.

"Give him a second chance. We all deserve one."

"I'm trying."

Camila pulled away from Van and returned to Lucia, encircling possessive arms around Lucia's waist.

"Let's go home," she said to Matias.

He stared at her for a suspended moment, sharing a private smile that lit up his face.

He was even more handsome than Lucia remembered, with his thick black hair, powerful frame, and hazel eyes glinting in the sunlight from the windows. Thank God, he and Camila had found each other again.

"The helicopter's ready." He gestured at the ceiling. "Head up to the roof. I need to talk to Cole for a—"

"I'm not going." Lucia stood taller, bracing for an argument.

"Oh." Camila stepped back, her expression etched with hurt and disappointment. "Okay... I... Well, we can get you back to Texas. I just thought—"

"I'm not leaving Venezuela without Tate." She wouldn't apologize for her feelings. They were real and honest, and Camila of all people would understand. "I love him."

A smile wobbled across Camila's lips. "I bet on my life he loves you, too." She gripped Lucia's hands. "But you need to see a doctor. You've been so sick."

Tate must've told Matias about her illness, but that would've been a week ago.

"I'm doing okay now." She rested a hand over her stomach. "I don't know why, but I haven't felt any of the symptoms."

Camila and Matias turned toward Cole Hartman, who leaned against the wall on the far side of the room. He straightened, shoved a hand through his hair, and approached.

"I intercepted the blood results Tate was waiting on," he said. "I had them reviewed by a doctor I trust."

She stopped breathing, and everything inside her went still. "What is it?"

Camila clutched her hand and squeezed. Clearly, everyone knew but her.

"There were traces of something like hemlock in your system." He held a fist against his brow, as if trying to think. "I don't have the report in front of me, but it was a poison that behaved like hemlock, derived from a plant the doctor couldn't identify. He found compounds or alkaloids or whatever that causes ascending muscular

307

paralysis. I guess it starts at the legs and works its way to the respiratory muscles. Did you experience that?"

"Yes. Exactly that." A sudden coldness hit her core. "What are you saying?"

"Tiago Badell was poisoning you with an unknown venomous plant. You had dinner with him every night, so I assume he put it in your food. Every morning, he injected you with an antivenom."

She swayed as the past few years came crashing down upon her. The mandatory dinners, the nighttime cramps and nausea, the instant relief after the medicine — it all fit. And she hadn't been sick since the last time she ate at his table.

"I don't have a terminal disease." She clutched her throat as she tried to absorb the impact. "I'm not going to die."

"Not today." Cole smiled. "As far as the doctor can tell, repeat exposure to the poison didn't cause lasting damage. Your overall blood work is healthy. But you need to have tests ran, a full examination. Not to mention your injury in Peru..."

His voice faded beneath the heavy thud of her heart. Tiago poisoned her. *For years.* That sick, disgusting, depraved son of a bitch. How could he do that? And now...

"He has Tate." Her pulse raced, and pain stabbed through her chest as she turned to Camila. "I need a loan. I'm sorry to ask this, but I just need some money for..." *Lodging, transportation, food, clothes, weapons — the list is endless.* "I have to find him, and I promise to pay you back."

"Lucia, calm down." Matias slid into her line of sight. "Cole will find him. He knows what he's doing and—"

"What would you do?" She moved around Matias and confronted her sister. "If Matias was taken by a man like Tiago, what would you do?"

"I'd put everything I had and everything I was into finding him." Camila's eyes dampened, and her voice broke. "I'll give you whatever you need."

"Stop." Cole pinched the bridge of his nose and cursed under his breath. "Here's the deal. I'm not babysitting you, and I'm not fucking kidnapping anyone."

"Okay." Lucia held her breath.

"Say your goodbyes." He rubbed the back of his neck and lowered his hand. "We leave in ten minutes."

CHAPTER 31

Standing on sturdy legs, Tate lifted a soaked sponge over his head and squeezed. Cool water sluiced down his nude body. It was neither refreshing nor painful. It was just…water. He plunged the sponge into the bucket and repeated the task with robotic movements.

Lift. Squeeze. Plunge. And don't forget to scrub beneath the ankle cuff.

They'd taken his clothes away when the doctor had stopped bathing him. It must've been weeks ago.

Was it weeks? Or months?

Time didn't exist within these walls. It didn't speed up or slow down. It didn't move at all. Because it was dead.

Sometimes his mind weakened, and he thought about the lost weeks. He could track them if he wanted to. He only needed to take inventory of his injuries. The stitches in his arm had been removed, and his hand had some mobility. His back didn't feel as tight when he paced the dirt floor, dragging the heavy chain behind him. Pain still lingered in his ribs, but it was muted. Dull.

Dull like the water trickling over his skin as he bathed.

Dull like the stew and porridge they brought every day.

Dull like the beat of his heart when he forced himself to face the truth.

She's dead.

He hurled the sponge into the water, snatched the bucket from the ground, and shoved it toward the guard waiting at the door.

It was always the same two silent scowling men. They were about as happy to be here as he was.

The guard reached for the bucket, and Tate yanked it back.

"Where's Lucia?" he demanded.

Always the same question. Always the same non-response.

When the man pinned his lips, Tate threw the bucket at his feet, splashing the man's trousers with water.

"Where is she?" he bellowed.

The guard's face turned red-hot. A beating would follow. A fist in the face. A boot in the ribs. Didn't matter if he taunted them or not. They seemed to get off on boxing a shackled man who was too weak to defend himself.

But Tate always fought back, and he was growing stronger. He fought until blood leaked into his eyes and clouded his vision. Until his lungs wheezed, and his ribs screamed in protest. Until the bastards knocked him out.

He fought because it made him feel alive.

Today would be no different.

The second guard entered the shack and cracked his knuckles. They never brought weapons in. Nothing Tate could use against them. If he managed to kill them bare handed, what would he do? His fucking ankle was chained to a fucking pike buried a mile into the fucking dirt floor. The damn thing wasn't budging. He'd bloodied his hands trying to dig it out.

He stepped to the center of the shack, as far as the chain would allow, and squared his shoulders.

But the guards didn't attack.

"Where's Lucia?" He gnashed his teeth.

When they didn't respond, he spat at their feet. "Fuck off then."

They didn't fuck off. Why were they just standing there?

A moment later, an electronic buzzing sound broke the silence.

Buzzing.

Like a phone.

One of the guards reached into his pocket and removed exactly that.

He hadn't seen a phone since the night he...

He tried not to think about that night.

His attention locked onto the phone as the guard connected the call on speaker and held it out of his reach.

"Hello, Tate." The deep voice sliced across his skin like the edge of a blade.

Tiago Badell.

He tried to step closer to the guard, but the chain jerked his leg back. "Where's—?"

"If you ask about her," Badell said, "the call ends and you'll never hear from me again. You'll spend the rest of your lonely existence locked away in that shack, wondering why I called and what I was going to say."

His molars clamped together so hard he felt the pain ripple through his skull. "I'm listening."

"I would be there in person, but I haven't been feeling well. I'm sure you know why."

Lucia thought she'd killed him. She must've injured him, and Tate hoped the bastard's dick had been removed during the attempt on his life.

"I wanted to offer you something," Badell said. "Let's call it a last request. Anything you want. This doesn't include information, and it must fit inside the shack."

What the fuck? "What is this? Like a last-meal request? Am I on death row?"

"I'm offering more than a meal, Tate. You can choose anything—a bed to sleep on, a girl to fuck, a drug to numb your mind. I'm sure you can come up with something creative."

"Why?" He paced the dirt floor, and the chain slithered after him. "What do you want?"

"I've already taken my payment. Consider this a thank you."

He slammed to a stop, and the pound of his heartbeat thrashed in his ears. "What did you *take*?"

"Not Lucia. I left her to die in prison. What's your last request, Tate?"

A hot ember formed in his throat and sank slowly, agonizingly into his chest, where it spread like fire, consuming him in excruciating heartache. His vision blurred, and despite the inferno charring him from the inside out, his skin felt cold, his limbs heavy, and his eyes gritty with hot sand.

He lowered to the blanket and stared at his empty hands. He had nothing. If she was truly gone, he wanted nothing. Yet his mouth moved, voicing the question before his brain caught up.

"Do you have a photo of Lucia?"

"Yes."

There was something. Something he could ask for, and as he closed his eyes, it was all he could see.

So he said it out loud.

He told Badell his final wish.

CHAPTER 32

Three months later…

"Stop the car." Lucia grabbed the binoculars, her pulse hammering and her mouth arid dry.

As Cole Hartman rolled the jeep to idle on the dirt road, she adjusted the focus on the lenses and scanned the parched horizon.

There weren't any big trees to provide a canopy in this part of Venezuela, and with the blistering temperatures, wavy heat lines distorted the landscape.

Where are you, Tate? I know you're out there.

Woody-stemmed shrubs dotted the salt-crusted earth. Between the widely spaced out cacti with their spiny slender arms, there was nothing but rocky sand and bare dirt as far as she could see.

"According to the old man," Cole said, leaning forward with an elbow propped on the steering wheel, "the monastery is supposed to be twenty kilometers the other way."

They'd already driven twenty kilometers in every direction, chasing one of the hundreds of possible locations where Tiago might've been holding Tate.

"This has to be it." Sweat beaded on her brow as

she shifted the binoculars and dialed in on an obscure formation in the distance.

"What are we doing, Lucia?" He grabbed a bottled water from the backseat. "We're wasting time on the musings of a senile man."

"He said there was a gate, and I'm not moving on until I find it."

With a scowl, he snatched the stack of papers from her lap and held them up. "There are two-hundred and seventeen places with gates. We'll never get through all of them."

Her desperation to find Tate might've pushed her past the point of insanity, but she wasn't stopping, wasn't budging. She would find him, dammit, and he would be alive. She refused to accept any other outcome.

"This one feels right." She glared at Cole's cocky aviator sunglasses and held her ground. "It's a hunch."

"You said that the last three times. This whole damn operation has dissolved into a *hunch*." He gulped back the water and tossed the capped bottle onto her lap. "This isn't how I do things."

Her chest constricted with pressure and insistence. "We spent three months doing things your way."

Three months chasing dead ends and all they knew was Tiago had left Caracas the day she attacked him. How he survived the head injury, where he went, and what he was doing—all of it was one big fat mystery.

Meanwhile, Tate was missing and alone, his body beaten and susceptible to infection. She couldn't stop obsessing over it, couldn't eat, couldn't breathe, couldn't think straight. Every second without him was another second he spent in misery.

Cole had hunted down the cops who had

apparently tossed Tate into the trunk of a car. But the corrupted police didn't know where he'd been taken or who'd been driving. Any clues leading to Tate had been so thoroughly buried not even Cole could bribe, threaten, or wrestle the information into the light.

But she knew Tiago, knew how his unshakable mind worked, and she couldn't stop thinking about the night Tate was tortured. It had been a trial, a disgusting experiment that put Tate's love to the test.

Over the past few months, she wondered if this was *her* test. Tiago wouldn't just throw her in a prison to die. His god complex demanded that he challenge, control, and weigh everyone around him, including her. He'd challenged Tate, and now it was her turn.

So many times, she replayed her conversation with Tiago right before she attacked him.

You have the power to give him what he wants most.
His survival is up to you.

There had been a lot of mumbo jumbo twisted into his words, including his suggestion that she move on. But there was something deeper at play. He never eluded to it, but he'd left her a clue.

He'd carved an image into Tate's back.
For her.

He tortured countless men that way, leaving scarred welts on the arms, chests, and legs of those who lived. But his designs tended to be more primitive — geometric lines, whorls, and simple shapes. What he'd sliced into Tate's skin was altogether different. It was a detailed illustration. Hours of gruesome cutting that painted a place with gates and a human-like figure floating through them.

Tiago had given her a way to find him. A depraved

challenge to test her determination and love. Yes, it was just a hunch, but it sat heavily and deeply in her gut, howling and bucking and refusing to be ignored.

Then she met the old man.

She and Cole had comprised most of their list of gated places by talking to people, such as historians at universities and locals in small villages. They'd traveled the breadth of the country, and that was how she met the elderly man in an impoverished town an hour's drive from here.

In thick Spanish, the man had told her about a monastery called *Medio del Corazón*. Translation: *Middle of the Heart.*

Abandoned a century ago, it was left in rubble and ruin. He said the gate still stood to protect the dark secrets that loomed behind its bars. Secrets about a high-ranking monk who had fallen in love with a village girl. The religious order condemned their relationship, separating them. But the lovers had found a way to steal a night together, and within the sacred walls of the monastery, they'd killed themselves.

The old man claimed the lovers could still be heard in the crumbling foundation. He called it *a silent, unified heartbeat in the midst of devastation.*

She knew it was just folklore. Whispered words among superstitious locals. But the story resonated with her. If Tiago put Tate behind gates, it would be those gates. She believed it down to the bottom of her soul.

Problem was, the old man wasn't exactly sure how to find it. He'd never been there, and his directions were approximations. She and Cole had been circling the desert for days.

"Find a road that goes that way." She pointed at

the formation on the horizon.

With a sigh, Cole handed the papers to her and shifted the jeep into gear.

An hour and several wrong turns later, he slowed along a rocky road that ended on a hill. At the top of the incline stood two towering pillars of stone. And between them hung a massive wrought iron double gate.

"This is it." Her heart slammed against her ribcage, and her hand shot out to grip Cole's arm. "Those pillars... I remember them on his back."

She couldn't breathe as she fumbled with the door handle, shaking all over with urgency.

"Lucia, wait." He caught her wrist, stopping her from scrambling out of the jeep. "If he's here —"

"He is!"

" — there will be guards. Security. We don't know what's up there, and they probably heard us approach."

With panting breaths, she opened the glove compartment and removed a 9mm gun.

"I'm going in alone." He drew a pistol from one of the many holsters he wore. "Stay in the car."

"Not happening."

After spending three months together, their power exchanges had fizzled into a laughable waste of time. He barked orders. She barked back. Then he stormed off, grumbling about how he should've never taken this job. Which he did now as he slid out of the jeep, tossed a backpack over his shoulder, and crept up the hill with his gun raised.

The sun beat down on her neck as she followed behind him. Then they separated, seeking the concealment of the pillars on either side of the gate. The gun rattled in her hands, and the atmosphere was so dry it burned her lungs.

Beyond the heavy black bars sat clumps of simplistic, boxy structures made of stone. A passage of archways cut through the largest building at the center. Two wings of corridors spread out from there, connecting smaller, one-room buildings. No doors. No bars or glass on the windows. And from this vantage, there didn't appear to be a roof on the main belfry.

She scanned the perimeter. No cars. No people. No signs of life whatsoever.

Her gaze locked with Cole's where he stood on the other side of the gate.

No one, she mouthed.

Muscles bounced along his jaw, and his shoulders loosened. The disappointment on his face made her stiffen. He'd already decided they had the wrong location.

"I'm not leaving until I look around." She stayed alert as she sidled through the two-foot opening in the sagging double gate.

Arms locked in front of her with the gun trained, she made her way to the ruins on silent feet. Cole trailed at a distance as she crept through the largest building.

The scent of dust and baked earth permeated the air. Loose gravel crunched beneath her boots, and birds took flight in the open rafters. Very few plants grew in this region, but something twiggy and leafless had vined its way up the stone walls toward the open sky.

The altars and benches and pots were long gone. There was nothing. No indication that anyone had been here in decades.

Desperate and tense, she continued moving, passing through the decaying corridors and rooms that would've slept rows of monks on spartan beds. A century later, this monastery only housed families of birds. Nests made of spindly shrubs lined what was left of the rooftops.

She searched everywhere for a hidden door, a basement, someplace that could house a prisoner. When her quest brought her back to the main tower, she let her head fall back on her shoulders and stared at the pale sky peeking through the rafters.

Why isn't he here?

She'd been so certain. So damn amped up with hope.

The thud of her heart drummed in her ears, growing stronger, louder in the silence.

A silent, unified heartbeat in the midst of devastation.

A tear trickled from her eye. Then more fell, tracing sluggish, crooked lines down her cheeks and clinging to her throat.

Goddammit, Tate. Where are you?

She wiped her face and lowered her chin. Then she saw it.

An arched corridor led to the rear of the monastery and opened to a barren landscape of shrubs and sand.

Standing at this angle, she could peer through the arches and see something in the distance. A small structure. Maybe fifty yards away.

"Cole." Her whisper echoed like a roar through the cavernous space.

"I see it." He stepped to her side and gripped her shoulder. "I'm right behind you."

She took off, sprinting over gravel and fallen rock in the passageway. The sun blinded her as she burst outside and raced across the field of sand and stone. Her legs burned. Her lungs heaved, and her muscles worked overtime to cover the distance.

As she grew closer she could make out a shed. A tiny, single-room shack made of rustic wood, with a steel bar across the door.

He's in there. He has to be.

But for how long? They were in the middle of nowhere. How did he eat? Who took care of him? What if he was left there to die?

Her pulse went crazy, and by the time she reached the door, her entire body was shaking uncontrollably.

Cole skidded to a stop beside her and helped her lift the steel bar from the supports.

As she moved to push open the door, he clamped his fingers around her arm, halting her. Then he cast her a look that said, *Brace yourself. You don't know what you'll find in there.*

A vicious battle erupted inside her, a tug-of-war that seesawed between terror and exaltation, ramming against her breastbone like an earth-shattering hurricane. This was it, the moment that could salvage her life or utterly destroy it.

She pulled her arm from his grip, drew in a ragged breath, and opened the door.

The next breath came in a gasp as her heart dropped out of her chest and tumbled across the dirt floor.

Tate stood near the back wall, with a dirty, paper-thin blanket tied around his waist. The rest of him was nude, his skin pale, his entire physique emaciated. A full beard covered his face, and his hair hung in clumped strands around his crystal blue eyes.

"Tate." The violence of her emotions and the

overwhelming happiness spiking through her staggered her forward steps.

He jerked back, bumping into the wall. "You're not real."

"I am." She covered her mouth with a hand to stifle her sob. "This is real."

Behind her, Cole spoke quietly into his phone, probably arranging transportation with Matias.

Trusting him to watch the door, she inched closer to Tate. He went rigid, lifting his chin at an angle and glaring at her with a menacing look in his eyes.

A metal cuff encircled his ankle, the skin beneath it torn and red. A chain connected the cuff to a spike. The hard, moistureless dirt floor had been dug away from it, revealing a block of concrete underneath.

He'd tried to escape at some point, and though he looked stunned and distrusting, he was still in there somewhere. She just needed to be patient.

"You're an angel," he rasped, his voice dry as dust. "Not real."

"Do angels have scars?"

His brows pulled together, and he shook his head.

With a trembling hand, she lifted the hem of her shirt to expose her abdomen.

"I doubt I'll be chosen for heaven, but if I am..." She traced a finger along the marred flesh from her breastbone to her hip. "I don't intend to take this with me."

He stared at her scar. The longer he stared, the faster his breaths came, until his chest heaved with whatever was building inside him.

She held impossibly still, waiting for him to make the first move, to say the word, to give her an indication that this moment was sinking in.

When he finally lifted his eyes and found hers, she saw him. He was right there, clear and bright and alive.

"Lucia." He swallowed and took a step forward.

The chain clanked against the ground, but he wouldn't need the length of it, because she was running, reaching. Her fingers tangled in his long hair, and she lifted on tiptoes to press her nose against the pocket of his throat.

He wrapped his arms around her back and held her tight against his chest. He felt different, so much thinner, but the embrace was the same—protective, strong, *possessive.*

"God, I missed you." She couldn't stop the tears from coming, couldn't hold back the whimpers or the clench of her fingers in his hair.

"The memory of you was the only thing that kept me alive." His deep voice whispered over her, threading with unimaginable pain. "How long has it been?"

"Three months." Cole crouched beside them and dug through his backpack. "It'll take me a second to pick the lock on your shackle. Are you expecting visitors?"

"Two guards bring food at nightfall." Tate dragged his nose through her hair. "How are you alive?"

"Long story." She stepped back and glided her hands up his arms. "Let's get you out of here first."

Her fingers bumped a patch of strangely rough skin on his bicep, drawing her attention to it.

What the—?

She'd been so focused on the drastic changes in his appearance—his beard, loss of weight, the healing skin on his injured arm—she didn't notice until now that his tattoo had grown, stretching above his elbow and covering part of his shoulder.

The inked roses he had before blurred into something new. A portrait of a woman with straight black hair, holding her finger against the profile of her lips.

Her breath caught. "Is that—?"

"You." He glanced at it and returned to her eyes with a flicker of light in the brilliant blue of his. "Badell gave me a last request. Since I couldn't have *you*, this was the next best thing."

He asked for a tattoo of my face on his arm?

Tingling warmth seeped through her limbs, sparking a sudden release of all tension. Her chest expanded. Her heart overflowed, and every whirling, erratic, out-of-control piece of her life snapped into place.

"Got it." Cole stood and tossed the chain away. "I'll run and get the jeep."

"I can walk." Tate twined his fingers with hers and strode to the door.

"It's rocky—" She was jerked forward by his grip on her hand and stumbled to keep up.

He crossed the hot, rugged terrain on bare feet with his free hand shielding his eyes. He didn't wince or slow, his gait matching Cole's in strong, efficient strides. The only thing he wore was a small blanket, and as her slower pace put her behind him, his back moved into her line of sight.

The image was just like she remembered, only cleaner, free of infection, and healed. The raised skin from each cut formed an artistic illustration of pillars along his sides, a double gate hanging between them, and a silhouette of a woman levitating in the opening with the arc of the sun behind her head.

It was terrible and beautiful, summoning extreme reactions from horrific agony to profound wonder.

"You're staring at it." He glanced at her over his shoulder.

"Have you seen it?"

"No." His tone held deep anger, and he tugged her forward.

Cole explained the history of the monastery as they passed the stone structures, including the tragic love story that had compelled her to come here.

She and Tate didn't speak, but they watched each other, their eyes sharing three months of loss, one night of lasting torture, and a future that didn't need to be defined. Wherever they went from here, they would go there together.

When they reached the gate, he stopped abruptly and released her hand.

"What's wrong?" she asked.

"That's..." He stared up at the towering wrought iron bars and reached behind him, sliding his fingers over the welts on his back. "I've felt this so many times, trying to figure out... That's it, isn't it? He carved those gates on my back?"

Her chin trembled as she nodded. "I think he did it to see if I would find you. That's why it took me so long. I've been searching for gates and—"

"There's something else." He moved his hand up his spine.

She edged back, watching as his fingers traced the feminine figure.

"It's a silhouette," she said on a serrated breath. "A woman."

"Show me." He pointed at the gates before him.

"Walk through them."

A swallow lodged in her throat. She glanced at Cole, who waited patiently behind her, surveying the perimeter. Then she moved to stand in the opening of the gate, facing Tate exactly as it was depicted on his back.

The sun sat high in the sky. If it were a few hours later, it would've been at the right height behind her head.

"It's…" His chest rose and fell with a deep breath. "Beautiful. You're absolutely stunning, Lucia." He twisted to look at Cole. "Is that what my back looks like?"

"Pretty much." Cole flicked his gaze between the gate and the illustration. "It's uncanny, really."

Tate regarded her for an endless moment before he lowered his head and stared at the ground.

"Okay." He anchored his hands on his hips and made a sharp sniffing sound that almost resembled a laugh. His lips twitched, and he met her eyes. "Let's go home."

"Where's home?" She reached her arm toward him, stretching her fingers.

He caught her hand and squeezed. "Wherever you are."

CHAPTER 33

Four days later, Tate exited the physician's room in Matias' extravagant estate in Colombia. His muscles twitched with restless energy, and something in his chest pinched, urging him to go look for Lucia.

He couldn't bear to be separated from her. Every time he left her side, it felt as though his limbs were being ripped from his body. He needed to get over that. Missing her was one thing. Smothering her was unhealthy.

He'd visited Picar, the old crusty resident doctor, three times now. But this meeting had been his last, because Picar had just given him a clean bill of health. No infections. No STDs. And other than the scarring on his back and the twinging discomfort in his arm, there was no permanent damage to his body.

He stepped onto the causeway and strolled through an open terrace sitting area. There was no one around, so he allowed himself a moment to enjoy the warm breeze and breathe in the aroma of loam and thriving vegetation.

The estate was expansive and luxurious, ensconced in the Amazon rainforest and protected by the best security available. He'd been here many times, and it always felt like paradise. But it wasn't home.

When Matias' helicopter picked them up in Venezuela, Lucia offered to go back to Texas with him. He would've preferred that, but she needed to spend time with Camila. She needed a reprieve from the bustle of reality. So he insisted they come here.

From the moment she floated into the shack like an angel, they'd been inseparable. But they hadn't spent much time alone, without others around. She had twelve years to catch up on with Camila, and he wanted that for her.

She was probably with Camila now, and as much as he craved her and ached to have her in his sights, maybe he needed a moment, too, just to...*be*.

The last four days had been a whirlwind of reunions and conversations. Everyone was here—Van and Amber, Liv and Josh, Livana and his roommates. Everyone except Kate.

Kate had disappeared the night he was tortured. A month ago, she called Liv from an untraceable number and said she didn't want to be found. She'd demanded that no one look for her.

Lucia had recalled Tiago Badell saying something about relocating. That he'd found a new interest he was pursuing.

Then there was Tate's phone conversation with him.

I've already taken my payment. Consider this a thank you.

What did you take?

Badell took Kate. There wasn't a doubt in Tate's mind. Cole Hartman was out there looking for her. Tate would've gone with him, but Lucia had begged. She'd pleaded with tears in her eyes for him to stay.

He would do what he could for Kate and help with the investigation. But Lucia came first. She didn't want him putting himself in harm's way, so he wouldn't.

Leaning against the railing of the causeway, he soaked in the sunlight. What he felt for Lucia was all-consuming. It itched and vibrated beneath his skin. His pulse soared, and his cock hardened just thinking about her, but they hadn't shared a single sexual moment since before that night in the basement.

They spent the majority of the past four days talking. They analyzed Badell's mental health, his cruel romanticism, and his motivation for bringing them together in such a brutal way. Tate told her everything he remembered during his time in the shack. She recounted her attack on Badell, their escape from the compound, the prison, and her three-month quest to find him.

She'd also spent some time with the cartel's cantankerous doctor. The poison Badell had been feeding her was completely gone from her system, but the crash in Peru had resulted in the removal of her uterus. She'd taken the news in stride, turning to Tate to say, "You were a child without a mother once. If you want a baby, I would love to save one."

Her tenacity and bravery awed him to no end. Several times, he found himself lying beside her on the bed in their room, face to face, content with simply staring at her as she stared back. Christ, he fucking loved her.

She slept beside him every night. She kissed his face when they were in the company of others. She caressed his back every time he removed his shirt. She held his hand when they strolled along the causeway. Every glance she cast in his direction made him want to shred her clothes like an animal and fuck her against the wall. But he held back.

His body didn't feel like his own. He'd shaved his face, cut his hair, and scrubbed his skin with scalding hot water. But he was wearing borrowed clothes and sleeping in a borrowed bed. He was still underweight, still overwhelmed, and so fucking out of sorts.

On the bright side, he'd completely lost the craving for cigarettes.

So he'd made use of Matias' gym. His strength would eventually return, but his mind... He wasn't broken. There was just something stuck there. Something he needed to un-stick.

Part of it had to do with his feelings of failure and the misery Lucia had gone through when he was too weak to protect her.

The rest of it had to do with Van. He'd seen the man around the estate and chatted with him about anything, everything, except what had happened that night in the basement.

He needed to talk to Van privately. And soon.

Decision made, he turned toward the common area to search for him.

"Tate." Camila's sweet voice drifted over his shoulder.

He pivoted, grinning instantly at the sight of her huge brown eyes. "Hey."

"Hey." She gave his clean-shaved face a quick caress. "Much better. I hated the beard."

"Yeah?" He rubbed his jaw, silently agreeing with her. "Where's Lucia?"

"Matias is showing her the citrus grove."

"Citrus grove?"

She bit down on her smile and hugged her waist. "He grew it for me a long, long time ago."

Because Matias loved her. He'd loved her his entire life, and apparently, Tate had to go through hell and back to truly understand the meaning of that.

"You know..." He gripped the back of his neck. "The feelings I had for you—"

"I know."

"It's different now."

"I know." Her eyes glistened as she smiled.

"You're my closest friend. That isn't going to change."

"Dammit, Tate." She pressed the heels of her hands against the corners of her eyes. "Don't make me cry."

"Come here."

He held his arms out, and she stepped in for a hug.

"Lucia's pretty fucking amazing, isn't she?" she mumbled against his chest.

"Yeah, she really is." He nudged her back and held her teary gaze. "We good?"

"Yeah," she said softly. "Thank you for finding her. Words can't express—"

"You're welcome." He appreciated her smile, but it wasn't the one he craved. His heart hammered, begging him to go find Lucia, but first... "Do you know where Van is?"

"Did you check his room?" She motioned toward the east wing. "He doesn't let Amber out of bed."

He chuckled. "Okay, I'll check there."

Ten minutes later, he stood at the door to Van's room, fist raised to knock and a million thoughts clashing in his head.

Just say what you need to say. In and out and move on.

He drew in a breath, slowly released it, and rapped on the door.

A few seconds passed before Van answered. Dressed in only a pair of jeans that weren't fully zipped, he glanced behind him before opening the door to let Tate in.

As Tate stepped through the doorway, he caught a glimpse of Amber crossing through the far side of the room, wrapped in a sheet and her hair a tangled mess of just-got-fucked.

Camila hadn't been joking.

"If I'm interrupting," Tate said, pausing in the entryway, "I can come back."

"Let's go out to the patio." Van turned and strolled toward the back door.

Tate followed him. The guest rooms were set up like hotel suites, with kitchenettes, sitting areas, private bathrooms, and artfully decorated beds and furnishings.

It never ceased to amaze him how much wealth could be amassed through corruption. He didn't know what the Restrepo cartel was involved in. No one knew but Camila. That said, Matias spent a great deal of time and money fighting a war against human slavery. Tate admired the man deeply for that.

The room reeked of sex. Several belts lay on the king-sized bed, and clothing scattered the floor as if they'd been stripped in a hurry.

A shiver crept up his spine as he entered the private patio and lowered onto the chair beside Van. It was blissfully hot outside, even at dusk. Moisture infused the air, so unlike the parched heat of the desert.

"How long will you stay?" he asked Van.

"Until I know my family will be safe in Texas."

That wouldn't be the case until Tiago Badell was six feet in the ground.

Matias had brought in a private teacher for Van's daughter, so she was probably getting a better education here. But Liv and Josh would lose their jobs if they stayed much longer.

"Spit it out, Tate." Van shifted his gaze from the tropical landscape and rested it on him.

Out of the corner of his eye, he saw Amber moving through the living area and decided to start there. "Does she know what happened?"

"Of course. I don't just fuck my wife. I confide in her, lean on her, and trust her. I tell her everything."

Tate nodded, letting that settle through his rioting nerves. "How did she take it?"

"She cried." Van's frown twisted into a smirk. "Then she demanded I talk to you when you returned."

"I'm not good at this." Tate leaned forward, bracing his elbows on knees. "I think what's been digging at me the most is the damage I might've done to you."

"Well, you have a huge goddamn cock, and I felt every inch—"

"You know what I mean."

"Right." Van heaved in a heavy breath and leaned back in the chair. "I was raped as a child. You don't really get over that, but you get *through* it. I've done that, and so have you." He removed a toothpick from his pocket and set it between his teeth. "What happened between us in that basement might not have been willing, but it wasn't violent or cruel. You didn't abuse me the way I abused you all those years ago. You understand the difference?"

"Yeah."

"The hardest part for me was betraying my wife."
Van twisted in the chair and tracked Amber's movements
through the window. "She sees me at my weakest, and
she still loves me."

"You weren't weak in Caracas. What you did for
me—"

"I was messed up in my head when I returned to
her, but she has this deep well of sympathy in her, an
ability to identify with how and why I do the things I
do." He rolled the toothpick between his lips. "Don't
know what I did to deserve her, but she's stuck with me,
for better or worse. So to address your concerns, there's
no damage on my end. What about you?"

He laughed uncomfortably. "The sex was the least
painful part of that night."

"But the most painful to come to terms with." Van
softened his voice. "Have you fucked her since you
returned?"

"No." He set his jaw. "I can't get out of my damn
head."

"Go fuck your girl, Tate. The second you're inside
her, controlling her in the way you both need, the mental
blocks will disappear." Van rose from the chair and held
out a hand. "No bad blood."

He stood, ignoring the offered handshake, and
pulled Van into a one-armed hug. "Thank you for
everything you did in Caracas. We're more than even. No
bad blood."

"Good to hear."

Tate left Van's room, hellbent on taking care of
Lucia in the way she deserved—deeply, passionately,
and thoroughly. The intimacy he'd wrongfully denied

her, the urgency to connect with her on every carnal level possible, and the cravings he felt every time she was near — it all swelled to hard, pulsating life.

The breath of his soul had been a distant whisper for so long he thought he'd lost it. But he heard it now, felt it growing closer, coming back to him. Maybe it hadn't been his body that was different, but rather his spirit. That was the part of him that had been severely wounded, reduced to damn-near nothingness.

He found her on the veranda, surrounded by Camila, Matias, and several men in the cartel he couldn't name.

As he approached Lucia's back, his emotional aches retreated, fading into the background of his thundering heartbeat.

He stopped behind her chair and brought his mouth to her ear, "Come with me."

She spun around with a huge grin, and the tabletop candlelight danced behind her, sharing his excitement.

A casual red dress molded to her curves and flirted with her knees as she stood.

His breath stuttered. Three months of poison-free health looked so fucking good on her. Sun-kissed skin, glossy black hair, full tits, a Latina ass that didn't know when to quit, and their room was a five-minute walk away. He was so fucking hard there was no way he'd make it there.

He clamped a hand around her arm and led her out of the dining area and toward the causeway.

The air around them sparked with hunger — his *and* hers. She didn't ask where they were going. She saw it in his expression and fed from it. He didn't have to be an empath to sense her desire. It materialized in the gasping hitch of her breath, the pebbling nipples beneath her dress, and the look in her eyes that didn't stray from his face.

He tried to focus on steps. One foot forward. Turn left at the next hall. Pass the kitchen. Watch the wet spot on the marble.

Wet spot. Short skirt. Long, sexy-as-fuck legs. Panties, pussy, tight heat...

Fuck this. He hooked an arm around her waist and shoved her back against the nearest wall. His hands went under her dress. His fingers found the satin crotch of her panties. Her mouth slotted against his, and they crashed into a frenzy of kissing, licking, biting need.

He ground his hips against her, letting her feel the swollen length of him. Then he yanked her panties down and buried his fingers inside her.

Her moan vibrated against his mouth, and goosebumps dotted her arms. The warm, wet clasp of her body sucked on his fingers, clenching and taunting as he imagined her sliding along his cock. Her pussy was the hottest thing he'd ever touched, and it was even hotter when she climaxed.

It'd been three months. Three harrowing months without the taste of her lips and the squeeze of her cunt.

He kept his tongue in her mouth, panting and feasting as he thrust his hand harder, faster, mindless in his pursuit to feel her come. He needed it. Goddamn, he'd missed her so much.

Footsteps approached the corridor, slowed to a stop, and moved on. He didn't care. Her nails scored his shoulders, and her moans intensified. Her orgasm was within reach.

"Give it to me, Lucia."

She quivered, ignited, and combusted on his hand, drenching his fingers and throbbing rhythmically. Her tits bounced with the heave of her chest, and her pupils dilated as she stared up at him, burned into him.

"You're so getting fucked right now." He unzipped and pulled himself out while fingering her and holding her on that euphoric edge.

She kicked her panties away and reached between her legs, sliding her fingers over his where they sank in and out of her.

"Hold on." He lifted her, pinned her back against the wall, and pushed inside her silky cunt in one motion.

"Fuck." He groaned, shaking with the deep-reaching flood of sensations. "Christ, your pussy... So fucking tight. Every bump and ridge is gripping me."

"There's nothing between us." She cupped his face, smiling as she searched his eyes.

No condom. He'd never had consensual sex without one. And as he kicked his hips to meet her body, he vowed to never wear one again.

Nothing felt like this. Nothing. It wasn't just the bareness between them. It was her. The staccato of her hungry whimpers, the submissive give of her body, and the love shining in her honey-brown eyes.

He pressed tighter against her chest and worked his mouth frantically against hers, his movements unhinged and desperate. It had been too long, and they'd been through too much to put restraints on this. He let his desire take over, driving his thrusts, drinking in her kisses, and digging his fingers into her beautiful skin.

The caress of her hand traveled over his ass, squeezing and kneading before dipping beneath the waistband to finger the cleft of his cheeks. Then it rose, slipping under his shirt to trace the scars he neither loved nor hated. They made her sad when she looked at them, but they'd brought them back together. They meant nothing to him. And everything.

Their lips slicked together, his tongue sliding over and around hers in a kiss that amplified every physical and emotional sensation vibrating through him. He was lost to her, a crazed and starving goner with everything he ever wanted in his arms.

His muscles were whipcord taut, his lungs pumping with the speed of his thrusts. Each stroke invigorated his body and nourished his heart. He couldn't get close enough to her, deep enough. He wanted to fuck her soul.

With his hands beneath her knees, he hitched them higher, wider, opening her to him as he pistoned between her legs, pounded her against the wall, and devoured her every gasp.

Then he broke the kiss to look deep into her eyes, gazing at her beautiful, healthy face. Her skin sheened under the dim lighting. Her lips parted, plump and wet, and her hair tousled around her graceful neck and shoulders. What a glorious sight.

Arousal loved her.

"Tate." A throaty, greedy whisper. The most seductive sound he'd ever heard.

"I love you." He drew his hips back and surged again and again, filling her, stretching her with an urgency that chopped his words into grunts. "Love you so damn much."

There was a natural rhythm between them, a pace and angle that had a way of bringing them to climax together. He didn't know how many times they'd had sex during their five days together, but he'd found their rhythm then and rediscovered it now.

His hips moved instinctively, impulsively, as he savored the slow build of yearning low in his back. Just the possibility of it, the relief of being inside her, and the knowledge that he would be here, in her, every day for the rest of his life — it was more than he could ever hope for.

He sensed the surge of pleasure inside her, the promise, the moment they reached for it at the same time.

Then he rode them over the edge, staring into her eyes and coming with her in powerful spurts that pounded his heart into a mold around hers. A unified heartbeat. It was the song in his ears and the barometer of their future.

She stared up at him, dazed and breathless. "We needed that."

Lowering her feet to the floor, he kissed her lips. "I won't ever deny us again. I'm sorry I—"

"Whatever you're about to say, stop." Her eyes flashed. She snatched her panties from the floor and pulled them on. "You endured things most men can't even think about, and you're apologizing for taking four days to heal?" She framed his face with her hands. "Take as long as you need, Tate. I'm not going anywhere."

He knew that, but hearing it from her lips freed something in his mind, un-sticking the final pieces of his mental baggage.

"What I need is *you*," he said, brushing a knuckle across her cheek, "and we've only just begun."

Ten minutes later, he stood by the bed in their room and ordered her to strip. Then he spread her gorgeous nude body across the mattress and worshiped every sensual inch of her skin. He kissed and licked until she bucked her hips, offering up his journey's end.

His body vibrated with need as he shifted between her legs. But he took his time, drawing out her panting breaths, making her wait for it. Her head snapped up, and when her eyes found his, he ran the tip of his finger with taunting slowness up the seam of her soaked pussy.

He teased her with his touch, stroking, rubbing, plunging in and out, all while imprisoning her with his eyes. She orgasmed on his hand. Then she orgasmed on his tongue. And he was nowhere near finished with her.

Kneeling between her thighs, he slid the head of his cock up and down her slit, torturing them both in the best way possible. He controlled her pleasure, and he didn't need chains or belts or any kind of physical restraint to do it.

She surrendered to him as he sank inside her. She yielded to the demands of his body. She relinquished her heart in connection of their lips.

He spent hours inside her, trying to slack a need that would never burn out. When they finally collapsed in a tangle of limbs, she laughed. She rolled to her back and laughed deep belly laughter with her knees pulled up and her arms around her waist.

He laughed with her, because fuck him, her smile. It was a huge, bursting, mystical entity inside him—an energetic, unpredictable live wire of happiness stretching out beneath his skin.

Snuggling up against her side, he tossed a leg over hers and cupped the side of her face. "What is it?"

"Joy." She met and held his gaze, glowing with life. "This feeling, you, us... It's laughter and soul-deep joy."

Her answer was everything. No matter where the

future took them, he would make sure she never stopped laughing.

"Tell me about your dreams." He circled a finger around the luscious curve of her breast. "Your fantasies, your hopes and aspirations."

Rolling toward him, she gave him a heart-melting smile. "It starts with you, a bottle of wine, and a Netflix subscription…"

CHAPTER 34

One month later...

Lucia reclined on the couch in Tate's house in Austin, flipping through the movie selections on Netflix. She smiled as the sounds of shuffling footsteps and heavy grunts drifted from the kitchen.

"Fucking hold still," Tate growled from around the corner.

Maybe she should go in there and help him, but it would only frustrate him more. The man loved to be in control.

When they left Colombia a few weeks ago, they made a stop in California wine country. The threat of Tiago lingered, and they kept their wits about them always, but deep down, she believed he'd moved on from Tate and her. He'd played out his mind games and got his revenge.

Whether she and Tate went after him was still up for discussion.

Tate's roommates had stayed in Colombia, working with Camila on her war against slavery. Cole was still searching for Kate.

Cole Hartman, as it turned out, was an interesting

man. She'd learned a lot about him during their three months on the road together. Hardworking and highly motivated, he lugged around a tragically broken heart. It gave him a perspective that few people could appreciate.

He never collected on the money Tate owed him, and she doubted he intended to bill Van and Matias. Cole had become part of their family, part of the Freedom Fighters.

The scamper of skidding feet tore out of the kitchen, and in the blink of an eye, her lap was filled with the long, awkward legs and huge muscled frame of an eight-year-old rescued greyhound.

Kingo stumbled and staggered like a newborn deer on her thighs, his feet slipping and tripping between the cushions, until he hopped off and collapsed onto his side on the floor.

"He got mud all over the kitchen." Tate stepped into the room and gave her a once-over. "And you."

She glanced down at her muddy clothes and shrugged. "He's still learning how to be a house dog."

They were fostering Kingo, until they were ready to make some permanent decisions. Stay in Texas, return to Colombia, search for Tiago Badell, explore the Venezuelan rainforest—all of it was on the table.

Tate disappeared in the kitchen and returned a second later with two glasses of wine from their trip. He set them on the coffee table and motioned for her to stand.

She did so with a smile, holding still as he removed her muddy shirt and jeans. Clad in a bra and panties, she sighed as he kissed her. His seeking tongue, his greedy hands on her body, and his clean, heady breath against her lips, he was so familiar and intoxicating and *hers*.

He was her everything.

He lowered her to the couch and positioned her where he wanted her. Then he stretched out behind her, tucking her backside against his groin and stroking his fingers through her hair.

Heaven.

As she sipped from her wine and cued up an action movie on Netflix, she felt a depth of joy that could only be earned through blood and tears.

There was a tilting, cracking, end-of-the-world transformation that happened inside of people who experienced extreme terror and hardship, abuse and tragedy, shame and forgiveness. Those who suffered the most held the greatest appreciation for movie subscriptions, rescued dogs, and a glass of red from wine country.

Maybe she and Tate would give up those things to pursue new quests together and reunite with old friends. But they would always remember what they'd endured and how they fell in love. They would always find solace in the dark and the pain, in a hand around the throat, or a last request in a shack, or a seedy sex club, or a ransom payment, as well as antivenom injections, scarification, Venezuelan prisons, monastery ruins, and tragic love stories.

Without the bad stuff—the trauma, the fall, and the crash—joy wouldn't exist. Maybe something like it would be in the background, like an echo of the real thing. But it wouldn't have strength and impact. It wouldn't be felt in every bone, tissue, and organ.

It was the bad stuff that breathed vivid life into the good.

Sorrow existed to breed happiness.

Pain gave rise to pleasure.

Loss brought about exploration.

Through a story of suicidal lovers and a gate carved into skin, it was grief that had led her to Tate.

They found each other in tragedy.

A silent, unified heartbeat in the midst of devastation.

The **DELIVER** series continues with:

TAKE (#5)
Kate's story

OTHER BOOKS
BY PAM GODWIN

LOVE TRIANGLE ROMANCE
TANGLED LIES TRILOGY
One is a Promise
Two is a Lie
Three is a War

DARK PARANORMAL ROMANCE
TRILOGY OF EVE
Dead of Eve #1
Heart of Eve #1.5
Blood of Eve #2
Dawn of Eve #3

STUDENT-TEACHER ROMANCE
Dark Notes

ROCK-STAR DARK ROMANCE
Beneath the Burn

ROMANTIC SUSPENSE
Dirty Ties

EROTIC ROMANCE
Incentive

ACKNOWLEDGMENTS

To my beta team - Angela Ann, Ann White, Shabnam Arora, Shea Moran, Tajana Cote, Author E.M. Abel, and Author Ellie Masters, you are my Freedom Fighters, my liberators of words and dirty minds. Your help with this book was priceless and precious, and you deserve all the toothpick kisses and breathless chokehold hugs. Seriously, I would be lost without you.

To the city of Caracas - I didn't paint your image in a pretty light, but I know you're rich in culture and beauty. Your people are strong and resilient, and one day, you'll rise above the corruption and shine through the fog. Much like my characters. Tortured, scarred, and sundered, you'll find your way, fight back, and achieve greatness. I'm rooting for you.

To my husband - Not gonna lie. You inspire my anti-heroes, you coarse alpha bastard. But that soft, squishy center you try to hide? Yeah, I know it's there. You're a good man, Mr. Godwin. And thorough. I love you.

ABOUT THE AUTHOR

New York Times and USA Today Bestselling author, Pam Godwin, lives in the Midwest with her husband, their two children, and a foulmouthed parrot. When she ran away, she traveled fourteen countries across five continents, attended three universities, and married the vocalist of her favorite rock band.

Java, tobacco, and dark romance novels are her favorite indulgences, and might be considered more unhealthy than her aversion to sleeping, eating meat, and dolls with blinking eyes.

EMAIL: pamgodwinauthor@gmail.com

Made in the USA
Lexington, KY
10 April 2018